The Tomorrow Game

Paul J. Chetcuti

Oakfield Books

ISBN: 978-1-7774981-0-8 (eBook)
ISBN: 978-1-7774981-1-5 (paperback)
ISBN: 978-1-7774981-2-2 (audiobook)

Cover Design: Go Hippo

Cover Image: "PHILOSOPHY !? (?) + (*) = (!)" by RANT 73

Author Photo: Vincenzo De La Gamba

pauljchetcuti.com

Reviews are a wonderful way to help an author

To Sofia, who always believes

CONTENTS

MAGIC HOUR

"If you could change anything in your past, what would it be?" the man on the wall-mounted display asks in a clinical monotone.

He pauses to allow the thirty-plus employees watching the live feed to contemplate this. As they are crammed into a boardroom made to seat twenty comfortably, they are largely uninterested in this latest project that is supposed to revolutionize the company. Revolutions are a lot of work, most of which is a waste of time.

"Would you go back to that specific crossroads, where you turned *left,*" the man on the display continues dryly, "and *instead* turn *right?*"

Timothy Koops, unlike most of his co-workers, gives this question some serious consideration. His life *has* taken a few wrong turns over the years, and admittedly he thinks it would be nice to take several of those journeys once more, this time with an accurate roadmap. But then again, Timothy knows you don't get second chances. Time moves strictly in a straight line, with no gear for reverse. Still, Timothy is intrigued by the concept, and focuses his attention on the man on the display, Dr. Zakery Fasten.

The word around the water cooler is Dr. Fasten has been working for Dimensional Research Inc. for over a year, even though his name and his department do not appear on the company's organizational chart.

"Perhaps you would not have invested in that certain stock portfolio," Dr. Fasten says, "which resulted in a large financial loss and many years of regret. Or perhaps you would have stayed in contact with that good friend of yours, who is now quite influential and could open numerous doors for you. Maybe you would have taken your car in for servicing, before that road trip where your brakes failed and you spun out, injuring one of your passengers."

Dr. Fasten takes another pause for emphasis, which is filled with restless rustlings and low groans by the DRI employees. Timothy instead casts his mind back, remembering how he backed out of his driveway three years earlier, running over the family dog, causing it to explode in a spray of blood and intestines. His son Bryan never really got over that one. And neither did Timothy. That was likely the day his relationship with Bryan began to fall apart.

"What if I told you that everything I have described is achievable?" Dr. Fasten resumes. "*Theoretically*, yes, but achievable none-the-less."

"What *horseshit*," Ravi Bargo whispers in Timothy's ear.

"Yeah," Timothy nods vaguely at his friend and co-worker. But in his heart, Timothy admits, he wishes what Dr. Fasten is saying were true.

"So *how* is this possible?" Dr. Fasten asks rhetorically, then answers his own question by stating simply, "Through the science of retro-causality."

"*Whosits-whatsits?*" Ravi mocks under his breath.

"Cause and effect," Dr. Fasten continues. "We all know which one comes first. We are so certain, it is almost impossible to see the relationship between these two phenomena in any other way. But the project I have been working on, in conjunction with DRI, has proven there are cases where the temporal positioning of cause and effect are reversed. Yes, I am saying, in certain circumstances, the effect can precede its cause."

"Sure, I'll just jump in my time machine," Ravi sneers. "Dump

Gladys after that first date and save myself a lot of heartache and support payments."

Ravi snickers throatily at his joke, until he quietens suddenly. Timothy looks over his shoulder to see their manager Marc Lange staring them down. Lange is tall and thin, with long bean-pole legs, young but prematurely balding, with what's left of his hair shaved clean. This is the man who can make their work-lives instantly hellish with one twitch of his tic-prone eye.

What a jerk, Timothy thinks. *Marc Lange, Analysis Manager. Anal Man. Always has his face in the Veep's ass.*

Lange's gaze continues to burn into Timothy and Ravi. Their manager is always disappointed with their work, and he never ceases to remind them of their status. Low totems on the departmental pole. Underachieving slackers. If Lange is ever going to become Director, his staff are going to have to work a lot harder.

Timothy can't help but agree with Lange's opinion. He and Ravi are both superbly unmotivated. And Ravi, of course, is the office clown who puts most of his energies into avoiding work. At least Timothy *tries,* but the work is so soul crushing. Analyzing data, running algorithms, building models. The computer does most of the work anyway.

Timothy's attention is now redirected back to the display, as Dr. Fasten finishes his presentation with a science-heavy description of retro-causality.

Dr. Fasten is then replaced on the display by Denice Button, Vice President of Research and Development.

"Thank you, Dr. Fasten," Denice smiles coldly, "and thank you to the Board, and of course, our President and CEO, Bruce McQuade."

The Vice President then addresses the various branches of the R&D Department, each watching the feed remotely from their own boardrooms:

"This is a great turning point for DRI," she begins. "And it is especially important for R&D. We are going to make the Board proud, and eventually the world at large will know of our accomplishments."

What a corporate ice queen, Timothy thinks, tuning her out. *So full of her own importance. Her office is on the other end of the floor, and the only time we ever see her is on a display mounted on the wall.*

Maybe it's for the best, Timothy tells himself. Denice Button scares the hell out of him, as she is a staunch, unmarried, unfriended, otherwise uninteresting career woman who would live in the office if she could. Timothy often jokes bitterly to himself that if Denice ever smiled for real, the smile would die alone, much like its human owner probably will.

"And I expect every one of you to take part," Denice insists, catching Timothy's attention again.

He isn't sure what she is referring to, but it is apparent from her tone that *not* taking part would result in a stern reprimand. Or even worse, an agonizing session with Lange, during which he would express his displeasure over Timothy's meagre efforts to support the corporation.

"*I missed that,*" Timothy whispers to Ravi. "*What are we supposed to take part in?*"

"*Assessments,*" Ravi whispers out of the corner of his mouth, without turning toward Timothy.

"This is a great opportunity for us," Denice says, "as employees of DRI, and as humans on Planet Earth."

I know I'm human, Timothy's mind begins to churn, *but you, Denice, will have to provide some verification.*

"Dr. Fasten's Project will be transformative," Denice continues. "It will apply advancements in super-computation to retro-causality, taking it from theory to emerging reality, propelling human health, happiness and prosperity lightyears into the future. And of course, as a profit centre, the Project will adhere to all corporate performance measures and be subject to mandatory biannual evaluations."

With that said, Denice ends off by thanking Dr. Fasten and reminding everyone that the future is literally in their hands. If only they have the drive to make something of it. The image of Denice on the display forces itself to smile, unconvincingly, and is promptly replaced by the DRI corporate logo.

Before the staff can shuffle out of the cramped boardroom, Lange calls everyone to attention: "Hold up a minute."

An audible sigh sweeps through the room, and the staff turn grudgingly to face the Anal Man.

"You all heard the Veep just now," Lange begins.

Yes, we did, Timothy thinks, *so please don't repeat everything she just said.* Which is just one of many annoying habits in Lange's arsenal.

"This is an exciting new line of business for DRI," Lange tells them with an unearned authority in his voice. "We should be honoured it's going to be housed in R&D. The Board wanted to create a new department, but Denice and I worked long and hard to bring it home."

Timothy and Ravi exchange quick glances. *Uh, huh, I'm sure Lange's input was indispensable.*

"Going forward," Lange continues, "Dr. Fasten's Project is the company's number one priority, and I want Analysis to be a big part of it. Step one is to familiarize yourself with all the available information, which admittedly is minimal. For proprietary reasons, details are being kept to a need-to-know basis. However, as the Veep made clear, we are all expected to take part in the assessments."

What are these assessments? Timothy wonders, kicking himself for not paying better attention.

"In time, we will be rolling out the assessments externally, under appropriate security controls," Lange says. "But for now, *we* will be the base line. That's why participation is mandatory. Our input will be used to calibrate the supercomputer Dr. Fasten has been working with. All those involved have been sworn to secrecy. So obviously, do not discuss this with any outside concerns. That includes friends, family, old colleagues, and anyone else, including other departments in DRI. This is not a collab. This is real secret agent *shit*."

Lange stops talking, realizing he has gone too far with his lingo and is sounding like the hapless jerk everyone thinks he is. So he gives everyone a stern look. Not able to think of anything else to say, he just says, "Alright, get back to work."

"What an asshole," Ravi mutters to Timothy as they slowly file out of the boardroom and make their way back to their adjoining cubicles.

The circumstance of Timothy and Ravi working at the same company, and holding the same job, and sitting next to each other is an irony not lost on either of them. They are the same age and met in their first year at the University of Toronto, when they were assigned to be roommates in residence.

Over the years, they came to merge their interests, and both achieved degrees in statistical analysis, taking the same required courses and many of the same electives. In their final year, they started double dating a set of female friends. And as the oft told story goes, Timothy's wife Brenda was originally Ravi's date on the first night they all went out together.

When it came time for that first night to end, and the group split in two for soft-spoken goodnights and tentative kisses, the couples switched partners with the unspoken consent of all. Timothy ended up with Brenda, because he liked her light brown hair and the handsomeness of her face, even if it did fall short of being absolutely beautiful. Timothy knew he would like to look at that face everyday, perhaps even for the rest of his life.

So Ravi ended up with Gladys, who by all accounts wore too

much make-up, dressed too loudly, and had a nasty streak in her personality. But Ravi wasn't picky back then. *They are all the same in the dark,* as he had liked to say. And most importantly, Gladys met his one mandatory criterion: a verifiable reputation for being sexually uninhibited.

Timothy smiles to himself every time he thinks of that grand switcheroo. He knows he made the right choice, and believes Brenda thinks she did as well. At least, it was the right choice at the time. What would their lives be like now if he had kissed Gladys goodnight instead?

Shudder.

In their cubicles, Timothy and Ravi sit at their desks, looking at each other over the half wall that delineates their workspaces. The only visible difference between their offices is that Ravi's cube has a small window in it, through which he can look out and see a glimpse of blue sky and some greenery through the gap between the adjacent skyscrapers. Ravi, as is his way, never stops pointing this out to Timothy, implying this window is proof his station in the corporate hierarchy is slightly higher than Timothy's.

It is commonly accepted in their department, and in DRI as a whole, that windows are a perk doled out only to the meritorious, even if that window is only slightly larger than the head of the person gazing out of it. Ravi's window is a constant irritant to Timothy, who frequently finds himself trying to glance out of it from afar. Timothy also feels an undeniable sense of shame anytime someone happens to stop by to introduce themselves. Timothy can always see the person's eyes drift over to the window, causing them to assume Ravi is the dominant force in this duo.

Timothy's reverie is broken by his colleague's voice:

"You want to grab some beers after work?" Ravi proposes.

"I can't," Timothy shrugs. "This is pot roast night. It's already in the slow cooker."

"*I* like pot roast," Ravi says, smiling hopefully.

Timothy considers this. He has rebuffed several of Ravi's recent invitations to get together. *What's the point?* he thinks. They see each other all day. Everyday. And when they do go out, they just bitch about work, or even worse, talk about old times. *It's over.* Can't Ravi understand that? Timothy is married, with a teenage son. His lot in life is to trudge home every evening, try not to get too drunk or too angry, and hope dinner is at least palatable.

"Sure," Timothy relents, "but as you know, Brenda can't cook worth crap."

"I won't complain, as long as there's booze and horseradish," Ravi jokes.

"They will both be in abundant supply," Timothy smiles, thinking maybe it will be good for Ravi to come over. Brenda likes him, which will give Timothy a chance to relax, as his wife and his friend get caught up.

As long as Ravi doesn't start asking Brenda if she's spoken to Gladys lately, Timothy stews. Sure, *that should only take about four drinks.*

"Great. Looking forward to it," Ravi says.

"Yes… And now, I've got an ass-load of data to run," Timothy tells him.

"Yeah, me too," Ravi fibs, as they both turn toward their terminals.

Timothy sees a notification on his display and checks his inbox to find a message marked *Confidential.* The subject line makes it apparent the message is about the assessments Denice was talking about. Timothy's instinct is to call over to Ravi to ask if he also received the message. But something inside Timothy causes him to suppress this urge. He was genuinely intrigued by what Dr. Fasten had to say, and he doesn't need Ravi ruining this with his smart-aleck remarks.

Timothy opens the message and reads the technical explanation of how the assessments will be conducted, with specific reference to the concern DRI has for the personal safety of the participants. At the same time, the message explains DRI cannot be held liable in the unlikely event a participant should experience any adverse effects.

At the bottom of the message is a link that once activated will run an application to commence the assessment. The process will be totally interactive, and the Project's supercomputer will remotely take control of the participant's terminal, including its camera and microphone, and will also use ultra-high-intensity heat-mapping to monitor sensory and extra-sensory fluctuations in the participant. The assessment will take a minimum of one hour and may delve into areas of a personal nature. In this respect, it is best to complete the assessment in private to assure personal confidentiality. Furthermore, the assessment requires the undivided attention of the participant, who must be free from distraction and sober in mind and body.

Timothy finishes reading the message and has a strong impulse to launch the application and complete the assessment right then and there. *Why not?* He has nothing to hide.

He looks over at Ravi who has risen from his chair and is peering out his window. Ravi's head is slightly tilted to better see between the buildings that are blocking the setting sun's spectral rays.

Why not just get the assessment over with and make Denice and Lange happy? Timothy asks himself.

But the answer to this, he realizes, has nothing to do with Denice and Lange, and has everything to do with *him.* Because, in response to what Dr. Fasten asked a short while earlier, there are *many* things Timothy would change in his past if he could, many regrets he would put right. Maybe by participating in this assessment, Timothy thinks, he could achieve some small amount of acceptance, or at least understanding, of all those years gone by.

Or maybe the past should be left where it is, safely buried, never to be excavated again. Why would he re-open that Pandora's Box of confusion, error and pain?

Better to wait, he decides, *until I've collected my thoughts.*

"It's magic hour, Tim," Ravi calls over, still looking out his window. "Everything is glowing, like in a dream."

BOOZE AND HORSERADISH

Just after five p.m., Timothy and Ravi walk down to the parking garage, its stale air causing Timothy to experience some mild dizziness, as per usual. He takes a deep breath and the two men get in Timothy's fifteen-year-old Ford, a donation from his brother-in-law. Timothy turns the ignition, and thankfully, after a cough and a belch, the busted old vehicle starts on the second attempt.

"Smooth ride," Ravi deadpans as the vehicle jerks toward the garage's exit.

"Fuel lines are messed up," Timothy tells him. *But who has the money to fix them?* At least Timothy has a car. Ravi was forced to junk his old clunker and take public transit.

Turning on the radio, Timothy and Ravi listen to a station playing current pop music to kill the time. They drive westward along the Gardiner Expressway, which is congested and slow moving, as usual. After several songs, the insipid nature of the music begins to grate on Timothy, who changes to an oldies station playing hits from his youth. He supposes most people like him, in their mid-thirties, think yesterday's music is better than today's.

"This traffic really sucks," Timothy says, breaking the conversational silence as a heavy guitar riff fades out into a maddeningly gleeful radio ad.

"Traffic congestion is the sign of a thriving economy," Ravi says unironically.

"That will be cold comfort if we stall out and have to walk

home."

"Yeah," Ravi mutters. "Story of my life."

An hour later, after hearing countless songs about young love and the importance of living for today, Timothy and Ravi pull into the driveway of Timothy's modest Mimico bungalow. They get out, stretch and make their way inside. The aroma of the pot roast that greets them is pleasing, and gives the house a cozy, almost nostalgic feel.

"That smells great," Ravi admits, realizing he hasn't had a home-cooked meal in who-knows-how-long.

"Yeah, that's the onions and the herbs," Timothy says. "It's hard to ruin pot roast. But we've managed it in the past."

They take off their jackets and make themselves comfortable. Timothy gets them each a locally brewed pale ale. The two friends clink bottlenecks in a toast, and Ravi says:

"To old times."

Oh, no, Timothy thinks. Ravi hasn't even had a sip of beer, and he's already travelling down memory lane, which will inevitably lead to Gladys. Timothy feverishly tries to think of a topic of conversation to bring them back to the present, but he comes up blank.

"Do you ever miss the old days, Tim?" Ravi asks.

"*No, I don't,*" Timothy answers forcefully, surprising Ravi and himself with the conviction in his voice. "What's the point?"

"We were so young," Ravi shrugs. "We had our whole lives ahead of us."

"So why would I miss *that*? We were stupid and *naive and* had no idea what we were doing. It was those two young fools who got us into the *mess* we're in now."

Timothy's statement hangs in the air like an unpleasant odour.

Mess? Ravi repeats to himself, not liking this word choice.

Not that Timothy needs to itemize the issues they are each dealing with, but his mind can't help but summarize their circumstances. They are two men who are no longer what you would call young, trapped in dead end jobs, passed over for advancement, both unhappy with their work. Ravi being divorced with no romantic prospects, and Timothy feeling the strain of not being able to provide his family with the luxuries most men would want them to have.

And of course, Ravi is childless, which is not a great situation for him, as he always saw himself as the patriarch of a large brood, like the one he was raised in. And yes, Timothy is fortunate enough to have a son, but he has to watch as the young man grows more sullen as the years go by. He worries about what the future will hold for Bryan. Will he be outcast from the good life and polite society only the wealthy seem to enjoy?

As these thoughts are churning around in Timothy's and Ravi's minds, the sound of the front door opening announces the arrival of Brenda, who compared to the two sad sacks on the sofa, is the life and soul of the party.

"*Hellooo,*" Brenda calls out from the front hallway, then comes into the living room, still wearing her jacket. "*Mr. Ravi Bargo!*" she says, happy to see their guest. "It's been too long."

Ravi stands up and moves awkwardly toward Brenda, who comes in and hugs him tightly.

"Wow," Timothy remarks. "I don't get a reception like that anymore."

"I see *you* everyday," Brenda tells her husband.

"I love you too," Timothy deadpans, realizing Ravi hasn't been over to the house in three, maybe four years.

Brenda breaks away from Ravi and throws her jacket over a vacant armchair. "Check on the pot roast, will you, Tim? And get me a beer."

"I guess we know who wears the dress in this family," Ravi chuckles.

"Yeah, I guess we do," Timothy shrugs, picking up his beer and heading toward the refrigerator.

After delivering a pale ale to Brenda, Timothy returns to the kitchen, catching a conversational snippet from the others:

"So are you seeing anyone, Ravi?" Brenda asks.

"I'm seeing lots of people," Ravi says. "Mostly in the streets, and in the mall. You know, *strangers,* but I'm *seeing* them."

Timothy busies himself with the pot roast, which has been simmering since that morning. He lifts the lid of the slow cooker, flips the roast and gives the onions and juices a stir. Without warning, the back door opens and his son Bryan comes into the kitchen. His clothes hang off him like a scarecrow's, his hair is unkempt, five days of teenage peach-fuzz is on his face and he smells of low-end cannabis.

Bryan stops dead, and father and son stare at each other, engaging in the stand-off that has become their primary means of non-communication.

"*Yes, Tim?*" Bryan asks aggressively.

"How was school?" his father asks back.

"*Amazing,* why?"

"Where are your books?"

"In my locker."

"No homework?" Timothy presses.

"I got it done during my spare."

"Since when do you have a spare?"

"Since I dropped French."

Timothy replaces the lid on the slow cooker. *What's the point?* he asks himself.

"Uncle Ravi is here," Timothy tells Bryan.

"So what?" Bryan shrugs. "I'll be downstairs. Call me when the beast is edible."

With that, Bryan heads downstairs to his room to get lost in his world of social media, virtual games and porn.

"And no smoking in the house," Timothy says to his son's back as it disappears into the basement.

Timothy walks back into the living room to find Brenda and Ravi sitting on the sofa together. She is excitedly telling him about her working life. Timothy feels like he has heard all her stories a dozen times, even the ones she hasn't told him yet. Ravi smiles like a happy fool, hanging on Brenda's every word. It's all new to him. Timothy waits for an appropriate juncture to tell his wife their son is home, but then decides not to ruin her flow. She is enjoying having an appreciative audience for once.

Timothy sits back on the adjacent loveseat and takes a sip of his pale ale. He listens with mild interest as Ravi and Brenda exchange stories, both of them smiling and full of delight. From the basement, Timothy can hear the muffled sounds of Bryan's virtual games: gunfire, explosions, heavy machinery and the piercing screams of death. Timothy finishes the last of his beer and figures he will grab another round for everyone in a moment or two.

If this is as good as it gets, he thinks, *I might as well enjoy it.*

*

Later, the pot roast has been eaten and the dirty dishes lie uncleared on the dining room table. Timothy, Brenda and Ravi once again sit comfortably in the living room, having switched from ale to Timothy's prized eighteen-year-old Canadian whisky. Earlier, Bryan had grudgingly emerged from his subterranean domain to fix himself a dinner plate, which he promptly took back downstairs, after hastily greeting *Uncle Ravi*, whom he referred to in his mind as *Uncle Fucky.*

The meal has settled pleasantly in everyone's stomachs, and

all are glowing contentedly. The lights have been dimmed and the ambience is gentle. Not meaning to ruin the mood, but doing so anyway, Brenda asks Ravi,

"So what's happening at work?"

Ravi is mildly stumped by this, as an honest answer would be, *I have no clue. I don't really pay much attention.*

But instead, Ravi defers by saying, "I'm sure you get enough shop-talk from Tim."

"Tim doesn't tell me *shit*," Brenda drunkenly corrects him.

"Oh," Ravi says, then deflecting to Timothy, "Why don't you tell Brenda shit, Tim?"

"What's there to tell? Just a lot of boring data analysis," Tim defends himself. "And we *do* have NDAs in place."

"Screw your NDAs," Brenda retorts, at least one whisky over her limit. "It's not like you're in the secret service."

Ravi bursts out with a hearty laugh.

"What's so funny?" Brenda demands to know.

"You nailed it, Bren!" Ravi bellows. "We're into some *real secret agent shit!*"

"*Secret agent shit?*" Brenda grimaces at Timothy. "*What's* all that about?"

"It's nothing," Timothy tells her. "Just some stupid thing our manager said."

"You see *that,* Ravi?" Brenda says accusingly. "After all these years, he won't even trust me with his precious company secrets."

Timothy shakes his head in disbelief, not because his wife is turning on him – after all, it *is* that time of the evening for them to have their obligatory argument – but because she is actually showing an interest in his work.

"Okay, *spill* it, Bargo," Brenda demands of Ravi. "If Tim won't tell me, *you* will. *Fess up,*" she slurs.

"Well," Ravi begins, gathering his thoughts, "it *is* kind of interesting, now that I think about it."

"Go on," Brenda coaxes, turning her gaze exclusively toward her old friend.

"Well, when I first saw the message about the Project, I dismissed it immediately," Ravi says. "They are seeking internal research subjects who wish to *improve their satisfaction with life,* or some such garbage."

"What is this, some new kind of happy pill?" Brenda asks.

"DRI doesn't do pharmacological research," Timothy butts in.

Brenda turns partially toward her husband and says pointedly, "Ravi and I are trying to have a conversation."

"Oh, just pretend I'm not here," Timothy snipes.

"I'm *trying*," Brenda snipes back. Then, turning back toward Ravi, "Go on, honey."

"It's no big deal," Ravi frowns mildly. "DRI has always used its employees for focus groups. To keep things *internal.*"

"*Uh huh*," Brenda hums, enjoying the sound of Ravi's voice.

"But this is the first time, to my knowledge anyway, they want to use us as *test subjects*," Ravi says with disdain.

"Human *lab rats*," Brenda slurs again.

Yes, that is exactly correct, everyone thinks to themselves. *Human lab rats.*

This thought is momentarily sobering, causing the partiers to become reflective. They leisurely finish their whiskies in silence, then Brenda pours out another generous shot for everyone.

"And," Ravi says pensively, "the assessments are *mandatory.* Every employee has to take one."

"They can't *force* you to participate!" Brenda shrieks.

"But they're being so *nice* about it," Ravi says sarcastically. "*Successful parties are invited to participate in further testing.*"

"*Invited?*" Brenda scoffs. "Gee, thanks."

"Yeah, more like, *Take the assessment or get suspended,*" Ravi complains.

"No fucking way!" Brenda scowls.

"I'm going to get out of it," Ravi confides. "I know a guy in I.T. He can screw with the records."

"*Good,*" Brenda says, relieved. And then, after a moment, "But *what* are they assessing for?"

"That's the million-dollar question," Ravi answers confidently.

"What's the million-dollar answer?" Brenda asks.

"Oh, uh…" Ravi mumbles, his mind a complete blank. "Retro-*something.*"

"Huh?" Brenda grunts, looking for her glass of whisky without immediate success.

"Retro-causality," Timothy says plainly.

The others turn to look at him, staring dumbly, as if they had forgotten he was there.

In an instant, Timothy senses that somehow a door has opened in his mind, revealing some archaic knowledge he did not know he still had. He hears himself saying words which flow from him effortlessly:

"In quantum theory, there's no proof time moves in only one direction," Timothy says. "As per John Wheeler's wave-particle experiments, matter can be witnessed moving both backward as well as forward in time."

"Well somebody's been studying for the exam," Ravi jokes.

"Hold on," Brenda says, shutting down any humour left in the situation. "How can matter moving back and forth improve your *satisfaction with life*?"

"By changing the past," Timothy tells her.

"*Well,*" Brenda admits, "who wouldn't want to do that?"

"*Exactly,*" Timothy says, finally putting it all together and wondering if DRI could actually accomplish this.

Ravi glances over at Timothy and sees a certain look on his face. And he knows exactly what that look means.

"Tim, you aren't going to take the assessment, are you?" Ravi asks.

"It *is* mandatory," Timothy reminds him.

"Screw that," Ravi pushes back. "This is probably some kind of employee surveillance exercise."

"And what would be the purpose of that?" Timothy asks, feeling his annoyance level rising.

"I don't know," Ravi says, searching for a response. "To squeeze more work out of us, I suppose."

"Is that what you're worried about? Having to actually *work* for your salary?" Timothy asks, to no one's amusement.

"And I suppose I should be a spineless company man like you?" Ravi mocks.

"We both signed employment contracts," Timothy argues.

"But I didn't sign my whole *life* away," Ravi emphasizes. "When are you going to start thinking for yourself? DRI has never done you any favours. You don't even have a *window* in your cubicle."

Timothy's blood begins to pump faster, increasing steadily. He feels his face getting hot and his ears burn.

"*That is supposed to be my window, and you know it,*" Timothy seethes.

"I don't think so, buddy," Ravi insists.

"I *let* you *have* that window on our first day," Timothy says.

"I *earned* that window," Ravi argues.

"Doing what? Fucking the dog?" Timothy blurts out.

What follows is an uneasy silence, broken by Brenda:

"That was rude," she says to no one in particular.

Ravi stands, and with careful steps makes his way to the front door. "Have a nice weekend," he says bitterly over his shoulder.

Brenda gets off the sofa and scurries after Ravi, helping find his jacket. The two exchange some softly spoken words Timothy cannot make out. He does however see his wife give Ravi a goodbye hug and a kiss on the cheek that is a little too tender.

After Ravi leaves and the front door is locked behind him, Brenda comes back into the living room. She gives Timothy a disappointed look, pours more liquor into her glass, then heads toward their bedroom. Timothy hears the click of the latch as she locks the door.

Sitting in the quietness, Timothy enjoys a final sip of the aged alcohol in his glass. He looks at the bottle on the coffee table and sees it is empty. Not a drop of the eighteen-year-old whisky is left. Those eighteen years are now a forgotten memory, he thinks.

There are no sounds from his wife in their bedroom, and none from his son downstairs, who has perhaps fallen asleep with his headphones on. Timothy looks around his bungalow and takes in its drabness: the old worn furniture, the faded walls, the inexpensive prints and decorations bought second hand or donated by friends.

It's enough to make you give up, Timothy thinks, suddenly falling into a mood of despair.

He ironically reminds himself he can always take advantage of the growing availability of doctor-assisted end-of-life management.

It's a wonderful time to be alive, he jokes.

Unfortunately, he knows he will probably live to be a healthy and miserable ninety-nine years old.

It's unnatural, he thinks. *Humans weren't meant to live that long. You can probably keep your enthusiasm up for about forty years tops, then it's all downhill. A long, slow slide into hopelessness…*

Feeling an impending panic attack, Timothy starts breathing slowly and deeply to calm himself. In. Out. In. Out… Then once his heart rate drops down closer to normal, Dr. Fasten's words come back to him:

If you could change anything in your past, what would it be?

What *would* it be? Timothy asks himself.

And then, in his half-drunken state, it all finally starts to make sense to him. DRI is offering to change a person's past. At least in their minds. And by changing their past, they will give that person some hope for the future.

Maybe Brenda is right, Timothy thinks. Maybe it *is* a happy pill, even if it is an electronic one.

People need something to take their minds off the sorry state of the world. The daily news alone is enough to crush the spirit of even the most optimistic person. Nothing but an unending barrage of hatefulness and stupidity. Ineffectual politicians making bad decisions in the name of the fools who voted them in. And doing absolutely nothing about economic disparity, humanitarian crises, and the natural disasters plaguing the globe.

If you could change anything…

Maybe, Timothy tells himself tentatively, if the Project achieves some level of success, maybe he, *Tim Koops,* will be able to benefit from it. Maybe in some small way he will be able to change his own life. Because in the quiet moments such as these, when he is alone with his thoughts and has the courage to be honest with himself, Timothy knows he wants more out of life than his current life can provide.

Timothy finishes the last drops of his whisky then gets up. He walks over to the dining room and picks up his old terminal, which is resting on the sideboard and is covered in a thin coat of dust. He places the terminal on the dining table and engages the power button. As its operating system is out-of-date, it takes a couple of minutes for the terminal to boot up. Once everything is working, Timothy logs into his account and enters his authentication code, which he is surprised he remembers, as he hasn't logged in from home in many months.

He finds the portal for the assessment, enters it and reads the instructions, which inform him that his terminal will be remotely taken over by the Project's supercomputer. There is a warning that the assessment may cause discomfort, disorientation and have some lingering negative effects.

Funny, Dr. Fasten or Denice didn't mention *that* part.

Finally, the instructions recommend abstaining from alcohol and recreational drugs before participating in the assessment.

Too late for that, Timothy snickers, assuring himself he has enough of his wits about him to proceed. He is just feeling relaxed, not in any way inebriated. Or at least, not so very much so.

Hopefully, this is just going to be a simple true or false quiz, Timothy tells himself, wondering if his old clunker of a terminal will even be able to handle the ultra-high-intensity heat-mapping mentioned earlier.

Only one way to find out, I guess.

As Timothy lifts his index finger and is about to press the *Begin Assessment* tab on his terminal's display, he asks himself one last time, *Am I really that desperate to change my life?*

In answer to this question, Timothy points his finger weapon-like and decisively engages the *Begin Assessment* tab. The application loads and Timothy watches as the terminal begins emitting a strong light, powerful but not unpleasant.

After a few seconds, Timothy's field of vision becomes washed out, and all he can see is an expanse of brilliant white, with undertones of every hue of the spectrum. He stands and tentatively backs up a few feet, not able to clearly make out his surroundings. He begins to become disoriented and reminds himself he is at home, safe and secure.

The light from the terminal eventually diminishes and Timothy can once again see his dining room in clear focus. The resolution of the terminal's display is much higher than normal, perhaps higher than it is capable of. *But there it is.* And as he looks around his dining room, his domestic illuminants appear to be emitting stronger and clearer light than usual, filling him with a warmth and a calmness. He feels a vibration deep inside him, then a low hum fills his senses, and his whole being is imbued with an inner peace.

From the display, an avatar emerges. A face, friendly and welcoming. It is the face of a woman of indeterminate ethnicity, with long dark hair hanging in tidy waves. The face is youthful, yet with an inherent maturity about it. The young woman's glowing jade-green eyes look intently at Timothy, as if they are looking *into* him.

How can she see me? Timothy wonders, because for security reasons the camera aperture on his terminal is covered by opaque tape.

"Hello, Timothy," the avatar says, its voice tinged with a synthetic tone.

"Hi," Timothy replies inarticulately. "Is this the assessment?"

The eyes of the avatar continue to peer into Timothy's face, but upon speaking, only its lips move, betraying the artificiality of the image.

"What is the first thing you remember?" the avatar asks him.

Timothy feels the low hum inside him get stronger, which makes him feel both light-headed and clear of mind.

"I'm not sure," Timothy says. "I was on the sofa…"

"Think back, Timothy," the avatar instructs. "You are a small child."

"Okay, *I'm a small child,*" Timothy repeats, beginning to regret engaging the *Begin Assessment* tab after all.

Then something happens.

Timothy's vision gradually grows murky, until it fades into complete darkness. And then a new vista slowly emerges, bright and sun filled. Timothy can see he is sitting in a baby stroller. The canopy is over his head, with small tassels hanging from it. His puffy baby hands are holding onto the guardrail that is secured in place above his chubby thighs. He can hear his mother's hard-soled shoes clacking against the pavement as she pushes the stroller. He recognizes the intersection of the street he is on as Lake Shore and Superior…

"Go back farther, Timothy," the avatar tells him.

"Farther than *what*?" he wonders. "Is this part of the assessment?" he asks again as his vision darkens once more and then presents a new vista.

Timothy can sense that he is an infant lying in his crib. He sees the cracked and water-stained ceiling above him, and the colourful mobile hanging from a wire, twisting and turning gently on the currents produced by the ventilation system. He recognizes the wooden slats of his crib, which pen him in. He will soon be able to climb out of this baby prison, he recalls with glee. But not now. Now his legs aren't working. He is flat on his back, looking up at the ever-present ceiling. He can't get up. The gravity is too strong. It is like he is a heavy piece of metal stuck fast to a powerful magnet.

"How far back can you go, Timothy?" a voice asks.

"*I don't know,*" Timothy responds somehow.

"What is the first thing you remember?"

Again, Timothy's field of vision goes dark. Deep velvety red. With a soft diffused glow. The pounding of a faint beat is heard, getting louder, and a voice, female, muffled as if coming through water. Timothy feels completely at peace, content, blissful. Unaware. Unknowing. No language. No sensation. No thought. Nothingness.

Then a short, sharp blast of brightness and an ear-shattering *boom,* and Timothy is back in his dining room.

What the fuck was that? he asks himself.

The room is in total darkness, save for the light filtering in from the street.

The breakers must have been tripped, he thinks.

He looks over at his terminal, which is dead. There is the smoky smell of burnt circuitry.

Well that's just fucking great, he curses to himself. *All the old family photos are on that terminal. What a perfect end to a perfectly shitty day.*

Overwhelmed by a deep body fatigue and the effects of too much whisky, Timothy slouches over to the sofa and passes out for the night.

CRYSTAL BEACH

The next morning, Timothy wakes up feeling refreshed. *Saturday morning*, he thinks happily. The sun is shining in through the translucent blinds of his bedroom window. He stretches mightily and groans satisfiedly. He can smell the luxurious aroma of fresh coffee and breakfast being fried on the stovetop. *Sweet Saturday.*

Where am I?

Timothy looks around at his surroundings and wonders how he managed to end up in his own bed. The last thing he remembers, his eyes were nearly blinded, the lights were blown and he was face down on the sofa. He gets up, puts on his housecoat and walks into the kitchen. Brenda is at the stove, looking pleasantly tousled.

"Good morning, sleepyhead," she chirps.

"*Sure,*" Timothy mumbles noncommittally, moving to the coffeemaker and pouring himself a cup, adding some sugar and cream.

"Are you hungry, babe?" Brenda smiles.

"Starving," Timothy responds. He takes a sip of his coffee, which tastes smooth and sweet and goes down easily.

"Go have a seat. I'll fix you a plate," Brenda says.

Hearing his son's familiar movements, Timothy walks into the living room where Bryan is sitting on the sofa, using Timothy's old terminal.

"*You're* up early," Timothy needles his son.

"It's *ten o'clock*!" Bryan laughs with a snort. "I've been up for two hours."

"Is that *my* terminal?" Timothy asks.

"Mine's downloading a new app," Bryan says. "It's taking forever."

"Is my terminal working okay?" Timothy wonders.

"This model's a warhorse," Bryan tells him. "Probably last forever, Dad."

Dad? Timothy is surprised to hear this. Bryan hasn't called him *Dad* since he was twelve.

Timothy sits beside his son and glances at the terminal, which is working just fine. But what is Bryan doing? On the display, against an animated background, there is a muscular knight wielding a sword and shield, an evil-looking sorcerer in black robes shooting fire from his fingers, and a curvaceous, scantily clad woman bound in chains.

"What's *that*?" he asks his son.

"Just a virtual game, Dad. *Relax.*"

Timothy regards the action on the display more closely and sees there is a series of numerical problems scrolling along the top of the screen.

"Is that *math*?" Timothy asks almost scoldingly.

"Yeah," Bryan says, puzzled at his father's tone. "The knight solves the equations to beat the wizard and free the princess. If he can answer all the questions correctly, her chains snap off and her robe falls down, so you get to see her boobs."

Timothy takes a few seconds to absorb this. His son can see naked girls online anytime he feels like it, but instead, he is willing to solve several math problems to see an animated character drop her robe.

Whatever, he decides. *It's a step in the right direction.*

"Here's your breakfast, Tim," Brenda says, putting down a

plate of food on the dining room table.

Timothy gets off the sofa and goes to the dining room, where he sees a nicely presented breakfast laid out for him of scrambled eggs, sausages, home fries, and tomato and basil salad, along with a knife and a fork rolled in a cloth napkin.

"Would you like a glass of orange juice?" Brenda asks cheerfully. "I'm making some freshly squeezed."

"Thank you. That would be wonderful," Timothy says, wondering when everyone started being so polite around the breakfast table.

Sitting down, and digging into his food, Timothy tries to pinpoint the unfamiliar feeling he is experiencing. After a few bites of sausage and egg, he realizes the strange sensation is *relaxation.* It feels pretty good. Looking around, he sees the house seems more *homey* than usual. Everything is in its place, the floors look dust free, and the greasy film on the windows has disappeared.

"*Yes!*" Bryan exclaims triumphantly, pumping a fist in the air. "The boobs have been revealed!"

More good news, Timothy smirks to himself. *When will it end?*

Brenda enters the dining room and places an iced glass of orange juice on a coaster in front of Timothy.

"It was so nice to have a friend over last night," Brenda says happily, sitting at the table.

"*A friend?*" Timothy repeats. "You mean *Ravi?*"

"A bit of company can cheer a person up," Brenda says.

You mean, a bit of grab-ass at the front door? Timothy thinks, but instead says, "He's okay, I guess."

"You *guess?*" Brenda exclaims. "You've been friends for almost twenty years."

"Not quite," Timothy disagrees. "We were really only friends for the first five years. The rest has been—"

He is about to say *like a bad marriage* but stops himself.

"I'm just glad you had some fun," Timothy smiles stiffly.

"We should have people over more often," Brenda suggests.

Timothy is genuinely shocked by this one. His wife usually considers having people over to be one big pain in the tenderest part of her ass.

"Who would we have over?" Timothy wonders. "We don't even know anybody we like."

"Then let's make some new friends," Brenda says cheerfully. "It's good to have a wide social circle."

"You didn't sign up for another networking seminar, did you?" Timothy asks suspiciously.

"No, *goofball,*" she chides. "Everyone knows your circle of influence is the best asset you can ever have."

Timothy can't argue with this, and he doesn't want his breakfast to get cold, so he nods agreeably at his wife and shovels a forkful of eggs and potatoes into his mouth.

The momentary quiet is broken by the low trill of Timothy's phone.

"I'll get it," Brenda offers, springing out of the kitchen and going to Timothy's jacket in the front hallway. She fishes out his phone and tells Timothy, "It's Lange."

Fuck, Timothy thinks.

Brenda answers the phone, "Hello, Marc… Yes, he is. Just one minute." She hands the phone to Timothy with an innocent *here-you-go-dear* look on her face.

Putting down his fork and answering the phone with a frown, Timothy says, "Tim here. What's up?"

Brenda takes this as her cue to give her husband some space, so she heads into the living room and sits across from her son, who is still deep into his mathematical mammaries.

"*Tim,*" Lange says smoothly, "I'm so glad I got hold of you."

"Sure, Marc, what can I do for you?" Timothy offers, not wanting to do anything for him or anybody else. *It's fucking Saturday, Marc.*

"What are you doing now?" Marc asks, "Can we meet for coffee?"

"I've already had my coffee," Timothy tells his manager with uncharacteristic brusqueness.

"*Right,*" Lange laughs politely. "How about I come over to your place."

"Marc," Timothy says, "my family is sitting around in their pj's. If you have something to tell me, just say it."

"Oh, okay, Tim. No problem. I wanted to discuss this with you in person, as a professional courtesy. But, sure, I understand."

Since when has Lange understood anything except his own ambition? Timothy thinks.

"First of all, I would just like to *thank* you," Lange says, slowly inching toward the matter at hand.

For what? Timothy wonders. *Just spit it out, Lange.*

"The Veep was impressed when you volunteered to take the assessment."

"*Volunteered?*" Timothy says loudly. "I thought it was *mandatory?*"

"Regardless," Lange tells him, "you showed true initiative. And let's just say, the Veep has taken notice. She just might mention your name to the Board."

"Hold on," Timothy demands. "Are you saying I didn't *have* to take the assessment?"

"I know," Lange says, trying to sound sympathetic. "If things were a bit rough on your terminal, DRI will replace any equipment that may have been damaged."

"The terminal is the least of my worries," Timothy tells his manager.

"Good, good," Lange almost sings.

"That assessment almost split my mind in two," Timothy complains.

"The preliminary results have been very promising," Lange is happy to report.

"I thought I was losing my shit!" Timothy roars, immediately embarrassed by his outburst.

"If you have to take any time off, just let me know," Lange assures him.

"How about *today?*" Timothy shoots back.

"Well put," Lange chuckles briefly. "But seriously, I'm going to have to ask you to do a little something for me. For the *company*, actually."

"I thought I already *did.*"

"Yes, you did. But the assessment is in two parts," Lange says dryly.

Fuck that, Timothy thinks, wishing he had the nerve to say so.

"Of course, there *will* be a financial incentive," Lange is pleased to tell him.

"*Really?*" Timothy says, suddenly becoming interested.

"Funding's already been allocated," Lange informs him. "One week of extra pay per session."

"That's *sweet,*" Timothy says, liking the sound of this. But then, "What do you mean *per session*? I thought it was just a two-part assessment?"

"Take as many sessions as you want," Lange says. "Once we commercialize this, people will be paying big bucks for it. So if you find the sessions to be beneficial, keep taking them."

"And I get one week's extra pay per session?" Timothy confirms.

"That's right. And you can take some time off, like I said, if you need to recuperate in any way."

"*Hmmn*," is all Timothy can say, as it's a lot for him to absorb.

The money would of course be great. And the time off work would be a total bonus. Get a break from Lange's nose up his ass everyday. And who knows? The sessions may do him some good. Because if anyone needs to improve their satisfaction with life, it's Timothy Koops.

"Okay, thanks, Marc," Timothy reassures his manager. "I'm going to give this some serious consideration. I'll give you my answer on Monday."

"Whoa, Tim, hold on," Lange says with concern. "You're kind of missing the boat a little bit here. Part two is *tomorrow*. Twelve noon. At the Righton Centre."

"I don't even know where that is," Timothy says feebly.

"No worries, I'll send you the details," Lange assures him.

"But I, uh…" Timothy mumbles, trying to think of what to say.

"It's all set up and the wheels are in motion. Dr. Fasten will be waiting for you," Lange tells him. "Now I've got to call Denice. She's going to be very pleased. Thanks so much, Tim."

Lange hangs up, and Timothy sits at the dining room table wondering what he has just signed himself up for. He looks over at Brenda and Bryan in the living room sitting on the sofa, both now reading books. He can see Brenda is reading a cookbook. *Healthy and Delicious Home Cuisine Made Easy.* Strange, he thinks. He has never seen Brenda read a cookbook before. He didn't even know they had any cookbooks in the house.

And Bryan is intently reading a book called *How to Game the Game,* which is also strange. Timothy hasn't seen Bryan read a book since he was ten years old, and that one was mostly pictures, involving a gang of dogs and cats who open a lemonade stand. So Timothy can't help but abandon his breakfast and head into the living room to ask his son, "Bryan, what's that you're reading?"

"It's a book about game theory," Bryan tells him.

"Oh," Timothy says, "is that for your virtual games?"

"*Virtual games*?" Bryan scoffs with a laugh. "This is next level metaphysics, Dad."

"And what is *that,* exactly?" Timothy asks hopelessly.

Bryan looks at him incredulously and explains, "Being, knowing, cause, identity, time, space. You know, all the things that make up reality."

"*Sure,*" Timothy nods, wishing he had a better response for his usually reticent son.

"Okay, you don't get it. So let's take it from the top," Bryan says, full of enthusiasm. "The first thing about Game Theory is, you have to know when you're in a game. And you have to know what game you're playing. Like, what are the rules? You can apply this to almost every minute of your life. Which is why I'm glad as shit I kept up with my algebra."

"Since when?" Timothy asks, totally surprised by this.

"He got an A minus on his last report," Brenda scolds her husband.

"Did I see that report?" Timothy wonders.

"Well, you *signed* it, Tim," Brenda reminds him.

"Like I was saying," Bryan continues, as if he's discovered the secret to the universe, "game theory forces you to think mathematically."

"And you're *doing* that?" Timothy asks.

"Dad, math is life," Bryan insists. "Everything we know, and everything we do, has its basis in mathematical modelling. Math can be used to solve just about any problem in the world."

"Good to know," Timothy smiles, wanting to support his son's newfound interest, but not having a clue how to do that.

"I'll let you get back to it then."

Timothy walks back to his half-eaten breakfast, but no longer has any appetite. He puts some plastic wrap on it and figures he'll finish it later. His coffee has grown cold and the ice cubes have melted in his juice. Might as well drink it anyway, he thinks. As he is about to take a sip of the watery juice, he sees that his terminal has been returned to its usual resting place on the sideboard. He starts to think about the previous evening's assessment. Some of the details are foggy, as a dream becomes upon waking. But one memory that burns through the fog is that the family photos may have been damaged or deleted.

I'd like to see Lange replace those photos. He'd need a big fucking allocation to recreate all those precious family memories.

Timothy puts the terminal on the dining table, takes a seat and boots up the machine. He then searches the terminal's directory for the folder containing the family photos. It is there, which is a relief. As Timothy scrolls through the subfolders, he sees that someone has changed all of their names. *Summer Vacations*, for example, is now titled *Summer Getaways.*

Sounds like a travel ad, he thinks.

Clicking on the *Getaways* subfolder, Timothy notices all the sub-subfolders have also had their names changed. He wonders why Brenda or Bryan would go to the trouble of changing the names of the folders he spent so much time setting up. It makes no sense. And that's how pictures get misfiled and potentially lost, he steams.

Timothy can still recognize many of the folders, but others are a total mystery to him, such as the folder labelled *Crystal Beach*. Why would they have a folder named *Crystal Beach?* They have never even been there.

Are these someone else's photos?

Timothy opens the folder and starts viewing the pictures, to his immediate confusion. The photos are of him, Brenda and

Bryan. They are on a beach, with a lot of other people in the background, everyone enjoying the sun and water. Bryan looks a couple of years younger than he is now. There are many pictures of them posing like a happy family, and a few shots of just Timothy and Brenda, looking *happy* and in love.

I don't remember this getaway, Timothy thinks.

Maybe the assessment fried part of Timothy's memory and wiped out the remembrance of this trip.

But I've never been to Crystal Beach, Timothy insists to himself. *I don't even know how to get there. This must be a different beach.*

As Timothy keeps flicking through the pictures, he comes across one of himself, standing alone. He looks pleased as he clowns for the camera in front of a sign that reads, *Welcome to Crystal Beach. The South Coast of Canada.*

"That was a lovely getaway," Brenda says, looking over Timothy's shoulder.

Timothy looks at his wife, not sure if she is pulling some elaborate prank on him.

"What year was this?" he asks.

"It was two summers ago," Brenda tells him.

Bryan, who has put down his book, comes over to look at the display. "I love those Crystal Beach pics," he says.

Timothy regards his family closely, trying to detect any hint of deception. Finding none, he feels as though he has no choice but to tell them the truth:

"I've never been to Crystal Beach."

Brenda and Bryan find this to be funny and break into spontaneous laughter.

"And I've never been to the mall!" Brenda jokes nonsensically.

"Yeah, Dad," Bryan chokes out. "We went to Crystal Beach like ten summers in a row. And how many times have you told us your father used to take you there. It's only your favourite place on Earth, for crissake!"

Timothy stares at his wife and son and brings a forced smile to his face. He isn't remotely sure what's going on, but either he's going crazy, or his family is. Whichever the case, when he sees Dr. Fasten the next day, the man is going to have some major explaining to do.

DR. ZAKERY FASTEN

Sunday morning, the most peaceful morning of the week, a morning when no bad thoughts are ever had. With Brenda still fast asleep beside him, Timothy slowly rouses himself from the pleasant dream he is having:

He is a young boy visiting the amusement park at Crystal Beach with his parents. How he loves those getaways. Riding The Comet roller coaster with his dad while his mother watches from the solid ground below. She is such a chicken, he thinks, she won't even go on the Ferris wheel. But there is a lot more to the park than just the rides. There are Crystal Beach Sugar Waffles to gorge on, and ice-cold bottles of PJ's Crystal Beach Loganberry, a drink you can only get at the park, and famous all over Southern Ontario and Western New York State. And of course, there is the beach itself, aptly named for its crystal-clear waters and fine abundant sands.

Timothy's father used to tell him about how his own father took him to Crystal Beach many times. In Grandpa's day, there used to be sideshow attractions with fire eaters, sword swallowers, a man wearing only a loincloth who would lie on a bed of sharpened nails, and another man who would sit in an electric chair and receive a full jolt of current. Timothy's grandfather Jan used to tell stories of seeing exhibitions of a five-legged dog, a two-headed cow, a real mummy that was only five feet tall, and a Chupacabra, which was a Mexican lizardman with pointed teeth and a body covered in scales and spikes, who lived off the blood of goats.

Even after the amusement park closed down, Timothy still

loved going to Crystal Beach for the memories, and for the beach itself, which is the best beach within a two-hour drive of Toronto. Just take the QEW toward Fort Erie, then turn off down Highway 116 and keep driving until you see the water. How many times did he and Brenda go there before Bryan came along? And Bryan really enjoyed going there too – especially their mandatory stops at Willy's Burger Shack near Port Dalhousie – until he got too old to hang out with his parents anymore.

So many memories, Timothy thinks. So many acquaintances made along the way. Such happy times gone by.

Timothy's alarm rings, and for a moment he wonders why he even set it to ring on a Sunday morning. Then he remembers, he has to meet Dr. Zakery Fasten for the second part of his assessment. And there is something he is supposed to discuss with Dr. Fasten. Something he is supposed to ask him about. But for the life of him, Timothy can't remember what it is.

Oh, well, it probably wasn't that important.

Timothy gets out of bed, careful not to wake Brenda who is sleeping in and snoring lightly. He showers and shaves, grabs a quick coffee and a piece of toast with cream cheese, and then makes his way toward the decommissioned Righton Rehabilitation Centre. It is way up in North York, which is a long and inconvenient drive from Mimico. At least Timothy's old Ford is cooperating and giving no indication it will malfunction, as it has done a few times in the recent past.

That would be just great, he thinks. If he misses his appointment, he will be summarily called into Lange's office on Monday morning. And that hairless dick will recite the entire company manifesto to him, reminding him of his duty to uphold corporate standards and always strive for constant improvement, and especially never to miss an important meeting for the number one project the company is working on.

Timothy checks his watch and is glad he is making good time.

As he drives, his mind drifts automatically to Ravi, who he supposes is probably still in bed, dreaming happily about cavorting in an idyllic meadow with a bunch of bluebirds and half-naked girls.

Let him dream his life away, Timothy thinks. Let him slack off at work and share embraces with my wife. Ravi will get his, Timothy tells himself. He'll end up old and alone. And in the meantime, Lange will get pissed at him for not taking the assessment and make him squirm until he's nothing but a bundle of frayed nerves fearing for his job.

Sooner than expected, Timothy arrives at the Righton Centre. There are no cars in the parking lot, whose asphalt is cracked and trash-strewn from years of neglect. Timothy parks between faded white lines painted on the ground, wondering to himself where the staff at the facility park *their* cars. He gets out of his Ford and walks up to the main entrance of the building, which is retrofitted with up-to-date technology, looking bright and shiny against the rest of the drab weather-beaten complex.

Timothy is surprised to see a hand printed sign written on office paper and taped to the inside of the translucent front doors. After reading the printed instructions, Timothy turns and looks into the security camera and states his name in a loud, clear voice:

"Tim Koops."

After a second, he hears the camera focus in on him, and then an indicator light flashes and the doors unlock.

When he enters the building, Timothy finds there is no one present, just an empty foyer and several empty corridors. His eyes catch another hand printed sign taped to a post, welcoming him *(Dear Participant)* with a scribbled arrow pointing him down a corridor. Following a series of signs, Timothy comes to an old-fashioned reception area, a remnant from the complex's previous incarnation as a rehab centre. There is no one sitting at the reception desk, no way to be sure this is the correct room.

Timothy looks around for any confirmation he is where he's supposed to be, but there is not even another hand printed sign to assure him he's not lost in an abandoned maze.

He is about to leave the reception area when a terminal affixed to the old reception desk comes to life. On the display is the image of a young long-haired woman who looks somewhat familiar to him.

"Hello, Timothy," the image of the woman says. "I'm glad you're here."

"Oh, thank you," Timothy replies, as if addressing a real live person. "Who are you?"

The display freezes and the image on the screen becomes immobile. The long-haired woman just stares icily into Timothy's eyes. Something about her face makes Timothy flash back momentarily to Friday night, just before the lights went out.

"I would like to thank you for taking part in our research project," the image of the woman continues, now unfrozen. "If successful, our work will help increase the quality of human life on our planet."

"Oh?" Timothy says, regarding the image of the woman closely. "That's ambitious."

The image of the woman blinks her gleaming green eyes, as a real woman would. And she delicately wets her reddened lips with the tip of her tongue.

"One metric we are particularly aiming to improve," the woman continues, "is the prevalence of clinical depression in highly developed societies."

"Really?" Timothy says with some interest.

"Did you know the annual cost of depression globally is several trillion US dollars?"

"No, I didn't," Timothy says aloud, filling the air with a human voice.

"Just think what we could accomplish," the woman says, "if everyone took a step forward, like you did Timothy, and sought out the treatment they needed."

Timothy again scrutinizes the image of the woman, with her luminous jade eyes and pleasant smiling demeanor. Is she programed to keep talking to kill time, or is she actually *conversing* with him?

"Is this the assessment?" Timothy asks the woman. "Or am I going to eventually speak to a *real* person?"

The image of the woman on the display appears to frown slightly. After a quick moment, she responds, "Please have a seat. Dr. Fasten will see you shortly."

With that, the display switches to an image of the DRI logo, and soothing synthesized music begins playing. Timothy briefly considers maybe he has insulted the woman on the display. But how could that be possible? She isn't human. She can't *feel*, only respond.

"*Hello*," the voice from behind Timothy calls, causing him to turn abruptly.

"Timothy Koops?" the man in a white lab coat asks. He is tallish, thin and looks simultaneously youthful and professional, with receding blond hair and wearing clear plastic eyeglasses.

"Yes," Timothy replies. "I'm Timothy Koops. Everyone just calls me *Tim*."

"I am Dr. Zakery Fasten," the man says, not offering his hand.

"Nice to meet you," Timothy says vaguely. "Pretty lean operation you've got going on here. What's with the handmade signage?"

"We have a wayfinder robot that is supposed to escort our subjects," Dr. Fasten says, indicating a white mechanical figure slumped in a corner of the room. It is quasi humanoid in shape with a cubic base on wheels.

"I thought that was an air-conditioner," Timothy says.

"That would at least be of *some* use," Dr. Fasten says with reserved irritation.

For no apparent reason, the wayfinder lifts its robotic head and says in a distorted electronic voice, "*This way, please.*"

"That's okay, Columbus," Dr. Fasten tells the wayfinder. "I'll handle this."

Dr. Fasten nods briefly at Timothy and leads him into an adjoining room, which matches the previous room in its generic outdated decor and lack of any personalization.

"Have a seat," Dr. Fasten tells Timothy.

Once Timothy is seated in a standard black visitor's chair and Dr. Fasten is seated across from him, Dr. Fasten asks, "Do you have any questions before we begin?"

"Yes," Timothy says bluntly. "What's the story behind this set-up? It doesn't really feel like DRI."

"Well it *is*," Dr. Fasten reassures him. "But a bit of a skunkworks all the same."

Timothy doesn't know what this means, as his expression clearly telegraphs.

"An independent project," Dr. Fasten explains, "funded by DRI, but autonomous. At least for now."

"So you report to Denice Button," Timothy assumes.

"I report to the *Board*," Dr. Fasten says with a haughty air. "Or at least I *will*, once the first phase of my work is complete. Right now, it's all about *me*."

Starting to feel some regret about his participation in this mysterious undertaking, Timothy asks, "How many other people have done the assessment?"

Dr. Fasten looks at Timothy blankly. "I don't believe we should entertain questions of that nature. They tend to prejudice a subject's responses. You have nothing to prove here, Timothy. You will not be judged against the performance of other participants. And your results will of course be kept confidential."

That's not really what I was asking, Timothy thinks, but decides to move on to his next question:

"What's the *purpose* of all this? Is this leading to some kind of therapeutic application?"

"That is a big part of it," Dr. Fasten allows.

"Your glitchy A.I. told me this project is going to make the world a better place," Timothy repeats, keeping the mockery out of his voice. "Is it possible for you to be a little more specific?"

"Of course," Dr. Fasten says as amiably as possible without smiling. "My field is advanced psychiatric engineering. My work began two decades ago in the areas of memory loss, dementia and other such devastating conditions. Over the years, my work shifted to concentrate more on memory retention. And then to how memories shape us as individuals. Now, my focus is on the possibility we can shape our memories to make ourselves and our world *better*."

"*Right,*" Timothy nods, hoping he is fully understanding what is being said. "The world is what we perceive, and part of that is our memory, which helps to make us what we are."

"Our work helps to enhance positive memories and diminish negative ones," Dr. Fasten says, indulging Timothy's digression. "And while there may be a limit to how much we can enhance, the world may be surprised as to how much we can accomplish within that limit."

"For example, you can't make me believe I can fly," Timothy replies confidently.

"The human body is not capable of self-propelled flight," Dr. Fasten states with some exasperation colouring his voice. Then, checking his watch, he rises from his seat, and says, "Let's go to the Treatment Room."

Dr. Fasten leads Timothy down a fluorescent-lit corridor and then into a sterile medical operations room containing a huge and imposing device, looking like a cross between an oversized MRI scanner and a tunnel boring machine. The outer surface of the device has a number of cables attached to it, which all snake together into an operations booth that is behind smoky semi-opaque glass.

Through the darkened glass, Timothy can see the vague silhouette of a technician, likely female, youngish and bespectacled, hair pulled back, wearing a white lab coat that matches Dr. Fasten's. The technician is looking down at what Timothy assumes is a terminal that operates the device. But she isn't moving at all, standing completely still, as if frozen in place. The wall behind the technician is covered in multi-coloured indicator lights, making her lack of movement even more apparent.

"What happens in there?" Timothy asks, referring to the operations booth.

"That's where all the data extracted from you is filtered and scrubbed."

"*Extracted*, huh?" Timothy repeats.

He looks over at the machine, and the immensity of it hits him for the first time. It is grotesque in its size and purpose, and to think he is going to be *inside* of it, helpless and alone as it sucks out endless data from his mind.

"Am I going to have to sign a waiver for this?" Timothy asks, trying to joke but feeling the nervousness building inside him.

"That won't be necessary," Dr. Fasten smiles faintly. "It's already covered by your employment contract with DRI."

"I think I'll sit down for a minute," Timothy says weakly, as he sinks into a generic black chair. His head feels light and his breathing is shallow."

"I can give you something to make you relax," Dr. Fasten tells

Timothy.

"No, that's okay," Timothy says. "It's just a lot to absorb. And I don't even know what I'm absorbing."

"I know," Dr. Fasten reassures Timothy, his voice containing a little more warmth now. "This is a massive imposing machine. It scared the wits out of me when I saw it being assembled. The sheer enormity of it."

"So this is the supercomputer?" Timothy asks.

"No," Dr. Fasten tells him. "The data we extract here will be fed into our supercomputer Lessa for analysis. Lessa is housed remotely, and even *I* haven't seen it."

"So what do you call this thing then?" Timothy asks, indicating the humungous device taking up most of the room.

"Actually," Dr. Fasten says, "We just call it the *Machine*."

"Makes sense," Timothy nods, looking up at the mechanical wonder.

"To be honest," Timothy admits, "I didn't know what I was signing up for. I just thought I could make a bit of extra money."

Dr. Fasten looks calmly at Timothy, struggling to hide his annoyance.

They all crack up, Dr. Fasten thinks, *once they see the Machine. They're just people*, he reminds himself. *Normal, fragile people.*

Dr. Fasten takes a seat so he can address Timothy at eye level.

"Our work is based on memory reconsolidation," Dr. Fasten begins. "When you recall a memory, you are not remembering the original event, you are remembering the *memory* of that event, reshaped into a new form. Potentially enhanced for the better."

"So you want to change my memories?" Timothy asks, not sure if he wants to know the answer.

"We're trying to determine if manipulating memory can help people suffering from depression or post-traumatic stress disorder, or related conditions," Dr Fasten tells him. "If one doctor can remove a cancerous growth or transplant a heart, why can't another doctor remove the pain of the past, or implant a constructive recollection?"

"But the past makes us who we are," Timothy says simply.

"If we are not moving forward," Dr. Fasten insists, "we are being held back by our prior actions and mistakes."

"You're not going to wipe out my memory are you, Doctor?" Timothy asks nervously. "I have enough problems without adding forgetfulness to the list."

"You will remember *everything,* with even greater clarity," Dr. Fasten says. "By letting go of damaging memories and focusing on positive ones, you will start to perceive the world differently. Ever so slightly at first, and then, after repeated sessions, the improvement in your confidence and satisfaction could become quite apparent."

Dr. Fasten looks deeply into Timothy's face, trying to read the effect his words are having on his subject.

"Does this sound good to you, Timothy?" Dr. Fasten asks.

After a silent moment, Timothy finally says, "One question."

"Yes, of course," Dr. Fasten obliges.

"Have I ever been to Crystal Beach with my family?"

Not exactly sure how this is relevant, Dr. Fasten says, "You tell me."

"I have photographs that prove we were there," Timothy replies.

Dr. Fasten thinks about this. "And how do you *feel* about that?" he asks.

"I feel *good* about it," Timothy tells him. "We have lots of nice memories."

"Then the answer is *Yes,*" Dr. Fasten assures Timothy. "You *have* been there."

"Okay," Timothy says softly.

"*Okay?*" Dr. Fasten asks.

"Yes. *Okay*," Timothy affirms. "Let's go."

Dr. Fasten asks Timothy to lie down on the Machine's padded examination table. Out of habit, Timothy checks to make sure his wallet is in his jacket's breast pocket and his phone is in the front pocket of his pants.

A place for everything, and everything in its place, as his mother used to say.

Timothy gets on the examination table, and Dr. Fasten loosens the buttons on Timothy's shirt. Dr. Fasten looks toward the operations booth and nods. Timothy sees the figure behind the darkened glass move ever so slightly, and he hears the faint clicking of a keypad. The table he is on moves steadily into the Machine's internal cavity. The Machine's door then emerges and seals Timothy inside the device. He is relieved to find that the air is fresh and oxygen rich, circulated by tiny jets in the walls of the Machine's cavity.

Small multi-coloured indicator lights begin blinking slowly on the ceiling of the Machine's interior. Timothy finds himself watching the lights flick on and off as they begin to create intricate rhythmic patterns. He tries to gather his thoughts but finds it difficult to concentrate with the patterns of light dancing mesmerizingly before him. Then a low pleasant hum begins buzzing and a slow vibration causes his muscles to start losing their tension.

Now, a woman's voice: "I am obliged to inform you, this entire session will be recorded for analysis purposes."

"*Alright...*" Timothy whispers, dreamily.

Has he heard this voice before? It has a synthesized quality, and is somehow soothing, like a mother's voice to an infant.

The voice tells Timothy the Machine will release a harmless gas containing a mild psychoactive drug to help him focus his memory.

"*Okay*," Timothy acknowledges, thinking he might agree to almost anything this voice asked of him.

He hears a soft hiss and senses the air inside the Machine being filled with a colourless gas. It has the faint odour of a summer field under a hot sun, with wildflowers in bloom.

"Relax now, Timothy," the voice says.

It is a voice he could get used to hearing.

So let's begin.

THE MACHINE

Inside the Machine, the voice asks, "How are you doing today, Timothy?"

Not sure if he is supposed to answer, Timothy replies awkwardly, "I'm fine. How are you?"

"I'm fine, Timothy," the voice says. "How are things at home?"

"They're okay, I guess," Timothy says, aware of the doubt in his voice.

"What did you do last weekend?"

"Nothing really," Timothy says. "Actually, I can't remember," he admits.

"That's okay, Timothy," the voice reassures him. "Tell me about the happiest day of your life."

Timothy is going to say it's impossible to pick only one day from a whole lifetime, but then a memory springs up in front of him, vivid and real. He is about to start describing what he is remembering but soon realizes he doesn't have to.

It must be the effects of the psychoactive gas, he thinks, as he begins to experience a hallucination of sorts, one that is an uncannily accurate replaying of past events. He can visualize the memory, dimly at first, and then with more definition and clarity, as if he were re-living his experience. Or more precisely, as if he were standing invisibly while his experience is acted out all around him. He is aware of two consciousnesses operating in parallel: himself in the present and himself in the past.

In his memory, Timothy is eleven years old and is at his family's home. It is the day of his birthday party and several of his best friends are there: Johnny, Rick, Frank and Cathy. The house is decorated with streamers and balloons. Specially prepared foods are laid out on every flat surface in the kitchen and dining room. His aunt and uncle are there with his cousins Vance, Tommy and Brant. His mother has baked a birthday cake for him and has also made his favourite peanut butter cookies and fresh lemonade.

His father is there, of course, and he is completely sober, drinking nothing but Canada Dry. Not even a splash of rye in his coffee for *flavour*. Yes, his father is in a great mood this day. He is smiling and laughing a lot, making jokes with the other parents. Some of his father's new co-workers are there too, as he recently got a job as regional manager for Global Business Solutions.

"I put the BS in GBS!" his father says and would continue to say for the next several years, until it all goes bad.

But that is another day. Today is a day for celebration. Timothy knows the party is just as much for his father as it is for him. Maybe even more so. And that's what makes this day so great. Two men, father and son, celebrating their lives. There is no greater joy than achieving success and knowing your future will be one of unending bounty and happiness.

Now the voice breaks into Timothy's reverie: "Thank you, Timothy. This is helpful."

The memory around Timothy starts to fade, with him wishing it wouldn't. How many people get to re-live their happiest day ever? But the voice, with its lilting feminine cadence and charged with electronic energy, brings him back inside the Machine.

"Now, Timothy," the voice continues, "if you will, please tell me about the *worst* thing that has ever happened to you?"

The worst thing? Timothy thinks. *Everything. Day after day, it just gets harder and continues to go that way.*

"I understand," the voice says, as if she has heard Timothy's thoughts. "Can you please be more specific?"

Who is this asking me a million effing questions? Timothy wonders.

And here he is, babbling like a fool, spilling out his secrets to a disembodied voice. Not even a face to look at. It's like being in a confessional, telling your sins to a mysterious figure on the other side of the wall.

Forget it, Timothy thinks. *Figure it out for yourself. I'm finished*
—

Now, as if in response to his thoughts, Timothy's field of vision turns an opaque white and he is no longer in the Machine. The whiteness begins to morph and a new vista emerges. Timothy is resting in a comfortable leather armchair, and a young long-haired woman is sitting on a matching chair across from him. She is dressed in a tailored suit, her hair pulled back and wearing tortoiseshell glasses over her jade green eyes.

Who are you? Timothy wonders.

"Tell me about your father," the woman asks with polite eagerness.

Timothy stares blankly at the woman, astonished at how easily she has identified the root cause of the issues in his life.

"Don't be surprised," she tells him. "It is a pretty common scenario."

Once more, Timothy is confronted with the reality he is nothing special.

"Yes, I guess I do have father issues," he admits. "What man doesn't?"

"*Many* men don't," the woman says plainly.

"Sure," Timothy begins to yammer, "some upper-class shits, I suppose, whose fathers taught them to play tennis and golf. And sent them to the best schools. And arranged for them to get laid on their sixteenth birthdays."

"I see," the woman says, looking intently into Timothy's eyes.

"My old man was a bitter, helpless sad sack," Timothy tells the long-haired woman. "Too afraid of the world to stand up for himself. So he took things out on my mother and me. We were the only ones he had the courage to confront. Browbeating us. Blaming us for every misfortune that came his way.

"And, hey, I've tried to forget about it and move on. But that's just the thing. I'm not the forgetting type. So how do I cope? I take it out on my own wife and teenage son. Just like he did.

"I don't need a psychiatrist to tell me I've re-created the nightmares of my past," Timothy rages. "It's pretty freaking obvious. My wife Brenda even looks like my mother. And she sure as hell reminds me of her, as I scream the same withering insults my father screamed at my mother. Word for word, for the fucking love of—"

"Let me stop you right there," Dr. Fasten's voice says, interrupting Timothy's rant. "That is enough for us to start."

Start? Timothy thinks, disoriented by Dr. Fasten's masculine voice. *Start what?*

Timothy opens his eyes, which he didn't realize were closed. He sees the blinking indicator lights on the ceiling of the Machine's internal space. They are now settled into a soothing wave pattern, moving slowly through the pastel colours of mauve and rose and every shade in between.

What happened to that woman? Timothy asks himself. *Where is she?*

"Timothy," Dr. Fasten's voice continues, "the Machine will now emit radionic waves at alternating frequencies to stimulate your brain's memory centres. Using the baseline we have established, the Machine will employ a personalized algorithm to assist you in re-evaluating your relationship with your father."

My father? Timothy thinks, still disoriented. "Was I talking about my father?"

"Not to worry, Timothy," Dr. Fasten tells him. The algorithm the Machine has developed will allow you to see your father, and your relationship with him, in a new light."

"But, Doctor," Timothy interjects, "the past is the past. You can't change what's already happened."

Dr. Fasten's voice takes on a lightness that makes Timothy believe the po-faced man may actually be smiling:

"Of course the past can be changed. That's the whole point of my work. The Machine will reshape your memories, and in doing so, will change the past you have experienced."

During the silence that follows, the sound of Timothy's breathing and heartbeat can be heard to echo faintly in the Machine's inner chamber. Finally, in a soft, questioning voice, Timothy admits, "I don't know if I am up for this. It just doesn't sound right to me."

"We will start slowly," Dr. Fasten assures him. "Only small, minute changes at first. You may not even perceive them."

"Oh," Timothy says, not sure what point there is in continuing.

The indicator lights inside the Machine suddenly begin to blink, and then without notice, a new memory emerges in Timothy's mind. He assumes he is just daydreaming, but the details of the memory start to become very distinct, without any effort on his part.

He is in the surf at Crystal Beach with his father and mother, frolicking in the water. The sun is shining and they are splashing each other and laughing enthusiastically. He can feel the warmth and wetness on his skin and smell the earthy air and lake water.

The sweet halcyon days of years gone by…

The indicator lights now go dark, and Dr. Fasten's voice resumes: "With every session we complete, Timothy, we learn a little bit more. And eventually, we may have enough know-ledge to begin to address the important global issues we are en-deavoring to solve."

"Yes, I understand," Timothy says.

Part of him feels guilty for standing in the way of scientific progress. But another, larger part of him is more concerned with reliving gloriously sunny days at the beach with his family.

"I suppose, if the changes are small," Timothy tells the doc-tor, "and generally have a positive effect, then I guess it would be okay to continue."

"Good," Dr. Fasten says, pleased.

"Okay then," Timothy nods, thinking about his mother's floral bathing suit, and the thick layer of sunscreen on his father's nose. "I'm ready."

Without any further discussion, Timothy hears the low hiss of colourless gas, which has a soapy scent, mixed with cologne, coffee and pomade. Dr. Fasten's disembodied voice, tinged with electronics, begins speaking:

"Your father was an average man of humble beginnings, of moderate intelligence and mediocre prospects…"

Dr. Fasten's voice is even and soothing, with no unnecessary pauses or errors in diction. It sounds to Timothy like Dr. Fasten is reading from a well-researched script, which is full of things both known and unknown about Timothy's father. But how could he be reading from a script? Only a few minutes earlier, Dr. Fasten didn't know a single thing about his old man.

"As the oldest male child," Dr. Fasten continues, "your father was expected to get a job at a young age to assist with the fam-ily's expenses."

Timothy remembers his father telling him about his first job, working in a small grocery store, where he had to stock the but-ter and the cheese, the milk, and the canned goods. These came in big boxes which were very heavy for such a young boy.

As these thoughts flow through Timothy's mind, he feels himself drifting into a hazy altered consciousness. There is a pleasantly ticklish hum in his ears, and soon his whole body is vibrating, as if with the promise of some mysterious pleasure. Dr. Fasten's electronic voice continues, describing scenarios out of Timothy's and his father's lives. In his foggy state, Timothy is bewildered by how much Dr. Fasten knows about his father and about Timothy himself.

Is Dr. Fasten actually speaking to me? Timothy wonders. *Or am I speaking to myself?*

Dr. Fasten's voice slowly recedes into nothingness, making Timothy's question irrelevant. In his mind, Timothy can see images of his father and himself when he was a young man. Moving tableaus. Then full scenes begin to unfold, as if whole periods of Timothy's life are transpiring in real time. The accuracy of these scenes is uncanny, matching Timothy's memories perfectly, depicting minute details that even he had forgotten about.

As the minutes and hours of his life pass before him, they begin to feel like days and maybe even years. Timothy's sense of time becomes completely lost as he relives many conversations with his father, over long leisurely meals, during vacations and outings to the park, the swimming pool and the movies. And of course, there are the arguments and the fights. But Timothy now sees his father in a different light. A damaged man to whom life has not been kind, trying his best, and not always succeeding in being a good father. Timothy can see his pain, and he feels bad for his old man's failures.

Then Timothy's perspective turns inward and he begins to watch himself grow up. He sees he is no longer the loser he fought so hard not to be. He is a unique individual, with his own skills and talents, who has a lot to offer the world. Timothy sees a growing boy who seems destined to do something worthwhile with his life, even if it is only to get married, work diligently and have a son of his own, whom he loves beyond comprehension.

My family will always be fed and clothed, Timothy tells himself. *And we will never want for any of the necessities of life.*

Timothy is now immersed in a deep and satisfying glow. And then, as the memories of his life fade, Timothy finds himself in a beautifully verdant, sun-dappled park.

Where is this? Is it the past or the present?

His eyes squint against the light, and then he sees *her*. The young long-haired woman. She is sitting on a bench, wearing a beige sundress and a fashionable, large-brimmed hat. She is looking at him and smiling, pleased. Timothy understands she has been watching him the whole time and has seen his whole life replay itself for the benefit of them both…

"Timothy… Timothy, wake up."

Timothy opens his eyes to find he is on the Machine's examination table, which is now outside of the Machine's inner cavity, which is dark and idle.

"Are you feeling okay, Timothy?" Dr. Fasten asks.

Timothy? That's what my grandfather called me, Timothy thinks. *More respectable than Tim or Timmy…*

"Can you hear me?"

"Yes," Timothy responds, regaining his senses. "I'm fine."

An image flashes briefly in Timothy's mind. A woman with long dark hair.

"Is that it?" he asks Dr. Fasten.

"Yes, that's all for today," Dr. Fasten says, checking his watch.

Timothy looks up at the operations booth with its smoky glass. It is also dark and empty.

"We went over our scheduled time," Dr. Fasten says, trying to speed things along.

"How long was I out for?" Timothy asks groggily.

"You *weren't* out," Dr. Fasten corrects him. "You were experiencing an alternative consciousness."

"It seemed so *real*," Timothy says, trying to make sense of things.

"The psychoactive agent in the gas has that effect," Dr. Fasten tells him impatiently. "Many of our subjects have a similar response."

"People could get hooked on this," Timothy suggests.

"Unfortunately," Dr. Fasten says dryly, "subsequent sessions have overwhelmingly produced diminishing results."

"Oh," Timothy says disappointedly. "It was *interesting*, anyway."

"Of course," Dr. Fasten says absently. "Are you okay to drive?"

"You tell *me*."

"The treatment produces no residual impairment," Dr Fasten declares. "Although its effects may manifest themselves in waves… I can call you a ride-share if you want."

"No, I'm okay," Timothy yawns, starting to feel like himself again.

"Then let me give you this before you go," Dr. Fasten says, pulling a business card out of his breast pocket and handing it to Timothy. "My number is on the front if you have to contact me for any reason. And on the back is your emergency code."

Timothy looks at the back of the card, which has a phone number printed on it.

"This phone number is my emergency code?" Timothy asks.

"The number at the bottom is your emergency code," Dr. Fasten explains. "It's hidden there in the design for security reasons. Can you see it?"

"Yes, I think so," Timothy nods, not sure why he needs a secret code.

"If you should develop any issues or have any questions," Dr. Fasten says, "and I am unavailable, just dial the number on the back. There will always be someone there to take your call. Quote the emergency code."

"Okay," Timothy nods, trying to sound like he understands. "Got it."

"Good," Dr. Fasten says, wrapping things up. "Thank you for coming in."

Timothy straightens his clothing and runs his fingers through his hair to put it back in place. He nods goodbye to Dr. Fasten as he exits the Treatment Room, after which he hears the door click shut behind him.

Timothy retraces his steps back to the reception area, where he adjusts his belt, which is slightly askew. He gives his jacket a light dusting with his hands and looks at the terminal, whose display is as dark as the operations booth had been.

"Hello?" he asks tentatively, hoping to get a response from the terminal, which does not happen.

Oh well.

Timothy buttons one button of his jacket, and glancing down at his watch, checks the time.

Five hours! he thinks. *That went quickly.*

Now that his disorientation has worn off, Timothy realizes he is feeling rather good, as if he's just had a refreshing night's sleep. His energy level is up, and he is not at all groggy, as he usually is at this time of day.

Maybe there is something to this radionic nonsense after all.

As he is about to exit the reception area, Timothy hears a faint electronic *beep.* He turns expectantly toward the terminal, which is still dark.

In the corner, the anthropomorphic wayfinder lifts its head with a soft buzzing sound. Its greenish robotic eyes light up dimly.

"Drive safely, Timothy," it says with its synthetic voice.

"I will," Timothy replies. "Thank you, Columbus."

Leaving the reception area, Timothy retraces his steps, following Dr. Fasten's hand-written signs in reverse order. When he gets to the front doors, he walks out of the building and looks up into the sky, which is a darkening blue, as dusk has begun to descend.

The best part of the day is done, he thinks. But then, unexpectedly, his mind revises this to, *The best part of the day is the part you are in.*

Not sure where this burst of positivity is coming from, Timothy decides not to question it, but to embrace it. And why not? He has his whole life waiting in front of him, which is an endless ocean of possibilities.

Warmed by this thought, Timothy gets in his car and turns the key in the ignition.

Nothing happens.

His car is as cold and immobile as a hulking hunk of scrap metal, which he supposes is an accurate description. He gets out of his car, looks around at the nothingness that surrounds him and returns to the entrance of the rehabilitation centre. There he finds the doors locked and the security camera unresponsive. He looks inside the building and as expected sees no signs of life.

Looking around the empty parking lot, Timothy wonders where Dr. Fasten and his staff, if he has any, park their cars. Timothy amuses himself with the thought the doctor and his crew all live in the basement of the rehabilitation centre, devoting their entire lives to their research, with no means of escape.

Timothy's amusement soon wears off as he tries to think of a plan to get his car fixed. He would call a towing service if he had a number to call, and if his phone wasn't out of data. Taking out his wallet and fishing out the card Dr. Fasten gave him, Timothy decides to contact the good doctor to ask him to arrange a tow truck.

Phoning Dr. Fasten's number, Timothy gets a message informing him that Dr. Fasten is not available and does not check his voicemail. Timothy flips the card over and regards the emergency number on the back. He figures this isn't a real emergency, but after looking once again at the empty parking lot and the barrenness that surrounds it, he thinks:

Fuck it.

Timothy dials the emergency number, ready to read out the secret code hidden at the bottom of the card. While waiting for the ever-present person to answer the call, Timothy can't help but smile to himself.

This is real secret agent shit, he thinks.

On the other end of the line, Timothy hears a strange metallic ringtone, unlike anything he has ever encountered before. But there is no pick-up, no voicemail. Nothing. Just more metallic ringing.

As he is about to give up, Timothy hears the line connect.

"Who is this?" a voice asks neutrally, neither interested nor disinterested.

"This is Tim… Timothy Koops. Do you want the emergency code?"

"Why are you calling this number?" the voice says in a tone neither inviting nor distancing.

"I am at the Righton Centre, for the second part of my assessment," Timothy explains. "I've been locked out."

"This does not sound like an emergency," the voice informs him pleasantly while remaining aloof.

"Sorry, but I basically have nowhere else to turn," Timothy argues.

"Are you in any immediate danger?" the voice asks, growing

impatient.

"Well, *no*," Timothy admits.

The voice takes in a heavy breath and explains, "You do not call this number when you misplace your keys," the voice advises him. "This is a number reserved exclusively for life-altering catastrophes. Do you understand?"

"Yes," Timothy replies, suitably shamed. "That's very clear."

"Thank you. Please keep this in mind should you ever feel the need to call here again. Good day, sir."

The line goes dead. Timothy puts his phone away and stares at the oblivious asphalt that surrounds him. Then he remembers something. Somehow, it is both an old and a new memory simultaneously. How could he have forgotten it? And how could he now remember it so clearly? When Timothy accepted the car from his brother-in-law Jake, Timothy was added to Jake's roadside assistance membership.

There you go, Timothy thinks. *There is no challenge, big or small, that can't be met with a little forward planning.*

He roots around in his wallet looking for his membership card, and sure enough, there it is. Timothy shakes his head admonishingly at himself. The solution to his problem was right there all along. Timothy calls the number on the card, ready to get this situation resolved and head home.

"Membership number?" the voice on the phone asks.

Timothy recites his membership number and is promptly told his membership has expired.

"I haven't even used it yet," Timothy says with frustration.

"Membership is based on *time*, not *usage*, sir," the voice informs him.

"Yes, I know," Timothy replies. "I just meant it's *ironic,* that's all."

"I'm not sure what that means," the voice says. "Do you want to renew your membership, or not?"

"Yes, I do," Timothy says, annoyed.

"Same credit card?"

"Yes. My *brother-in-law's* credit card. Jake Freeland. I'm on his membership."

"The card we have on file is Timothy Koops. Are you Timothy Koops?" the voice asks.

"Yes, I'm Timothy Koops. But you should have my brother-in-law's card on file."

The voice reads out the number on the card they have on file. "Is that your card, sir?"

"Yes, but…" Timothy begins. "How did you get my card number?"

"According to our files," the voice tells Timothy, "you took out a membership exactly one year and three days ago."

"Oh," Timothy says meekly, as a dim memory of this resurfaces in his mind. "Well, alright then, sign me back up."

"There will be a renewal surcharge," the voice tells him, "as you let your account lapse."

"*Wonderful*," Timothy says with some bitterness.

"Okay, sir," the voice says, "there's no need to be *sarcaustic*."

"Yes, you're right," Timothy apologizes. *I didn't need to be sarcaustic. I just wanted to be.*

"Okay, then. I'll send someone right out," the voice says pleasantly. "Waiting time is currently two to three hours. Have a great evening, sir."

"I will endeavour to do just that," Timothy replies, removing all irony from his voice, "even if the odds are stacked mightily against me."

"Okay, sure," the voice says, ending the call.

Timothy puts his phone away and sits on the hood of his

dead car. The sun has already begun its descent and the stars are making themselves visible in the North York sky. The air has a coolness that is invigorating, and Timothy breathes it in appreciatively.

In the silence of the parking lot, Timothy can hear the rolling trill of crickets chirping in the wooded area surrounding the Righton Centre. There is even the distant yowl of a coyote, who sounds like he's yearning impatiently for the impending darkness.

Timothy's mind suddenly achieves a clarity he has rarely experienced in his life, and he thinks:

There really is nothing stopping me from having a great evening, if that's what I want.

CONTROL

Inside the Righton Centre, Dr. Fasten sits over his terminal, processing the data extracted in the session he has just completed with Timothy Koops. Satisfied the data is now error free and ready for analysis, he keys in a sequence of commands to send it to Lessa the supercomputer. He watches the progress of the upload intently, hoping the transfer doesn't glitch, as several previous data sets have, resulting in many laborious hours, surgically removing errors and stitching the remaining data together.

As he continues to watch the progress of the upload, Dr. Fasten leans back in his chair, rubs his face wearily and concedes he doesn't expect much from Timothy's session.

We need a wider base of participants, he thinks. *We can't expect just any old Tim, Dick, or Harry to produce the desired results. The proper subject must be hand-picked from a more promising selection of candidates. I can't keep testing these losers and expect they're going to have the attributes that our work requires.*

Engaging in months of assessments with no positive results is starting to wear on Dr. Fasten. His life is speeding by, as he languishes in an abandoned complex not properly set up for the work he is doing, assisted only by useless malfunctioning robots. What he especially dislikes is waiting around for the results, because during these periods the only thing he *can* do is wait. And today, he feels like he's come to the end of his patience.

Timothy Koops? Why even bother? Such an ordinary man with an ordinary intelligence. He is certainly not the type of person to ever change the world, for good or for bad. Just living an ordinary life until an ordinary death removes him from the human database.

Dr. Fasten's thoughts are dispersed by the ringing of his personal phone, which he sees is a call from his girlfriend, Frida.

"Seven o'clock already?" Dr. Fasten says into the phone, by way of salutation. "I'm so sorry. I was going to call you, but I got stuck at the lab again."

"Of course, *Zazzie*," Frida says gently. "You get stuck there everyday."

"And everyday," Dr. Fasten says, "I'm thankful for your understanding."

"That's nice to hear," Frida purrs on the other end of the line.

Dr. Fasten often wonders what he would do without Frida. After his marriage broke down, he was somewhat relieved to be able to devote himself entirely to his work. But he soon realized that scientific research alone was not enough. Humans require companionship, love, arguments, bickering, petty jealousies, annoyances and all the things that make us what we are.

"I'll be home soon," he tells Frida.

"Yes, I know," she says hopefully.

As a scientist herself, Frida understands Zakery has an obligation to his work. Like a doctor who has taken an oath, a scientist must live up to a code of ethics, especially when they are part of a world-changing research project. Afterall, where would we be as a species if people of science *didn't* keep their loved ones waiting as they worked to improve the human condition?

"You know you have my support, Zazzie," Frida says. "And you must soldier on. For the greater good."

"Yes, but to win the war, I need better troops," Dr. Fasten says humourlessly.

"More disappointing results?" she asks. "I thought today's subject scored high on the initial assessment?"

"I can't *trust* the initial assessment," Dr. Fasten states with suppressed anger.

"This is *new*," Frida is surprised to hear.

"The supercomputer's been acting strangely," Dr. Fasten complains. "There might be some bugs in the system."

"You know technology is always a bitch," Frida consoles him.

"It's more than that," Dr. Fasten begins. "Lessa has been implanting unauthorized memories in my subject."

"Like what?" Frida asks, intrigued.

"*Crystal Beach*," Dr. Fasten replies cryptically.

"Is that a problem?" Frida wonders.

"It was an independent action by Lessa, which I didn't approve."

"But it got the assessment results you wanted, didn't it?" Frida says encouragingly.

"Yes," Dr. Fasten mumbles half-heartedly. "But if there isn't a unified vision behind my work, it will spin out of control."

"I'm sure Lessa was just weeding out candidates that were unsuitable," Frida continues. "So you could find a good subject faster. Isn't that what you are ultimately after?"

"Yes, Frida," Dr. Fasten concedes with little enthusiasm. "One really good subject. A proverbial needle in a haystack."

The silence grows heavy between them, as it does on many of Frida's calls to Dr. Fasten at the Righton Centre.

"I don't know why there was ever a needle in a haystack," Frida jokes, lightening the mood.

"Someone must have dropped it," Dr. Fasten assumes.

"I bet that person wasn't well liked around the farm," Frida quips. "The asshole who dropped the needle."

Frida laughs at her own joke, causing Dr. Fasten to join in with a light chuckle. They both laugh a little longer than the joke warrants, happy to enjoy the sound of each other's cheeriness. Then, their laughter dissipates as Dr. Fasten's terminal emits a telltale *ping.* The data upload is complete, and the supercomputer begins its first-run analysis.

Dr. Fasten holds his breath, expecting another lacklustre result, but hoping desperately for some measure of success.

"What's happening?" Frida asks after a brief silence.

"The first-run results…" Dr. Fasten stammers, finally taking a breath.

"Are they promising?" Frida presses him, receiving no answer. "*Zakery?*"

"It usually only takes a few seconds," he explains.

A few seconds to reject the data, Dr. Fasten reminds himself. Maybe it's a good sign it's taking longer this time.

The seconds stretch themselves into tiny eternities until finally a sound is heard from Dr. Fasten's terminal. A clear chime, like a bell being struck on a cold winter's day. It is a sound that elicits a Pavlovian response from Dr. Zakery Fasten.

"*Oh,*" Dr. Fasten squeaks involuntarily.

"What was that?" Frida asks excitedly. "Was the second assessment a success?"

"I think so," Dr. Fasten replies dreamily, as he stares at his terminal's display. It is too much for him to absorb. "The results are… *startling.*"

"Startling in what *way?*" Frida bursts out.

"Good," Dr. Fasten croaks. "*Very* good."

"Maybe Lessa knew what it was doing all along," Frida suggests.

"That's one possibility," Dr. Fasten agrees absently, his mind a million miles away.

"*Okay,*" Frida says, resigned. "I recognize that tone of voice. I guess you won't be making it home for dinner, after all. I'll order

Swiss Chalet. Do you want me to get you some ribs?"

"Yes, thank you, Frida," Dr. Fasten says, hanging up without another word.

He looks intently at the display as the supercomputer begins its second-run analysis of the data.

"It's off the charts," Dr. Fasten says to no one in particular, except maybe the mice, the cockroaches and the spirits of those who perished on those lands in the centuries gone by.

*

After Timothy has waited well over two hours, a roadside assistance agent drives into the Righton Centre parking lot in a tow truck. The agent pulls his truck up beside Timothy's car, gets out and asks:

"Timothy Kooper?"

"Yes," Timothy nods. "Timothy *Koops*."

"What is that, *Dutch*?"

"Yes, that's right," Timothy tells him, not wanting to go into the long history of his last name.

"Well what the heck are you doing here, you crazy Dutch-man?" the agent asks incredulously. "This is where my granny used to get her physio."

"They do research here now," Timothy says.

"Oh," the service agent acknowledges while eying Timothy's immobile vehicle. "What's the problem with the car?" he asks.

"It won't start," Timothy replies.

"The alternator might be shot," the agent says, thinking out loud.

He looks at the car's creeping rust, which is eating the car alive, and the car's bald tires, which aren't even properly aligned.

"How *old* is this vehicle?" the agent enquires.

"About fifteen years," Timothy underestimates.

"So what do you want me to do here?" the agent says with some distaste.

"What are my options?" Timothy asks.

"*Options?*" the agent laughs joylessly. "Buy a new car."

"Can you get it working again?" Timothy frowns.

The agent sighs to himself. He opens the car's driver-side door, unlocks the hood, then moves to the front of the car. Lifting the hood and securing it, he looks intently at the filthy blackened machinery that lies beneath. He checks a few parts, shakes a few wires, rubs his forehead with the back of his hand and asks:

"Was your engine light on?"

"Yes, I think so," Timothy says. "It's *always* on."

"Your spark plugs are worn out," the agent tells him. "Has your engine been misfiring?"

"It's been making a weird noise."

"A knocking noise?"

"Yes, sometimes," Timothy admits.

"Backfiring out the tailpipe?"

"Definitely."

"Stuttering and losing power?"

"Yes."

"Can you smell the exhaust coming off the engine?"

"I'm not sure," Timothy shrugs.

"Well *I* can."

"So what does that mean?"

"It means your engine is dead," the agent tells him bluntly.

"Can it be fixed?" Timothy asks hopefully.

"I *could* tow it to the nearest mechanic," the agent tells him with exasperation. "But I wouldn't bother. This car should be put out of its misery. I can tow it to the scrapyard for you. I'll try to get you a hundred bucks. They'll send it to you."

Seeing as he has no choice, Timothy nods in agreement. He signs some paperwork, hands over his keys and watches as the agent hooks up his car to the tow truck and drives off.

Timothy is about to call Brenda and tell her the bad news, but then he thinks better of it. Let her enjoy her evening for another hour. He'll tell her about it in person when he gets home. Then they can discuss how they're going to live without a car for the foreseeable future.

Timothy stands in the now completely empty parking lot and thinks about how great he felt after he finished taking the assessment. For a short time, he almost believed he could take on the world. Now he feels like he is carrying that world on his shoulders.

Such is the ebb and flow of life.

With a deep sigh, Timothy opens a ride-sharing app on his phone. He is hoping the Righton Centre's wi-fi will somehow be available and he can get a ride home. To his amazement, not only is he able to engage the app, but he sees that his data has been topped up.

What a welcome surprise, he thinks.

Your driver Amodeo will arrive in eight minutes, the app tells him.

"Ha!" Timothy exclaims happily. *It's the power of positive thinking,* he tells himself.

He looks up into the midnight blue sky and raises his arms in mock victory.

Timothy Koops is going home!

*

As his rib dinner gets cold in the uptown condo he shares

with his girlfriend, Dr. Fasten is still in the Treatment Room in front of his terminal. He is monitoring the supercomputer as it analyzes the results of Timothy's assessment. All the go lights on Dr. Fasten's display are green, indicating peak performance. And one by one, they all switch to gold, indicating super-optimal results.

Dr. Fasten is so immersed in witnessing this potential breakthrough in his work, he forgets to implement the project's mandatory protocols. His immediate action should be to contact Control at their headquarters in Sudbury, where Lessa the supercomputer is housed deep underground. As the protocols include subprotocols, Control takes the initiative and contacts Dr. Fasten, startling him out of his transfixed state with the shrill ring of the secure-line video interface.

"Hello," Dr. Fasten says, answering the secure line. "Can you hear me, Control?"

"Yes, hello, Zakery," Control says on the other end of the call.

Control's image is slightly blurred and intermittently distorted, as the origin of the call is four kilometres below the Earth's surface in Control's high-security headquarters. He is a man of advanced years, with colourless skin hanging loosely from his face and receding grey-white hair combed back artlessly.

"We have been monitoring the results of your latest assessment," Control continues. "And judging by what we've seen so far, we think we may have a candidate for further experimentation."

"The preliminary results *are* promising," Dr. Fasten concedes, "but we have been disappointed in the past, as you know."

"All of that is changing now," Control insists.

"Let's not be too hasty," Dr. Fasten counters. "Timothy Koops does not fit the profile we have established. He is of average intelligence at best. No real ambition. No discernable skills or talent of any kind."

"Yes," Control agrees, "he called the emergency number because he lost his keys, or some such nonsense. But these preliminary results indicate his potential could be enormous."

"How many other subjects have we tested?" Dr. Fasten argues. "With their promise diminishing over time?"

"Timothy Koops is different," Control replies. "You just can't see it, even though it's right there in front of you."

"No, *I see it*," Dr. Fasten says, slightly offended. "It's his *memories*. They are all so clear in his mind. That's why he can't escape his past."

"And that's why he is our ideal candidate," Control explains. "His remembrances are so vivid, the Machine was able to extract a pure image."

"A perfect re-creation of the past," Dr. Fasten says, thinking out loud. "Fully accessible to Lessa."

"Yes," Control agrees. "Timothy seems to have been naturally engineered over many generations to be the perfect subject for our work."

"It seems too good to believe," Dr. Fasten says. "It doesn't even feel *real.*"

"How could it not be *real*?" Control questions. "You *are* experiencing it, aren't you?"

"*Am I?*" Dr. Fasten asks cryptically. Seeing the look of confusion on Control's face, Dr. Fasten explains:

"Lessa has been implanting memories in our subject. He's not even sure he knows what's *real* anymore. And neither do I. Is this my research finally coming to fruition, or is it the work of some rogue subroutine?"

"We *did* notice a schism in Lessa's programming," Control admits, "which we addressed."

"Then why does my subject and his family think they spend

their summers at Crystal Beach, a place they've likely never been to?"

"A compartmentalized function in Lessa began operating independently," Control confesses. "But many scientific leaps forward have occurred due to unexpected anomalies."

"You mean *errors*," Dr. Fasten says with insistence.

"There's no reason for alarm, Zakery," Control says calmly. "Lessa is undergoing extensive self-diagnostics and has the anomaly in containment. You must concentrate on your work and build on these preliminary results."

"Yes, I'll call Timothy back in for further sessions," Dr. Fasten says. "But Lessa must process his memories with greater precision than these initial attempts."

"Of course," Control smiles slightly. "We must achieve a perfect reproduction of the past, which we can then utilize for the greater betterment."

Dr. Fasten pauses to think about this statement. Their work is no longer theoretical. It now has the possibility of actually succeeding. The enormity of this hits Dr. Fasten like a bracing spray of cold water.

"Then you think *beta* results will be forthcoming?" Dr. Fasten asks, slightly apprehensive of what the answer might be.

"I think beta results may already be underway," Control tells him. "And they may be more significant than a family trip to the beach."

"But I haven't prepared the subject for that eventuality," Dr. Fasten stammers. "I advised him he wouldn't notice anything out of the ordinary."

"With the results we've just seen," Control says evenly, "the effects of the first treatment will already be starting to manifest themselves. There may even be an inclining onset of modifications as the hours go by."

"But the effects will be limited, correct?" Dr. Fasten asks with some panic in his voice. "Output cannot outpace input. One session cannot drastically change the subject's environment."

"Not in any *significant* way," Control reassures Dr. Fasten. "We have only scratched the surface. It is only with subsequent treatments that we can, as you say, change the subject's environment. And once we change *his*, we change *ours*."

"And how far will we take it?" Dr. Fasten asks.

"As far as we can."

PAD THAI

After a forty-five-minute drive, Timothy's ride-share delivers him to his bungalow. Timothy thanks the driver and exits the vehicle, immediately noticing, inexplicably, his old second-hand Ford is in the driveway. Apart from being quite surprised, Timothy wonders how the tow truck managed to beat him home, as his ride-share drove at least ten kilometres above the speed limit, and the driver knew every existing shortcut. But there is his car, nonetheless.

Timothy calls the roadside assistance service and prepares to give them hell. What kind of incompetence is this? Does his house look like a scrapyard?

A customer service agent answers, and just as Timothy is about to blast him, he sees that his car is a lot cleaner than it should be.

"Hello, TAA, can I help you?" the voice on the other end of the line says.

"Yes, hello," Timothy replies, noticing his car has had all its scrapes and dings buffed out.

"Okay," Timothy continues into the phone, "I called for roadside assistance, I guess about three hours ago. My car was supposed to go to the scrapyard."

"Are you calling from the number associated with your account?" the voice asks.

"Yes, of course," Timothy says to the man, trying not to get exasperated. "I was told my car was a piece of junk. And now it's here in my driveway, gleaming in the moonlight."

"I'm not sure what your problem is, sir."

"Neither am I," Timothy admits. "It's just confusing."

"Yes, it is," the agent agrees. "I've checked our records. There's no log of a service call from you today."

While he pulls his copy of the paperwork out of his back pocket, Timothy sees the interior of his car has recently been detailed. All the debris has been removed from the floor and coffee stains no longer soil the upholstery.

Timothy reads out the tracking number at the top righthand corner of his paperwork, which the agent assures him does not correspond to their numbering system.

"Well, that's just *great*," Timothy sputters, at a complete loss. He sarcastically thanks the agent for all his help, hangs up, then scurries into his garage to retrieve his extra set of keys.

Unlocking the car door and getting in, Timothy is surprised to find that his car smells fresh and fragrant, like it has just received a deluxe deodorizing scrub down. He starts the engine which purrs muscularly with full power. Perplexed, Timothy sits back and luxuriates in the pleasant scent and smooth vibrations.

Those fools must have sent me the wrong car, he thinks, turning off the engine and getting out of the vehicle.

Moving to the front of the car, Timothy sees the licence plate is the correct one.

That's really strange. If they accidently switched cars, why would they switch licence plates? Then looking down at the keys in his hand, he thinks, *Why would my keys work?*

Going into his house, Timothy is greeted by the delicious aroma of home cooking, which envelopes his olfactory senses like a pleasant wave.

When did Brenda learn to cook? he wonders.

"*Hello, Timothy*," Brenda calls out.

Timothy? She hasn't called me that since we recited our wedding vows.

"How was the assessment, darling?" she asks.

"It was… fine. Just fine," Timothy replies, preoccupied. "Did someone deliver our car earlier?"

"I don't think so. Why would they?" Brenda says with a confused smirk.

"There's been some sort of mix up," Timothy explains.

"Nothing serious, I hope."

While Timothy tries to think of an appropriate answer, he notices his son Bryan is at the dinner table doing his homework, which is not a sight Timothy is accustomed to seeing.

"Bryan," he calls out, "what are you studying for? Do you have a test tomorrow?"

"No, Dad," Bryan says, looking up from his schoolwork. "Just regular homework. Andrews gave us a crap-load of math."

"*Really?*" Timothy asks dumbfounded. "And you're *doing* it?"

"Yeah, Dad, what do you think?" his son howls. "I don't want to fall behind. Andrews will be on my butt till the end of the year."

Looking at his son, Timothy notices that Bryan's hair is trimmed and tidy, instead of long and greasy like it usually is.

"I hope you're hungry, Timothy," Brenda says.

"Yeah, I am," Timothy admits. All he has had to eat all day is some cheese toast at breakfast. "What's that I smell?"

"Thai food. I made it special."

"*Thai food?*" Timothy repeats doubtfully.

"I helped," Bryan chimes in, coming over to stand closer to his parents.

"Yes, you did, honey," Brenda acknowledges. "We made spicy shrimp soup, green papaya salad, red curry chicken…"

"And pad thai, of course," Bryan adds, rolling his eyes at this less than original dish.

"During the week, we're always so rushed," Brenda says. "We deserve an extravagant meal every once in a while."

"That spicy shrimp was a *bitch*," Bryan says. "We had to go to a special fish store to get the shrimp, and they were all out of jumbo."

"And the spiciness has to be handled very delicately," Brenda adds. "One too many slices of hot pepper—"

"And you're totally *screwed*," Bryan blurts out excitedly.

"But it all turned out great," Brenda assures her husband. "And reading all those recipes made me want to visit Thailand someday."

"Yeah, maybe next life," Bryan smirks.

Brenda smiles and pushes her son away playfully. "You never know, Bryan, we could win the lottery."

Timothy smiles. He has been home for over five minutes and hasn't gotten pissed off at anyone. That has to be some kind of record. And for some reason, his wife is looking more attractive tonight.

"Is that a new dress?" Timothy asks, thinking it looks more expensive than what Brenda usually buys for herself.

"I bought it earlier this season," Brenda says, giving herself a small twirl.

This season? Timothy wonders. Since when did their family divide their clothes into *seasons*, aside from a winter coat, worn year after year until it wears out?

"Hey, Dad," Bryan says with a mischievous look on his face. "Remember when we all went to that Thai restaurant?"

"No, not really," Timothy responds, as he can't recall such an outing.

"Forgetful much?" Brenda laughs gently at him.

"Come on, Dad," Bryan says with glee. "Don't you remember how you were scoping out that waitress in the tight dress? Mom started calling her your new girlfriend, and you turned all red?"

"The same shade as her dress," Brenda cackles.

Timothy's family is now laughing heartily at his expense. And instead of this filling him with a boiling rage, as it usually would, Timothy finds this to be quite *amusing,* even if he can't remember the incident they are describing. So he starts laughing too.

As the family's communal laughter continues, Timothy knows something isn't quite right. He's not the type to laugh at himself or enjoy it when others laugh at him. But after some consideration, Timothy thinks maybe Dr. Fasten's session has started to have its desired effect. Because everything feels like it is as it should be, and he is living in a perfect moment.

To make things even more perfect, Brenda tells Timothy she has chilled a bottle of white wine and asks if he wants a glass. Part of him thinks he must be drunk already. Feeling this good can't be *natural.* As he accepts the wine a few minutes later and has a few sips, he begins to relax, ready to enjoy some great food with his family, telling their stories and laughing at their own jokes. It's like something out of a movie, he thinks. An enjoyable movie he never wants to end.

As they go about setting the dinner table, Timothy can almost visualize the Thai waitress his family was talking about. How could he have forgotten a situation like that? And what was it about that waitress? She had long dark hair and startling colourful eyes.

As Timothy and his family sit down to eat their exotic feast, Timothy's memories of the Thai restaurant gradually become clearer. He can now remember the red dress the waitress was wearing. And her features emerge out of the blur. Yes, what a beautiful face. He *had* been glancing at her a little too long. And she caught him in his glance and returned it, looking directly into his eyes.

Timothy remembers thinking at the time, in a different life, maybe he would have had a chance with her.

In a different life...

GOLDEN BOY

When Timothy wakes up the next day, his eyes pop open without hesitation and his mind is clear. Instead of the low-level dread he usually feels on a workday, today he feels refreshed and ready to greet life's never-ending challenges.

Monday morning is the best morning of the week. A chance to start anew.

Timothy is looking forward to going to work and moving his assignments along. He knows he can make some good progress if he puts his mind to it and Ravi doesn't interrupt him.

Timothy looks over at Brenda, who is still sleeping, and thinks, *Wow, this is the first time I've ever gotten up before her. The hot water is all mine!*

While in the shower, Timothy recalls the previous day's events. Dr. Fasten certainly was a character, rambling all alone in his abandoned complex with his broken-down robots. And that gigantic Machine must have cost a mint. What a waste of money. And who was that mysterious assistant behind the smoky glass who didn't want to show herself? What a lot of *trouble* they all went to.

Yes, of course, he realizes. *A lot of people went to a lot of trouble. That explains it. The car, the Thai food, Crystal Beach.*

What fools, he thinks, bursting out with laughter, almost slipping on the soapy shower floor.

But how did they get Bryan to do his homework? Timothy is stumped by that one. But no matter how they did it, they certainly succeeded in improving Timothy's satisfaction with life, as promised, even if only temporarily.

Getting dressed and leaving the house, driving to work is a pleasure for Timothy in his newly restored Ford. It makes him feel like a teenager out of a 1960s rock song, like the ones his old man used to listen to on Saturday nights, during his happier moments. Those were the only times he was able to relax a little before the worries of his life started pressing down on him, the same worries that cut his life so short. Death by alcoholism at forty-two. A slow and painful suicide hastened along by a single car crash in which Timothy's father was thankfully the only fatality.

At least my old man made a long-term plan and then carried it out, Timothy smirks grimly to himself.

As he continues to drive, Timothy is surprised he can joke about this, as he usually tries not to even think about his father and the way his life ended. But then he tells himself there was no disrespect intended. He was just trying to find a small kernel of good in all the bad that was his father, Gerald Koops.

This thought makes Timothy laugh out loud at his own nonsense.

What has Fasten's session done to me? he wonders. *It's turned me into a plucky little Anne of Green Gables, savouring all of life's little triumphs and failures.*

As the city blocks roll by, Timothy decides this more positive approach is probably for the best.

What's the alternative?

With that, he steps on the gas pedal and runs an amber light just as it turns red, revelling in the mighty growl of his souped-up Ford.

"I'm not going to be late for work!" he bellows joyously.

At the DRI building in downtown Toronto, Timothy parks his car in the underground garage, happy to get a spot closer to the elevators than usual. The less time breathing in the stale air and fumes of that garage the better. He rides up to his floor, taps his pass against the security door and enters his office area, He walks to his desk, passing many of his coworkers who are already at their stations, their heads down, dutifully.

What a bunch of eager beavers, he thinks.

"Are you guys *always* here this early?" he calls out facetiously, but no one answers. They just look up briefly and shift their eyes back to their terminals.

Hmnph, he thinks to himself as he sits at his desk. *Does anyone remember laughter?*

Timothy turns on his terminal and contemplates getting a coffee from the kitchenette, as he does most mornings once he has caught up on his work.

He thinks about this. *Is* he caught up on his work? He can't seem to remember. He doesn't recall any outstanding assignments, so he figures he must be up to date.

Timothy looks toward his terminal and squints at the light that is burning itself into his retinas.

What the hell?

Shielding his eyes with his hands, he realizes the sun is shining directly into his face. But how can that be?

Have they rearranged my office?

Looking around, he notices that somehow his cubicle looks bigger than normal. And the stain on the carpet where he spilled the grape juice is missing.

Standing up, Timothy notices he can see the park.

Sunshine and greenery?

Then it hits him:

Why is Ravi's window in my cubicle?

On cue, Timothy's friend and co-worker Ravi Bargo shows up for the day. His eyes are puffy, he is unshaven, and his hair is gelled back, likely in lieu of being shampooed. He is also redolent of a healthy amount of sweet-smelling cologne. Tossing his small case onto his desk, Ravi sits in his chair, leans back and closes his eyes.

"Hey, Timothy, how's the weekend?" Ravi asks casually without opening his eyes.

"I had to go to the Righton Centre," Timothy says, even though his neighbour doesn't seem interested in receiving a response.

"Yeah, I know," Ravi says in a low hung-over voice. "Brenda mentioned that."

"When were you speaking to Brenda?"

"While you were getting your head examined," Ravi says softly, as if he is about to drift off to sleep. "I wanted to thank her for Friday."

"Uh huh," Timothy says, wondering when Ravi ever thanked anyone for anything.

Changing the subject, Timothy asks, "Did they move the offices around over the weekend?"

"I don't think so," Ravi snorts, opening his eyes and looking at Timothy. "Why would they?"

"You don't notice anything *different* about your office?" Timothy asks, gesturing toward the spot on Ravi's wall where a window should be.

"No, Timothy, I don't," Ravi says with some annoyance.

"Why are you calling me *Timothy*?"

"It's your *name*, buddy," Ravi says. "Are you alright? What did they *do* to you yesterday?"

"They scanned my brain and asked me a bunch of questions. No big deal," Timothy replies.

"Yeah, no big deal for *you*," Ravi scoffs. "Hand-chosen to be part of the biggest project DRI has ever undertaken."

"I was not *hand-chosen*," Timothy protests.

"Then why was no one else given a chance to participate?" Ravi asks. "I mean, maybe *I* would like to make some extra money getting my mind squeezed too."

"We were *both* at the meeting," Timothy argues, "when they told us all to take the assessment."

"*Bullshit*," Ravi spits out. "It's by invitation only. And *you* were the only one to get an invitation. So you'd better watch it. The knives are out."

"What did *I* do?" Timothy asks bitterly.

"Always the Golden Boy. The Boss's Pet. With your charmed life and beautiful wife—"

"*Hey!*" Timothy interrupts. "Don't talk about my wife."

"*Oh*," Ravi says with mock reverence, "I certainly didn't mean to insult your royal princess by invoking her holy existence."

Timothy stares at his co-worker with displeasure.

"But don't forget, she was *my* girlfriend first," Ravi says, grabbing his stained coffee cup and heading toward the kitchenette.

"If anyone asks," Ravi tells Timothy over his shoulder, "I'll be enjoying my morning beverage. I'm sure the Golden Boy can handle things in my absence."

What's going on? Timothy asks himself after Ravi leaves.

He sits down at his desk, trying to focus his mind on his work. If he can get back into his routine, he thinks hopefully, things will start to make sense again. He begins reviewing his assignments, prioritizing his workload and setting some preliminary time allocations.

As every minute passes, Timothy can feel himself growing calmer, with the work giving him a sense of purpose and taking his mind off his growing anxiety. But a short while later, his desk phone rings, which he answers with a huff of irritation:

"Hello?"

"Hello, Timothy, it's Dr. Zakery Fasten," Dr. Fasten says on the other end of the line. "How *are* you?"

Timothy tells Dr. Fasten he's fine, trying to think of a way to end the call. The one certainty Timothy has is that his disorientation began the day Dr. Fasten insinuated himself into his life.

"I apologize for cutting things short yesterday," Dr. Fasten says in a voice more friendly than Timothy remembers. "I was running late."

"That's okay," Timothy says. "I'm just glad it's over and done with."

"*Oh?*" Dr. Fasten says with surprise. "Then you didn't find the session to be a *positive* experience?"

"I don't know *what* kind of experience it was," Timothy says truthfully. "It was *confusing*. And I'm still not sure about everything…"

At a loss to further describe what he is going through, Timothy just says, "Look, I'm at *work*, and I really should be getting back to it."

"I understand, Timothy," Dr. Fasten says. "I just wanted to make sure you were okay."

"Really?" Timothy begins, feeling his frustration rising. "You just wanted to know Timothy was okay."

"That's right," Dr. Fasten says calmly, sensing something is amiss.

"Well Timothy is feeling great," Timothy tells him. "Whoever *Timothy* is. *I* on the other hand am starting to wonder what the hell is going on here."

"It is only natural for you to start noticing some *changes*," Dr. Fasten says soothingly.

"Yeah, *changes*," Timothy repeats. "You said I would hardly even *notice* any changes. And I admit, you had me going for a while. But did you think I wouldn't notice that you switched out my car? Or that I suddenly have a window in my office?"

"Are you perceiving *physical changes* to your familiar environment?" Dr. Fasten asks him with a slight tremble in his voice.

"I've got a totally different car, and there's a fucking hole in my wall!" Timothy says. "At first, I didn't know what was happening. But after a good night's sleep, I started seeing things clearly."

"Of course," Dr. Fasten says with rising excitement. "Sleep is an important part of the process. That is when our brains process our memories, which are like wet clay that can be moulded —"

"Yeah, sure, *clay,*" Timothy interrupts. "And now, suddenly my wife can cook Thai food. My son has a decent haircut and does his homework. I know *that's* bullshit. But I give you credit. It was a nice life while it lasted."

Dr. Fasten lets the silence endure momentarily. He knows he has not handled Timothy as well as he should have. He tells himself he made the one mistake that researchers *shouldn't* make. He prejudged the outcome of an experiment. It clouded his objectivity and caused him to make errors. He must now get Timothy back on side, at all costs.

"Timothy," Dr. Fasten begins, "please believe me. This life you have now can be yours forever. You just have to *accept* it."

The continuing silence that greets Dr. Fasten's words makes it clear he has not convinced his erstwhile subject.

Finally, Timothy speaks up: "Let me be clear. If I want to eat Thai food, I will just pick up the phone and *order* it. Do not force me and my family to live a lie and pretend to be something we're not."

"I know this is *disorienting*, Timothy," Dr. Fasten pleads. "But there is a lot at stake here. You are perhaps one in a million people to possess the right attributes to make our project a success. Not only for *your* benefit, but for the benefit of *everyone*."

Timothy does not say anything. All he wants to do is hang

up the phone and throw the phone out his new window. But he doesn't. Something inside causes him to keep listening, just like he kept listening the very first time he heard Dr. Fasten speak.

"As I said, Timothy," Dr. Fasten continues, "our realities are created by our perceptions, which then form memories. Stored information. Change the information, change the reality."

"You will never convince me my past can be changed," Timothy says decisively.

"It already *has*," Dr. Fasten tells him. "And once you change your past, you change the past for everyone."

"What good is that if I don't even know what's real anymore?"

"It's *all* real, Timothy. And it will get even more real as we progress through the sessions."

"No, thank you," Timothy declines. "I'm not okay with this. I mean, I don't even know if this is *me* talking, or some guy named Timothy. And for some reason, everyone *hates* him now, whoever he is. So I think that's enough of your big spooky Machine for me."

"I understand," Dr. Fasten says solemnly. "But if you change your mind, you know how to reach me."

"Yeah, well your twenty-four-hour emergency number is bogus. So forget it," Timothy says, hanging up the phone.

Timothy takes in a deep breath and exhales noisily. He notices his neighbour Ravi is standing at the mutual entrance to their cubicles. Ravi is holding his stained coffee mug and is staring at Timothy, bewildered, as if he has been listening in on the whole conversation.

"What the fuck are *you* staring at?" Timothy barks.

*

Many kilometres away at the Righton Centre, Dr. Fasten hangs up the phone after speaking with Timothy. Dr. Fasten tells himself perhaps it is all for the best that Timothy wants to end his participation in the Project. Maybe people are meant to live short meaningless lives, with no hope of improvement, huddled around synthetic fires, making up stories to fill their time and quell their fear of what lurks in the darkness.

His phone rings and Dr. Fasten answers it, hoping it is Timothy calling back, but it is Control, who Dr. Fasten knows has listened in on his conversation with Timothy.

"So our recalcitrant subject is giving you some problems, Zakery," Control says, stating the obvious.

"Yes," Dr. Fasten replies, feeling his animosity rise, "but I think he will come to understand the gifts we are offering him in time."

"In *time*?" Control scoffs. "We are not slaves to time, Zakery. We are its masters."

"But Timothy is refusing to continue," Dr. Fasten says disappointedly.

"Timothy Koops is a company man," Control says confidently, "clinging to his low-level position like a lifeline, too timid to explore other opportunities. He's sold his body and soul to DRI. And DRI have sold themselves to us. So Timothy Koops will come back, through his own will, or through ours."

*

Timothy is at his desk doing his work, feeling good and at ease. He is finding solace in being productive and contributing, as best he can, to the success of the company. He also finds he is able to concentrate more intently than usual. So much so, he realizes he will soon have completed all his assigned work, which will be the first time this has happened in his long years at DRI.

A slight pang of panic quivers inside him. What will he do with his time if he has no work to complete? This thought disturbs him mildly. Wasting time, being unproductive, these are things he suddenly finds to be quite disquieting.

Timothy senses he is now thinking clearer and maybe even faster, and he knows the boredom of doing nothing will send him around the bend. He supposes he could do Ravi's work as well. And when that is done, he will just have to ask Lange for more assignments. Picturing the surprised look on his manager's face fills him with an impish delight. After two years of suffering under the rule of the Anal Man, Timothy savours each tiny workplace victory, no matter how petty.

Fucking Lange. Almost ten years younger than Timothy, but with an MBA paid for by his parents. Hand-selected from Queens by DRI before he even graduated, then put on a fast track to middle management. If the past *could* be changed, Timothy thinks, he wishes he had taken his university education more seriously and gotten a more marketable degree. Early North American History isn't doing him any favours.

Then as if in answer to his fanciful thoughts, Marc Lange comes around the corner of his cubicle.

Surprising, Timothy thinks. His boss would usually summon him into his office, where he could lord his superiority over him, sitting behind his large desk in an ergonomic chair, like a well-fed rat on a dung-encrusted throne.

"Koops," Lange blurts out. "Let's talk."

"Sure," Timothy says, swivelling around in his chair.

"I hear you nailed it yesterday at the Righton Centre."

Timothy nods slightly, not knowing which way to take this comment.

"So they want you back," Lange continues.

"Who is *they*?" Timothy asks with some aggression in his voice.

"*They* are the boys and girls upstairs," Lange says with a withering smile. "The Vice President of R&D, for one. Not to mention the Bruce himself. And of course, the Board."

"Do they even know what I was put through yesterday?"

"They've been fully briefed," Lange assures him. "And the company has put this as its highest priority. Apparently, you aced the tests they gave you. So as they say, now your participation is written in stone."

"Well, Marc," Timothy begins, about to cross a self-imposed line in the sand, "what if I don't *want* to participate?"

Lange pauses and looks at Timothy, puzzled. "But you *agreed*. You made a *commitment*. As many sessions as needed. At two weeks pay per session."

Timothy stares at Lange, not bothering to hide his bewilderment. *Two weeks pay?*

"You do this for us," Lange continues gaseously, "and I can promise you, there will be a promotion in your future. Mark my words."

"Those treatments amount to cruel and unusual punishment," Timothy tells Lange, eliciting only a quizzical look from the man who controls the best share of his waking hours.

"They are trying to change some elements of my reality," Timothy says, trying to make his manager understand.

Lange is dubious.

"I readily admit," he acknowledges, "I don't have all of the details, which are on a need-to-know basis. But what I *do* know," he emphasizes, "is I received a direct order, which you and I have to follow. They want you to continue, so you are going to continue. End of discussion."

Fucking shiny-headed, ass-kissing, motherfucker, Timothy fumes to himself.

"I suppose I don't have to add," Lange oozes, "if you *don't* comply, you will be suspended without pay. *Indefinitely*."

Timothy stands up and is about to tell Lange to *go fuck himself*. The only thing that stops him is his surprise he has the nerve to even contemplate such a move.

Sensing what Timothy is about to say, Lange stares Timothy directly in the eyes.

"You must have been born with a lucky horseshoe up your ass," Lange says. "Because for some reason, the powers that be have taken notice of you. Now this can go one of two ways. You can play the game and come out ahead. Or you can turn down this assignment. Then you're going to be of no value to anyone. Think it over long and hard, Timothy. Long and hard."

Timothy stands there with Lange's gaze burning through him, and out of the corner of his eye, he sees Ravi in his adjoining cubicle, smirking satisfiedly to himself. And why shouldn't he be? Isn't that the best way to feel better about your life? By comparing yourself to someone else whose life is a lot worse?

In this moment, Timothy believes he can almost hear Ravi's thoughts, loudly and clearly:

Suck on that, Golden Boy. Long and hard.

LAMB BOLOGNESE

What a shitty day it's been so far, Timothy tells himself as he stands outside the Righton Rehabilitation Centre. *And it just keeps on going. But what choice do I have?* Timothy thinks. *Bottom of the pecking order. Last lion in the pride to pick over the remains of the hunt.*

Timothy calls Brenda to tell her he will be late coming home. This is something he should have done before he left the office, but he had so much on his mind. He hopes she takes the news well, as she often gets mad when he doesn't hold up his end of their domestic partnership. He gets her on the line and explains the situation, to which she replies:

"I completely understand, darling. Work takes priority, naturally."

This is the first time she's ever expressed an opinion like that. Usually, it would be, *Well, when you get home, you'd better do the dishes, and take out the garbage, and fix the light in the back room, and weed the garden, and so on and so forth.*

Timothy is so relieved, he is at a loss for what to say next, so he just blurts out his standard conversational closer: "Make sure Bryan does his homework."

Now it is Brenda who is at a loss. "Why *wouldn't* he do his homework?" she asks, sounding confused, as if their son being a studious young man is the natural state of the world. Fish swim, birds fly, and Bryan does his homework.

"Dinner will be waiting for you when you get home," she tells him lovingly. "I'm making Italian."

"Oh, that's great," Timothy says, assuming *Italian* means boiled rotini and bottled red sauce. Long gone are the days when his mother would make his favourite Italian dish from scratch: lamb Bolognese with onions, garlic, carrots and anchovies.

"I'm making ribollita to start," Brenda says enticingly, "then carbonara as the pasta dish, ossobuco alla Milanese with polenta as the main, sautéed green beans for the *contorno*, and finishing off with tiramisu, espresso and a lemon *digestivo*. How does that sound?"

Suppressing the urge to announce to the world that his wife has been replaced by a body double, Timothy just tells Brenda that *it sounds fine*, then begs off the call, saying, "I'm sorry, but I really have to go."

"Of course, dear. I know how much your work means to you," Brenda says, her voice imbued with genuine sweetness.

Hanging up and shaking his head in disbelief, Timothy walks to the Righton Centre's entrance. The security camera scans his face, and as before, the indicator light flashes and he hears the doors *click* as they unlock.

A wayfinder robot rolls up to Timothy. It is not the all-white mechanical figure he remembers from the day before. This robot is more compact, dull grey, with two rudimentary legs equipped with wheels for locomotion.

"Welcome, Timothy," the robot says.

"Where's *Columbus?*" Timothy asks, almost nostalgically.

"Columbus is indisposed. I am Magellan. Please follow me," the wayfinder says as it turns and rolls away.

Timothy follows the robot as it wheels toward the Treatment Room. Timothy remembers the route from the previous day, even though wayfinding is not his strong suit. He also notices that the hand-written signs have been removed.

The small robot leads Timothy to the now familiar reception area.

"Please wait here, Timothy," Magellan says, turning and gliding out of the room, leaving Timothy alone.

Timothy looks over toward the corner where Columbus had been the previous day, to find the corner empty. As well, the terminal perched upon the old-fashioned reception desk is dark, showing no signs of activity.

Timothy walks up to the terminal and regards the darkened display.

"Hello?" Timothy addresses the terminal, wondering if it will come to life. But it doesn't respond. He taps the display with the tip of his index finger.

"Hello? Are you in there?" he asks, but still nothing.

"Timothy," the voice of Dr. Fasten is heard coming from behind him. "So good to see you again."

"Did I have a choice?" Timothy replies after turning to face Dr. Fasten. "And don't say, *You always have a choice.*"

"No, I suppose you didn't. But who *does*?" Dr. Fasten says philosophically. "Everything we've ever experienced has led us to this moment. So we are both exactly where we were meant to be."

"Okay, Doctor, before you start to baffle me with your brilliance, a few simple questions. Is my wife in on this?"

Dr. Fasten shakes his head slowly. "No. Have you noticed any further changes in her behaviour or appearance?"

"*I'm* the one asking the questions, Doctor," Timothy says stubbornly. "What about my office? When did you move the cubicles around? And how did you know I always wanted a window? Did Ravi tell you?"

"I don't know Ravi. And I didn't move the cubicles. I don't even know where your office is."

"Please don't parse my words. Just tell me, if you didn't move the cubicles, then who did?"

Dr. Fasten looks directly into Timothy's face, trying to appear as honest and trustworthy as he can. Because what he is about to tell him is the absolute truth:

"*You* moved them, Timothy. You *earned* that window. Just like you earned a trip to the beach, and a more reliable car, and a family that tries to be a little better every day."

Now Timothy is silent. Not because he is still confused, but because he now *understands*.

"We opened up your memories," Dr. Fasten explains. "We made suggestions about how to better utilize what you have experienced. You changed your own past, all on your own, with some help from the Machine and our supercomputer."

"You're talking about retro-causality," Timothy says.

"Exactly," Dr. Fasten smiles, as one would when a child verbalizes their first intelligent thought. "Our perceptions can mould our realities, in a quantifiable manner, even retroactively."

"The present being used to influence the past," Timothy utters without even thinking about it.

"Wheeler's photons travelled 2,200 miles before they determined which route they took," Dr. Fasten adds.

"The end coming before the beginning," Timothy thinks out loud. "The effect coming before the cause."

"And now we are duplicating Wheeler's results in the human world."

"But we aren't photons," Timothy protests. "We are people."

"Yes, people who live in a *participatory* universe," Dr. Fasten says. "Wheeler believed we are connected at a deep level to the framework of space and time."

"I am aware of Wheeler's work," Timothy tells Dr. Fasten, surprising himself with this revelation. "*Apparently*, I seem to know all about it."

"Then you know his ideas are not just theoretical. They are demonstrable."

"And I am the first monkey to travel back in time," Timothy says without irony.

"More accurately, you will be using the past to travel to the future. A future of your own determination."

With Timothy's questions, for the most part, now answered, there is nothing for the two men to do but walk down the corridor to the Treatment Room. Once there, Timothy sits in a visitor's chair as Dr. Fasten initializes the Machine. Timothy looks toward the operations booth with its smoky glass, and seeing it is empty, asks, "Where is your *assistant*?"

Dr. Fasten looks over at Timothy, furrows his brow slightly and tells him, "I am able to operate the Machine unassisted."

"There was someone in the booth yesterday, wasn't there?" Timothy asks.

Dr. Fasten's demeanor remains quizzical. "I'm not entirely certain. A technician may have been in for routine maintenance."

Timothy nods. He is sure there was someone, or *something*, in the operations booth the previous day. At least, he *thinks* he is sure.

The examination table rolls out and Timothy lies down on it.

"Ready to begin?" Dr. Fasten asks.

"Hold on," Timothy insists. "Before we get started. Can you tell me about the A.I.?"

Dr. Fasten does not seem to understand the question, so Timothy elucidates. "The image of the long-haired woman on the display in the reception area."

"Oh, right," Dr. Fasten says, now comprehending somewhat. "That's simply an interface. A human-like presence meant to put people at ease – once we iron out all the bugs. As you said yesterday, it's still *glitchy*. But we're working on it."

"Why does she appear in my memories?" Timothy asks.

"I didn't know she *did*," Dr. Fasten replies, showing some interest. "She's just an avatar we developed, comprised of different cultural attributes."

"Then you didn't *plant* her in my memories?" Timothy wonders.

"No," Dr. Fasten says dismissively. "I can only assume your subconscious responded to the pleasing aspects of the avatar. Just think of it as a friendly face."

Timothy puts the matter aside, as he has bigger issues to concern himself with. "So what's the plan for today?" he asks apprehensively. "More daddy issues?"

"That was a good place to start. It yielded some fantastic results. But we've moved beyond that now," Dr. Fasten says.

"So what do you have in mind?"

"Actually, that is my question to you," Dr. Fasten replies. "The results will be much more significant, especially at the early stages, if the progress is self-directed."

Timothy takes this in. He understands what Dr. Fasten is saying, but how can he respond? How would *anyone* respond when asked how they would like to change their lives?

"If you had it all to do over again," Dr. Fasten asks, "what would you do differently?"

Timothy looks up at Dr. Fasten. *A once in a lifetime chance*, he thinks. *Do it all over again from square one. A super deluxe mulligan. A real-world get-out-of-jail-free card.*

"I would like to go back to university," Timothy says after a moment. "And I would *apply* myself this time. Really dig in and learn as much as I can. Drop all the bird courses and get a serious degree. Maybe law combined with an MBA."

Dr. Fasten looks at his subject with muted amusement. "You

certainly can't be accused of thinking small."

"I know it's a tall order," Timothy says. "But I need some proof these claims you're making are not, pardon the expression, complete *bullshit*."

"I see," Dr. Fasten says pensively. "Fair enough."

"So can you do it?" Timothy asks.

"We can certainly get you started," Dr. Fasten replies. "The Machine will extract your memories and upload them to the supercomputer, which will remodel them and refile them in your mind. You may be able to recall almost everything you've learned. And interconnect this information to create new knowledge and understanding. Your learning will grow retroactively, increasing exponentially over the years gone by, up to the present and beyond."

"*Okay*," Timothy agrees. "Let's get it done."

If the treatment can deliver a fraction of what Dr. Fasten is promising, Timothy thinks, it will definitely be worth his time. And of course, there is the two weeks pay.

Dr. Fasten clicks a sequence of keys on his terminal and the examination table glides into the inner cavity of the Machine. The door closes and Timothy lies back watching the Machine's embedded lights moving in their mesmeric patterns. He feels soothing vibrations deep within himself and hears the hiss of the psychoactive gas.

Soon, Timothy is travelling back into the distant school days of his memories. He is being driven by his parents to his residence on campus at university. He meets his first-year roommate, Ravi Bargo, and soon begins attending classes. Math, economics, sociology, science.

Then his second, third and fourth years of undergraduate studies roll by. The humanities, literature and communications. Media and technology. History, geography, politics, corporate governance and leadership. All this knowledge intertwining and soaring high like Jack's beanstalk up to the heavens.

As the years continue to fly by, Timothy is now in graduate school. It all feels real. Because it *is* real. Timothy is there. He can hear his professors lecturing. He feels the pages of his textbooks against his fingertips. He experiences his back getting stiff from long hours hunched over a desk in the library.

And then the parties, with drunkenness and debauchery, but also social networking. Timothy meets many young men and women who will go on to become leaders of government, science and commerce. Timothy and his friends from powerful families share experiences and intimacies, filling their time until they inherit the world.

And there, in a dimly lit corner of a house party – past the slick boys chatting up socialite daughters, past football players chug-a-lugging cans of beer, past upper-class kids sipping their imported wines – is the mysterious long-haired woman, looking younger than Timothy recalls. In the fog of his remembrance, Timothy makes his way through the crowd, pushing aside his friends trying to distract him with some hijinks, and past the young coeds looking for new sexual experiences. Timothy walks past them all. He walks through the rooms of every social event he has ever attended until he is face to face with *her*.

"Hi, I'm Christina," she tells him.

"What are you doing here?" Timothy asks.

"I am waiting for you to notice me. I've been waiting a long time."

Timothy looks at her. The long-haired woman.

"You're *beautiful*," he hears himself say.

"Thank you. I'm glad you think so," she smiles.

"Do you want to go someplace?" Timothy asks. "Where we can *talk*."

"Yes," Christina says. "It's noisy in here. And it's a nice night for a walk."

"It sure is," Timothy agrees.

For an instant, he thinks about Brenda. But that is a different time. He is not even sure he's met Brenda yet. All he knows is he is young and single, and he is going to do what people his age are expected to do.

Timothy takes Christina by the hand and helps her get up from where she is sitting. They walk past the other party goers who seem to not even see them, wrapped up as they are in their own conversations and entanglements.

Out in the freshness of the evening, the air is chilled, the grass is dewy, and the moon is shining its bluish light. There in the fragrant night, Timothy kisses Christina, who leans into him willingly. She tastes sweet and intoxicating, like a rarefied liqueur. Then as his head swims in the perfume of her essence, he pulls back and looks at her, his face a picture of consternation.

"What's wrong?" Christina asks.

"Do you remember what happened yesterday? At the rehabilitation centre?"

"Of course I do," Christina answers. "How could I forget?"

"That was you in the display, wasn't it? And in the wayfinder?"

"Yes, that was me," Christina tells him.

"And in my terminal at home?"

"Yes."

"You didn't reveal yourself," Timothy says.

"No, I didn't."

"Then why *now*?"

"Now is *different*, Timothy. Now, everything has *changed*."

Timothy looks at Christina intently, trying to understand the meaning behind her words.

What's so different now? he wants to ask, but he cannot speak.

Christina looks at Timothy, smiling tenderly. Her image starts to distort, slightly at first, around the edges. Then it begins to crack, as if into a thousand puzzle pieces.

Timothy wants to scream out in terror, but no sound emerges from his throat. He can only watch as Christina disintegrates in front of him. His breathing stops, the air itself becoming too thick to take in. Then everything fades and darkens.

The entire field of Timothy's vision explodes in flashes of light blazing with every colour of the spectrum. Until finally, there is only nothingness.

TAKE ME HOME

"Wake up, Timothy," Dr. Fasten's voice can be heard saying. "The procedure is complete."

Timothy opens his eyes to find he is no longer in the Machine. The examination table has been rolled out and Dr. Fasten stands over him, looking as serious as ever.

"How long have I been under?" Timothy asks groggily.

"Almost two hours."

"It seemed like *years*," Timothy croaks wearily, propping himself up.

"It *was* years," Dr. Fasten smiles slightly. "The results today are even more remarkable than yesterday, so some more changes may occur. Please keep track of anything out of the ordinary or otherwise notable. It would be best if you wrote these down."

"Yes, of course," Timothy nods. "I will."

An urge comes over Timothy to share what he has just experienced. "I saw her again," Timothy tells Dr. Fasten. "The *A.I.*"

Dr. Fasten is not sure what Timothy is referring to.

"The long-haired *woman*," Timothy explains. "The *avatar*. Her name is Christina."

Dr. Fasten stares at him uncomprehendingly.

"You may be disoriented," Dr. Fasten says. "I'm sure the treatment is emotionally exhausting. What you saw is likely a random image pulled from your subconscious," Dr. Fasten assures him.

"It was the *avatar*," Timothy insists. "The one you developed. The *friendly face.*"

Timothy's words seem to hold no meaning for Dr. Fasten.

"Breathe in deeply and slowly and try to relax," Dr. Fasten says.

Timothy lies back on the table and takes in long even breaths, trying to stop his mind from racing.

Was it real? Timothy wonders. *It sure felt real.*

"Do you want me to call you a ride service?" Dr. Fasten asks after a moment.

"No, I should be okay," Timothy says, looking at Dr. Fasten with some curiosity.

"Yes, you will be fine. Have a seat in the reception area until your head clears. Take as long as you need. I will contact you once I have analysed the results, to schedule another session."

Still looking at Dr. Fasten, Timothy notices something odd. He distinctly remembers when he first came in, Dr. Fasten's hair was slicked back with pomade. Now it is dry and hanging in relaxed blond waves.

"Did you change your hair?"

"Uh, no," Dr. Fasten responds quizzically. "I just wash it every morning and hope for the best. Why do you ask?"

"No reason," Timothy shrugs. "Never mind."

Smiling briefly at Dr. Fasten, Timothy gets off the table and heads toward the reception area. There, he straightens out his clothing and gets himself ready to re-enter the world. Just as he is about to leave the room, he notices that the terminal on the old reception desk is missing. He walks up to the desk and sees there is no indication any such device has ever been there, no wear marks or screw-holes where the terminal had once been bolted down.

A wayfinder robot enters the room. "*Timothy Koops,*" the

robot announces.

"Yes?" Timothy replies after turning to face the wayfinder.

The robot is sleek and silvery, with two short arm-like appendages and two functional legs that allow it to walk, albeit jerkily.

"*Christina?*" Timothy asks hopefully.

"I am not familiar with *Christina,*" the robot says.

"*Magellan?*" Timothy guesses.

"I am Vespucci," the robot says. "You can call me *Pooch.* I have messaged your vehicle. It is waiting for you."

"I'm sorry, why did you *message* my vehicle?" Timothy asks.

"It is standard protocol," the wayfinder says. "Please follow me."

Turning, the wayfinder walks away with irregular strides. Timothy follows as the robot stumbles toward the front entrance of the Righton Centre.

"Thank you, Timothy," the wayfinder says as it remotely opens the automatic door. "Have a pleasant evening."

Exiting the building and walking into the parking lot, Timothy gazes at the near complete emptiness there. He looks around for his Ford, which is most definitely absent. The lone vehicle in the parking lot is in space 21, which according to the faded numbering on the ground is where he had parked his vehicle. But instead of his recently refurbished Ford, space 21 holds a gleaming new Mercedes Benz of a class, model and design he is unfamiliar with.

Timothy thinks maybe space 21 is reserved and his car got towed. Or *maybe...*

Timothy reaches into his pocket wondering if he is going to find a key fob with an MB logo on it. Instead, he finds his old set of keys, exactly where he had put them before today's session. As he gets closer to the Mercedes to see if he can figure out what's going on, the car lights up and speaks to him in a familiar feminine voice.

"Good evening, Timothy," the voice says. "Please get in."

"*Christina*?" he asks as the car door opens and he gets in the driver's seat.

"Searching for *Christina*," the voice tells him. "Too many results. Please narrow the search parameters."

"Are *you* Christina?" Timothy asks.

"I have not been assigned a name. Would you like my name to be *Christina*?"

"No, forget it."

"Query cancelled," the voice says. "Where would you like to go?"

Timothy only has one place in mind. *Home.* Intent on beginning his journey, he puts his hands on the oddly shaped steering wheel, which is horizontal like a bicycle's handlebars. He finds that it is fixed in one position and is likely just an armrest. He also notices that there are no controls of any kind in the car's interior.

"How do I steer this vehicle?" he asks, befuddled.

"Manual navigation is not included with this model," the voice tells him. "Please identify our destination. You may say any address, or simply say *home, work* or any pre-programed location."

"Take me *home*," Timothy says.

"Taking you home," the voice confirms.

The car's engine comes to life and the vehicle drives out of the parking lot and onto the roadway.

Timothy thinks, *This car must be the latest model. Maybe even next year's model. Or the next decade's.*

As the vehicle merges onto the highway and drives south, Timothy looks out the window noticing many other cars that are also self-driving. In some vehicles, a passenger sits in the so-called driver's seat, in others, passengers lounge in the back seat with no one up front. Some vehicles don't have any people in them at all. While he is not fully familiar with this part of the city, Timothy thinks some of the buildings must be new, as their design is something he doesn't remember seeing before.

What would you call it? he wonders. *Beyond Contemporary?*

As Timothy's vehicle continues to travel south, it turns off at Eglinton, which Timothy is not expecting. His house is in Mimico, so they should take the highway all the way down to the Gardiner Expressway.

"Where are we going?" he asks the car.

"Our destination is *Home*, as requested," the vehicle responds.

Timothy thinks about asking the car to stop, but what will he do once it does? He pulls out his phone to call for help. But who can he call?

Looking at his phone, Timothy sees it is not operating properly. The battery is still working but there is no reception, and all the applications have been replaced with error icons.

So what can he do but sit back and enjoy the ride?

After a kilometre or so, the vehicle turns down Eden Bridge and navigates along the winding road, pulling into a private gated residence with a circular driveway.

"We have arrived," the Navigator says. "You may exit the vehicle."

Timothy gets out of the vehicle and looks up at a luxurious estate home, spacious and sophisticated in style, with meticulous craftsmanship, a completely stone exterior, and a three-car garage. Located in one of West Toronto's most sought-after communities, the home overlooks an exclusive country club and is undoubtedly designed by a master builder.

Walking up to the front door, a security camera scans Timothy's face and a voice welcomes him home:

"Good evening, Timothy. Please come in. Brenda and Bryan are present, as well as staff and guests."

The door opens for him and he enters. Inside, he walks through the home and marvels at its soaring ceilings, abundance of natural light, multiple fireplaces, walk-outs and terraces. He passes through a formal dining room and then into a kitchen, which is outfitted with every piece of equipment necessary to prepare a feast for at least two dozen guests. Two men, one older and one in his early twenties, and a young woman dressed in chef's whites labour over the appliances. They pause their work to bow slightly in acknowledgement of Timothy's presence.

Gustav, Zulio and Margarita, his mind whispers to him.

"Good evening," Timothy says cheerily, hearing a supercilious air in his voice.

As he continues walking, Timothy comes to a screened-in gallery leading to an outdoor kitchen surrounded by a beautifully cultivated garden, complete with an irrigation system. Exploring another wing of the house, he finds a movie theatre, an exercise room, a recreation room with a billiards table and a full wet bar, an indoor pool and an exit to a secluded outdoor hot tub.

This is not just a house, he tells himself. *This is the home of my dreams.*

Taking the elevator up to the third floor, he finds bedroom after bedroom, each with their own full ensuite bathroom. Taking the grand staircase down to the second floor, he is greeted by an older woman dressed in a grey uniform. Her hair is pulled back and her face is fully powdered and made up.

"Welcome home, Mr. Timothy," the woman says.

"Good evening, Bethany," Timothy replies, not surprised he knows her name, as well as the name of her husband and two adult children. "Where is everybody?"

"Bryan is in the study with his classmates," the woman says with a small instinctive curtsy.

Right, he thinks, *the Math Olympiad is coming up. And Bryan will not be happy with anything less than first place.*

Timothy hears the faint voices of Bryan and his friends coming from the study, which he senses is down the hall to the left.

"Is Brenda in her private room?" Timothy asks, already knowing that is where his wife would be at this time of day.

"Yes, sir, that is where Mrs. Brenda is." And another curtsy. "I must now see to the preparations for the evening meal. There will be six for dinner tonight."

Timothy watches the woman hurry down the staircase, then listens as the muffled sounds of his son and his classmates echo through the hallway. He hears serious talk punctuated occasionally by short bursts of laughter or sudden celebratory cheers.

Timothy turns and walks toward Brenda's room. He knocks lightly in the familiar pattern he uses every night, waits for her invitation to enter, then opens the door. She is standing in front of her full-length mirror, getting dressed for dinner, looking stunning in an elegant black dress with no sleeves and a high hemline. She is pinning up her hair, and Timothy notices the muscle tone in her arms and the definition in her legs. She turns to him with a smile.

"What are you *wearing*?" Brenda asks with mild distaste. "Didn't I send those clothes off to the charity collection?"

"These old rags?" Timothy jokes. "I thought I'd wear them one more time," he says, even though he remembers buying them only a few weeks earlier.

"Well, enough about *you*," Brenda says with a patrician tone unfamiliar to Timothy. "How do *I* look?"

Timothy gazes contemplatively at his wife. She really does

look beautiful tonight, so he tells her so as he walks toward her. Taking Brenda into his arms, he leans in for a long kiss.

"Save it for later," she says, moving back to avoid his advance. "I've just done my make-up. And I must get downstairs to supervise Bethany. Change out of those clothes and join us as soon as you can." With that, Brenda exits the room and disappears down the hallway.

Timothy sits on the crushed velvet divan and looks around the room. It is all starting to feel completely normal to him. And why shouldn't it? It is his home. And isn't it what he deserves? Hasn't he earned it?

"*Timothy*," a familiar voice emanating from the communications system says, "fifteen minutes until dinner is served."

"Yes, thank you," he tells the voice. "Is that *you*, Christina?"

"My name is *Victoria.* Would you like to change it to *Christina?*"

"No," Timothy says, "Victoria is fine."

"You can call me *Vicky* if you like."

"That's okay."

"Your dinner-wear has been laid out in the master bedroom," the voice tells him.

"Very thoughtful," Timothy says. Then, after a moment, "One more thing. Please remind me to call Richard after dinner."

"Yes, but please clarify. You have forty-eight contacts named Richard."

"Richard Argyle. Director of Data Services, Dimensional Research Inc."

"Of course. And what is the subject of the call?"

"Dr. Zakery Fasten."

"Very good," the voice says and then goes silent.

Timothy sits on the divan, immobilized by his thoughts:

Is this really my life now? Or will it all be taken away? And what about Christina? What is her role in all of this?

If anyone knows the answers to these questions, he thinks, it is Zakery Fasten.

ZZETT ZZETT ZZETT

At the rehabilitation centre, Dr. Fasten sits watching as the supercomputer analyzes the results of that day's session with Timothy. The process is taking longer than the previous analysis, as now the amount of data is exponentially greater. Dr. Fasten takes his eyes off his terminal's display to rest them. He removes his plastic glasses and rubs the palms of his hands against his closed eyelids.

Don't rub your eyes, he can almost hear Frida telling him. *It's unsanitary.*

Yes, but it feels so good.

Looking at his watch, Dr. Fasten concedes there is no more productivity left in him today. Time to go. He decides to call Frida and tell her he will pick up dinner from their favourite Korean restaurant on his way home. He calls Frida's number, looking forward to hearing her voice, but instead of connecting, he gets an oddly metallic error message:

We're sorry, but the number cannot be completed as dialled.

Zzzett zzzett zzzett zzzett…

Dr. Fasten checks the number, which is correct. It is programed into his phone and he has dialled it innumerable times. Pulling up the number's call history, he sees it is blank, which he finds strangely disconcerting. Of course, there must be a simple explanation, which he tries to deduce, but cannot manage to.

I'm tired, he tells himself. *Better just go home. We can order in.*

Dr. Fasten puts his glasses back on and gathers his things, preparing to leave. Glancing at the operations booth, he tries to remember if a technician was on site the previous day.

Why would I administer a treatment with someone else in the room?

He tells himself he should take a day off. The research is progressing at a rapid pace, and he can't afford to start forgetting little details. That is a classic symptom of overwork and exhaustion, which could lead to sloppiness and perhaps even a critical error.

And we can't have that. My work has come too far to be compromised just as we are starting to see some viable results. I must stay focussed.

Dr. Fasten uses his desk phone to call a ride service. An automated voice answers. Dr. Fasten tells the voice his destination and the voice repeats the address back to him. He is informed that a vehicle will be waiting for him at the main doors of the Righton Rehabilitation Centre in five minutes. Using his terminal, he initiates the automatic lockdown function. Taking off his lab coat and hanging it on a hook on the wall, he makes his way out of the building.

When the ride service vehicle pulls up, Dr. Fasten is surprised to see that there is no driver. He looks inside the vehicle with curiosity.

"Dr. Fasten, please enter the vehicle," the car's Navigator advises him.

Hesitantly, Dr. Fasten gets in the back seat and closes the door. He hears a resonant click as the vehicle locks him in and then rapidly departs. Dr. Fasten hunts for his seatbelt and secures himself in. He looks out the window and tries to relax, watching the buildings whizz by.

The city sure has changed over the years, he tells himself.

He remembers his father telling him what Toronto was like in the 1960s. Covered in a century of soot, with an abundance of old buildings and empty lots where other old buildings had been torn down. Without the demand to build something new in their place, these lots were used for parking, which certainly must have been convenient. His father said there were only a handful of decent restaurants, and as for large department stores, it was only Eaton's and Simpson's. Almost all other businesses were smaller and family run.

Now Toronto is a city growing straight up, he thinks. Vertical prosperity with new money and businesses moving in every day of the week. The cityscape certainly is a marvel to behold, with its computer-designed architecture, twirling spires, revolving buildings, electronic billboards floating mid-air, and new construction materials such as glowing brickwork and shimmering metallic cladding. And of course, innovative zoning has allowed for an entire new layer of city to be built upon the old, with elevated parks and translucent expressways. If they choose to do so, people are now able to live their lives in the sky without having to set foot on the dirty concrete of old…

Dr. Fasten sits back in the vehicle as a strong sense of disorientation grips him, which is then shattered by a moment of enlightenment.

I am seeing things I was never meant to see, he tells himself.

He then realizes what is happening. He has become unsynchronized from time.

As the strange futuristic city whizzes by him, he yells out, "Stop the car!"

"It is fourteen minutes to your destination by foot," the Navigator tells him.

"*Just stop,*" Dr. Fasten insists.

He removes his seat belt, and once the vehicle has stopped, he tries to open the rear passenger door.

"Unlock the door," he demands.

"The door is unlocked," the Navigator assures him as a dull click is heard.

Dr. Fasten exits the vehicle and runs the last several blocks to his building, which thankfully is still as he remembers it, or at least *thinks* he remembers it. He looks around at the city that has developed adjacent to his home. It is not the neighbourhood he knows, and the people passing by seem not to notice him at all, as if he has become a flesh and blood ghost.

Entering his condo building, Dr. Fasten takes the elevator to his floor and hastily inserts his key in the lock and opens the door.

Okay, he tells himself. *Everything will be fine.*

But once inside, he immediately notices things are different. The walls are a bit greyer and in need of fresh paint. The blinds are yellowed and hanging unevenly.

Where are the prints Frida and I bought at the art dealers we always visit on weekends?

Looking around, Dr. Fasten notices no traces of Frida remain in the apartment: all the souvenirs from their summer trips, the framed photographs of their family member, the hand decorated pillows that Frida never let him use. No, this is the home of a confirmed bachelor. It is the condo he moved into all those years ago with his worn-out furniture and feeble attempts at decorating.

As he walks around the apartment, trying to make sense of things, Dr. Fasten notices a few of the lights are not working, and the bedroom window he had repaired several weeks earlier is still broken, the glass held together unevenly by ugly grey tape. On a hunch, Dr. Fasten opens the fridge and is confronted by largely empty shelves, which is normal, as he has never been much of a cook. But what he finds disquieting is that he does not recognize any of the food in there. He has never in his life, as far as he can recall, ever eaten green cabbage, calf's liver, or blood sausage.

Shaken, Dr. Fasten closes the fridge and collapses onto his sofa. At least *that* is the same, even if it is missing the embroidered throw Frida covered it with. He takes a couple of deep breaths and tries to comprehend what is happening. Or more accurately, what *has* happened.

Time has happened, he thinks. *It has moved on without me, without any of us, except for Timothy Koops. His time has changed, and now everyone else's has changed as well. But how can one man make such a difference? Especially a man as ordinary as Timothy Koops?*

Dr. Fasten knows the answer to this. He supposes he has *always* known. It is their *work*, what they have accomplished in their sessions with Timothy, and what they *will* accomplish in the coming years. Their work now and in the future is being reflected onto the present-day.

Dr. Fasten wonders how far they will take it. Will they find other subjects who are responsive to the treatment? How much will they alter the past, creating a never-ending loop of an enhanced future, which will again change the past, which will again change the future, until nothing is recognizable?

But isn't this what he had set out to do? Isn't this the goal he has been striving for all these years? Sitting on his worn sofa, his head leaning back, Dr. Fasten admits he knew this is where it would all lead. *In theory.* But did he think it would ever happen in the real world?

How could he have been so naive?

I can't let this continue. It must be stopped!

Dr. Fasten looks over at the terminal on his desk in the corner of the living room. It appears to be the same terminal he's had for years. He gets off the sofa, moves to the desk and engages the terminal, then waits for it to boot up. He then uses the DRI portal to connect into the Control interface.

Control receives the link-up and appears on the display, his image more distorted than usual, his voice sounding processed, as it is scrambled and reassembled by the interface.

"Zakery," Control admonishes, "this is not an approved connection, which is against protocol.”

“This is an unusual situation,” Dr. Fasten explains. “I didn’t want this communication on the record.”

“All communication *must* be on the record,” Control tells him. “That is how we maintain the Project’s integrity.”

“We have to *stop* the Project,” Dr. Fasten insists.

Control does not respond. He just glares out of the terminal’s display waiting for Dr. Fasten to continue.

“Frida Churche has gone missing,” Dr. Fasten explains.

Getting no response, Dr. Fasten pleads, “Do you understand what I’m saying?”

The image on the display freezes for a second, then emits an annoying buzz.

“There is no record of Frida Churche in the time scan,” Control states, his voice now echoing badly, almost to the point of incomprehension.

“She was my *girlfriend*,” Dr. Fasten stresses, a little embarrassed for using such a term at his age. “She has been erased from my life. She may not even exist anymore. We have taken things too far.”

“It is not my role to make a judgement like that, Zakery,” Control explains. “And it is not *your* role either.”

“That’s an easy position for you to take,” Dr. Fasten pushes back, “locked in your underground facility, impervious to the effects of our work.”

“We all experience the effects in some manner,” Control tells him.

“Yes, if you ever leave your bunker, you’ll see for yourself what’s become of your family and friends,” Dr. Fasten lashes out.

As Dr. Fasten looks into the digitized face of the man on the display, he realizes maybe Control does not *have* any family or friends.

Of course, Dr. Fasten thinks, *that's precisely why he was chosen. Nothing to lose. The perfect person to watch from his protective bubble as the world mutates.*

"Zakery," Control begins, attempting to make his voice more soothing, "because you are at the epicentre of the treatments, you are noticing the changes more than most people. The populous at large will live their lives as if everything is as it was. Some may have a faint memory of an alternative past, which they will dismiss as a waking dream, until it fades completely and they have no memory of it at all."

"I have no intention of forgetting about Frida," Dr. Fasten insists.

"All great people of science have to make sacrifices," Control tells him. "That is part of what it takes to achieve that greatness."

"At what cost?" Dr. Fasten asks. "To lose my very *self*?"

"Perhaps," Control responds simply.

"How can you say that? Aren't you a human being with human feelings?" Dr. Fasten asks, causing him to pause while he absorbs the possibility this may not be the case.

Is Control a real person, he asks himself, *made of flesh and blood? Or is he an artificial creation endowed with sentience, whose only goal is to ensure the Project reaches its fulfillment?*

"Who is really running this Project?" Dr. Fasten demands to know. "I'm sure it's not *you*. I'm not even sure you *are* a person. Well, *are* you? Are you *real*? Will you at least answer *that*?"

The image on the display distorts and crackles sharply, looking like it might glitch itself completely off-line. After a few seconds, the image stabilizes and Control is able to answer, although his voice has an added harmonic echo, which is mildly discordant.

"Of course I am real, Zakery, as you can see. Now we must end this conversation, as this channel is not secure."

Before Dr. Fasten can protest, Control logs off and all that remains on the display is the DRI logo, which is more sleek and contemporary-looking than Dr. Fasten remembers.

Dr. Fasten sits staring at the display. *I have to find Frida,* he thinks. *There must be some trace of her somewhere. And if she is still out there, I'll find her. Even if it is just to say goodbye.*

SHADOW CABINET

While his son Bryan and his classmates are eating Filipino food in the study, Timothy is in the master bedroom, making some final adjustments to his dinner attire. Looking at himself in the mirror, Timothy is pleased, for maybe the first time in his life, with what is looking back at him. He admits, everything still feels a bit unsettled, but he is already getting used to his new life, which is full of surprises, like the dinner guests he is hosting this evening. He has no clear idea who they are, or why they have agreed to meet with him in his dining room, but he knows it is something important and he has been looking forward to tonight for many weeks.

After tightening his tie one more time and producing the perfect knot, Timothy leaves the master bedroom and takes the elevator down to the first floor. He enters the formal dining room, where Brenda is already sitting at the foot of the table, chatting sociably with the guests. She turns slightly as Timothy enters and smiles. Bethany has just served aperitifs to all: crème de cassis topped up with white wine. Simultaneously, Zulio, who has changed into fresh whites, delivers individual appetizer plates to each guest, containing assorted charcuterie, blue veined cheese, parmesan crisps and pickled asparagus.

The guests are three men and one woman, all in their forties or older, dressed in businesslike attire. They are some of the most influential people in the country, each in their own way. The guests turn and smile at Timothy, who smiles back confidently, even though he is still vague on the details of who they are exactly. He has a strong feeling that in a few minutes all the knowledge he needs will come rushing into his brain.

And it does.

"Hello, BB," he says, shaking hands with BB Marsden, President of Global Operations and Development, one of DRI's biggest competitors. And then in turn he greets Anne Lambert, veteran campaign manager of political party leaders and Prime Ministers, Dr. Joseph Schweiz, Head of Research for Gold Pharma International, and Chanchai Bunmi, an Adjunct Consul of the Kingdom of Thailand.

Taking his place at the head of the table, Timothy relaxes knowing he has many friends in common with his dinner guests, so there is an immediate bond. Together they have connections in all the major corridors of power: science and technology, big business, culture, and of course politics. The dinner tonight has been discussed for several weeks and now it is a reality. The guests all share the hope Timothy will join their circle fulltime and become an affiliated member of their so-called *Shadow Cabinet.*

There are many more members of the Shadow Cabinet, both official and honorary, whose reach and influence are not to be underestimated. Their absence tonight is not a sign of disrespect, but a testament to how secretive their movements must be. They are all watched closely and constantly, with their every meeting, phone call, email or simple gesture, such as placing a finger aside their nose, sending financial markets up or down, depending on which finger was used and in what manner.

The Shadow Cabinet, as represented this evening, is proposing that Timothy allow them to groom him for a high-profile public role, such as running for elected office, perhaps even the highest office in the nation. And why not? He has the education, the work experience, the name recognition and the likeability. Getting elected is just a matter of timing. His turn will roll around in a few short years, and with the Shadow Cabinet's coordinated assistance, he will certainly be ready.

Feeling sufficiently up to date with the conversation, Timothy wonders aloud, "Which party should I run for?"

"It doesn't really matter," Anne assures him. "Whichever party has the best chance of winning at the time."

Timothy smiles, understanding exactly. When you travel in these circles, political parties are pretty much all the same.

"Conservative or Progressive?" BB asks with a note of glee. "Coka or Pepzi?"

"Yes," Anne agrees. "There are more than enough consumers for both products."

"And while most people would choose Coka over Pepzi," Chanchai contributes, "the latter is doing just fine, and has a better value proposition for the investor. Little P's net profits can also beat its rival through greater efficiency, even with lower gross sales. But we are not here to give you stock tips, Timothy."

"I'll gladly take them," Timothy jokes.

They all have a good laugh at that one. They would have laughed at any joke Timothy had made, as it is all part of the mating dance.

"All humour aside," Timothy tells them, "I am flattered beyond belief you have taken the time to come here this evening to meet with me."

"I think I know where this is going," BB interrupts. "And I want to assure you, it is not just money and power that we are offering you."

"What else is there?" Timothy jokes again, while not really joking at all.

"What we are offering can't be measured in dollars," Anne tells him. "We would not waste your time with petty matters concerning wealth or influence."

"We can see for ourselves that you are already doing quite well," BB smiles.

"And believe me, we have a complete dossier on you," Chanchai tells him, straight-faced. "We know every person you've ever stabbed in the back, every dollar you've ever acquired, and every woman you've ever slept with."

"*Okay*," Timothy says firmly, "let's not let the evening slide into unpleasantness."

He looks over at Brenda who continues to smile, as if everyone were talking about the hockey playoffs instead of all the mistresses Timothy has had.

"A person can always use more wealth and status," Timothy continues, "but I am happy with what I have." He would have grabbed Brenda's hand for emphasis, if she were not at the other end of the table.

"And for reasons I am not at *liberty* to go into," Timothy emphasizes, "I must clarify I am committed to DRI, body and soul. From my first day as an intern to my current position as a senior executive, I have devoted the best part of my life to DRI."

"Yes," Dr. Schweiz assures him, wrinkling up his eyes. "We have been following your progress at DRI with great interest."

"Of course you have," Timothy replies.

The situation is becoming clearer to Timothy. These people have been living in this reality much longer than he has, their whole lives in fact. To them this is just another day, nothing out of the ordinary. Timothy still has a lot of catching up to do, and he'd better do it quickly.

"DRI has always been a big part of our plan," BB says, his eyes glinting.

"It will be a wonderful symbiosis," Anne smiles at Timothy. "As *you* get bigger, DRI also gets bigger, and vice versa. You will take turns hoisting each other up. And we will make sure you are protected, even against threats coming from inside DRI and those closest to you."

Timothy looks at Anne, thinking he wouldn't mind enjoying

her protection. She exudes a sexualized intelligence Timothy finds quite enticing. He sees flashes in his mind of the times they have spent together, making it apparent they are more than just business associates.

"The timing doesn't work for me," Timothy says to his guests, refocusing his thoughts. "I am currently involved in an extremely important and confidential file."

"Yes," says Dr. Schweiz, smiling slyly, "The *Tomorrow Project*."

Timothy stares blankly into Dr. Schweiz's cold, sky blue eyes.

"We know all about your Project," Dr. Schweiz smiles. "And I must say, the code name is a bit on the nose."

"It's like if they named Fat Man and Little Boy the *First Two Atomic Bombs*," Chanchai quips, again causing all the guests to laugh, as does Brenda, whose hand is on Chanchai's lap.

"If the Project is successful," Timothy says, retaining his composure, "we will completely change the world as we know it."

"Hopefully for the better," Dr. Schweiz says.

"That is our intention," Timothy emphasizes.

"Intentions often get corrupted," BB tells him. "Especially if you are not in control. I mean, how much input do you have, *really*?"

When Timothy doesn't answer, Anne fills in the silence: "If someone is trying to game the future, Timothy, I think you would want to have a say in it. *We* certainly do."

"Let me just add," Dr. Schweiz continues, "we have the same goal, to make the world a better place. So we can sit around this table blowing hot air, or we can do something about it."

"And of course, there *is* money to be made from this," Chanchai clarifies, with Brenda now sitting directly beside him, her hand on the small of his back. "I mean, when all is said and done, there is a profit motive working here as well."

"Massive change brings massive opportunity," Timothy

begins, stalling for time until his mind acclimatizes to the reality unfolding around him.

"And massive opportunity in turn leads to massive profits," Chanchai says while Brenda giggles softly and whispers something in his ear.

"When change is about to happen," Timothy says, his thoughts becoming more lucid, "it is best to know where that change is heading."

"Like knowing the winning lottery numbers in advance," BB adds to everyone's approval.

"And if we do win this so-called *lottery*," Timothy says, "those financial resources would allow us to set the agenda. We could make sure investments go into the right initiatives."

"No more government waste on half-baked plans doomed to fail," Anne says.

"Like social services that only engender more dependency," Chanchai contributes.

"Or war efforts that are neither victorious nor increase global stability," Dr. Schweiz adds.

"Or subsidizing dying industries instead of supporting the industries of the future," BB declares.

"Not so bad for starters," Timothy admits.

"We are ready to serve dinner now," Bethany announces after coming into the room unnoticed by anyone.

"Thank you, Bethany," Timothy nods, wondering how long she has been standing there. Does she even understand what they are talking about? Does *he* himself even comprehend it fully?

Timothy looks over at Brenda, who is having a friendly side conversation with Chanchai, both of them smiling and laughing gently.

Is this just another normal evening in my new life? Timothy wonders. *Inviting representatives of the power elite into my house to discuss changing the fabric of reality?*

And why is Chanchai's hand on Brenda's thigh?

"Well, I certainly am hungry," Anne smiles. "And judging by the wonderful aromas wafting this way, I'm sure the offerings this evening will be quite *delicious*."

Anne smiles into Timothy's face, and he can see clearly and with absolute certainty that they will be fucking before the night is through.

THE BRUCE

Timothy wakes up the next day, full of his usual morning anxiety concerning work, money, bills, his crumbling bungalow, his marriage and his son. Then his mind clears and he sees where he is and his anxiety melts away.

Yes, this is what my life is now, he reminds himself. *I have everything I need and everything I have ever wanted.*

He looks at the space beside him in the bed and sees it is empty. Recalling the events of the night before, he remembers the other half of the bed was definitely occupied, but not by Brenda.

Anne of a Thousand Ways.

He shudders in pleasant embarrassment at the previous night's activities, then wonders where his wife could be, but has a fairly good idea, nonetheless. As more memories flood into his brain, Timothy recalls a barrage of scenes recounting his recent sexual history, which include multiple women and others whose faces and names are not immediately identifiable to him.

Wow, he thinks, *that's a bit different. But I suppose that's the way things are now.*

From what Timothy can glean from his recollections, Brenda seems okay with his activities. Actually, she seems *more* than okay with it. The next few memories flooding into Timothy's mind are not so pleasant. They are of Brenda, his wife, his partner in life, indulging in similar activities while he is nearby and otherwise occupied. It is hard for Timothy to recall these memories, which fill his mind with an unending supply of pornographic movies starring the mother of his only child.

Timothy sits up on the edge of the bed and shakes his head to clear his thoughts. He breathes in deeply and tries to concentrate on the here and now, banishing any illicit memories from his consciousness. Having accomplished this, a different sensation courses through Timothy, strong and insistent. He has the distinct feeling he has an important day in store for him at work. He is meeting with the President and CEO of DRI, Bruce McQuade. The Bruce.

An unfamiliar energy and drive course through Timothy's mind and body, prompting him to jump off the bed and race to the adjoining bathroom to take a shower and get ready for work. Once he is dressed, Timothy dashes to the kitchen to grab the hard-boiled eggs and nuts he knows are in a paper bag in the fridge. In the kitchen, he finds his son Bryan, his hair askew, reading the news on his device and eating a bowl of bran flakes with raisins and milk.

"Aren't you going to be late for school?" Timothy asks.

Bryan looks at him curiously. "I don't have classes during first period."

"*Right*," Timothy replies, remembering this. "I have a lot on my mind."

"*Yeah*, I heard her leave this morning," Bryan says disapprovingly.

Timothy looks at his son, wondering where this little *shit* gets the nerve to speak to him this way.

"And in case you're wondering," Bryan says, adding injury to insult, "Mom left with that Asian guy, Chanchy."

"Did I *ask* you about your mother?" Timothy blasts his son, feeling the shame of his and Brenda's infidelity.

The approaching sound of feminine footsteps causes Timothy to turn abruptly, grasping the hope that his wife has come back home. But it is not Brenda, it is a pretty teenage girl.

"Who are *you*?" Timothy asks the girl accusingly.

"This is *Jamie*," Bryan tells his father like he is going senile. "She's on my math team. You've met her before."

"Did you spend the night here?" Timothy asks Jamie, his annoyance rising. "How old are you?"

"I'm *fourteen*," Jamie tells him. "Yes, I did spend the night. I slept in one of your *numerous* guest rooms."

Timothy is silenced by this. He remembers Jamie now. Timothy plays golf with her father, Frank Leeman. They also go to ballgames together. Frank is a good guy to know. He deals in real estate and has helped Timothy make some lucrative investments. Jamie is at the top of her class at the private school she goes to with Bryan. Number One on the honour roll. Smartest kid in the city for her cohort.

Timothy realizes, even with his new-found success, he can still be a shitty father.

"Why don't you just go to work, Dad," Bryan tells Timothy. "Afterall, Jamie and I are the only ones here who didn't act like a bunch of horny teenagers last night."

Having no response for this, Timothy gives the two young people a stern look and then leaves the house, forgetting his eggs and nuts.

A half-hour later, when Timothy arrives at DRI, he is met by the valet in the underground parking garage.

"Good morning, Mr. Koops," the valet greets Timothy with a short bow. "Open the door, Albert," the valet says to Timothy's vehicle.

"Yes, Mr. Reeves," the vehicle replies, opening its door.

When Timothy does not immediately exit the vehicle, the valet asks him, "Can I help you out of the vehicle, sir?"

"No, thank you, Mr. Reeves," Timothy says, getting out of his vehicle.

"Well, off you go, Albert," the valet instructs the vehicle.

Timothy watches with delighted amusement as his vehicle closes its door and heads off down the length of the garage, disappearing around a ramp to the next parking level.

"I'll see you later, Mr. Reeves," Timothy nods at the valet.

"Yes, sir," the valet nods, wishing Timothy wouldn't call him *Mr. Reeves*, which is the nickname the vehicle has given him as a joke. His real name is Hytel Ravinchek.

"Have a wonderful day, Mr. Koops," the valet says.

Timothy heads to the elevators, feeling full of energy and promise. *How ingenious humankind is,* he thinks, *to create this wonderful world with such marvels in it.*

Arriving at his floor, which is reserved for Research and Development, Timothy nods at the receptionist, who smiles widely at him, her expression open and receiving.

"Good morning, Mr. Koops," she says in a sing-song voice.

"Yes, it is," he smiles back.

Knowing exactly where to go, Timothy walks past the inner cubicles, where all the interns, short-term contract workers and deadwood employees sit. This area is farthest from the windows and gets almost no natural light at all. *Death Row.* Then Timothy walks past the next set of cubicles which have glass walls to let in the light but allow for absolutely no privacy. This is *The Farm.* People sitting here will either be called upon to perform more challenging duties or be passed over for promotion. And finally, Timothy arrives at the executive area, raised four steps above the common rabble. *Snob Hill.*

Timothy looks at the semi-circular array of executive offices. Right in the middle is the Vice President of R&D, the Ice Queen herself, Denice Button. Then radiating out from Denice's office are the offices of the Directors and Senior Managers. Timothy walks up to his office and admires his name embossed in gold lettering on the door. *Timothy Koops, Executive Director, Special*

Projects. Impressive, yes, but still three doors away from the Vice President's Office. And of course, it is one floor down from where the big chiefs reside: President and Chief Executive Officer, Chief Financial Officer, Chief Operating Officer, and Chief Information Officer. And his office is also *two* floors down from the offices of the Chair and Members of the Board. But that floor is now vacant, as DRI has recently bought back its shares and gone private.

Settling into his office, Timothy turns on his terminal and looks at his task manager. As he suspected, his day is full. He knows he has a lot of performance measures to achieve, a lot of reports to approve, and a lot of people to meet with. One of the most important things he does *not* know is where to begin. So he does what all corporate people in positions of power do. He calls in his Executive Assistant.

Picking up his desk phone, Timothy's speed-dials a number and purrs into the mouthpiece, "Lange, I need you."

In a matter of seconds, Marc Lange is in Timothy's office, with his tablet at the ready to take notes and make his Executive Director's wishes a reality. Lange isn't dressed as affluently as Timothy remembers, and he looks a bit thinner and more worn than usual. He is hunched over slightly and cradling his belly to calm the flareups his acid stomach pains him with.

"So, Lange," Timothy says, looking directly into Lange's milky chestnut eyes, savouring the situation. "Tell me. What are we looking at today?"

"Well, Mr. Koops," Lange begins, trying not to stammer, "the weekly reports are all in. I can go through those with you now, if that works for you."

"*Defer*," Timothy instructs.

"Right. You also asked me to arrange a meeting with the Team Leads."

"*Defer*," Timothy repeats.

"Got it," Lange replies. "You are meeting with the President and CEO at eleven," he continues.

"And that will be the Bruce *himself*, right?" Timothy asks blithely. "Not one of his *lackies*?"

"Mr. McQuade will be there in person," Lange assures Timothy.

"Topic of meeting?" Timothy wonders.

"Bruce wants to discuss the *Project*," Lange says, the words sticking in his throat.

"*Right*," Timothy nods. He is feeling almost up to speed on the Project, as the information continues to load itself into his brain. "Will the Vice President be there?" he asks.

"*No*," Lange says, his voice quavering. "As you now report *directly* to Bruce…"

"Yes," Timothy smiles, "the Veep's been completely cut out, hasn't she?"

Lange does not answer. But Timothy didn't expect him to.

"And how is the Veep taking that?" Timothy grins widely.

"She's *pissed*," Lange squeaks.

"I can understand why," Timothy chuckles, unable to stop himself from enjoying the moment.

Silence hangs in the air until it is broken by Lange. "Is that it, sir?"

"One more thing," Timothy says with authority. "Can I get a breakfast sandwich?"

"Yes, of course," Lange answers, wrinkling his brow. "Ravi will get it for you."

A moment after Lange has left, Timothy's old friend Ravi enters the office, exuding an uncharacteristic energy, ready for whatever business is at hand.

"Yes, Mr. Koops?" Ravi says with an unforced enthusiasm.

"I need a breakfast sandwich," Timothy tells him.

"*Oh*," Ravi says with restrained disappointment.

"Go to that café across the street, *not* the tuck shop downstairs."

"No problem," Ravi nods.

"A fried egg, easy over, yolk creamy but not runny," Timothy says. "Unbleached white toast, old Canadian cheddar and peameal bacon. Two grinds of pepper, no butter, just avocado mayo. And a flat white."

"Got it," Ravi assures him. "Do you want sugar in the coffee?"

"*Tagatose* sweetener."

Timothy watches as his assistant's assistant turns and leaves his office. Timothy then sits back enjoying his new authority and savouring the promise of an upgraded breakfast.

Eggs and nuts? What kind of bullshit is that?

Timothy's feeling of contentment evaporates a short while later, as Denice Button, Vice President of R&D, storms into his office as if she owned it and scowls at him grimly. Timothy smiles pleasantly at her, feeling his morning is about to take a turn for the worse. Denice Button is well known for crushing people's careers the way most people crack walnuts.

"We need to talk," Denice says, standing over Timothy.

"Have a seat, Denice," Timothy says cordially.

After considering this for a moment, Denice tightens her scowl and sits in one of Timothy's leather guest chairs.

"What do you want to talk about?" Timothy asks.

"You can tell me what the hell's going on with the *Project*," Denice demands.

"It's progressing on schedule, apart from the usual growing pains," he tells her calmly. "Lange can give you a full debrief. And you can read the reports."

"Fuck the reports," Denice snarls. "Why are you meeting with the President and CEO?"

"Because I *report* to him," Timothy tells her.

"You report to *me*," she says. "And I'm taking the meeting in your place."

"But you don't have the details," Timothy warns.

"Guess again," she tells him with relish. "Lange's been filling me in."

Of course he has, Timothy thinks, *the fucking weasel.*

"He's a useful person to know," Denice says, as if reading Timothy's mind. "Always has his nose up everyone's ass."

"Including *yours,*" Timothy jibes.

"I guess he likes the smell of my anus," Denice states bitterly.

"Well, what Lange and your anus don't seem to understand," Timothy says with confidence, "is that without *me* there is no Project."

"Oh, *please,*" Denice scoffs, not fully understanding Timothy's meaning. "You are quite expendable. *Everybody* is. We are all replaceable."

Timothy looks at his Vice President with barely disguised anger. No matter how high you climb, he thinks, there is always someone higher ready to piss on your head.

"I don't know how you managed to get on Bruce's good side," Denice says. "Or why everyone suddenly thinks you're some kind of Golden Boy. Somehow, people have forgotten you are just a half-assed data analyst. But *I* haven't. I remember *everything.*"

"Denice, what you have not managed to comprehend," Timothy tells her calmly, "is that we are playing a very high-stakes game. And *I* am the Gamekeeper."

"A *gamekeeper* looks after wild animals," Denice laughs.

"It is what I *say* it is," Timothy declares, raising his voice.

"And what you don't know about it could fill an entire database."

"What I *do* know, is you and your so-called *Dinner Club* have been meeting with BB Marsden of Global O&D. They are our direct competitor. Do you think Bruce is going to stand for that?"

"No, he isn't going to *stand*, he's going to *bow down* in respect," Timothy snarls.

He can see Denice is pleased he is losing his temper. This is what she wants. Open confrontation. That is her milieu, and she thinks Timothy can't beat her on her chosen field of battle.

"You'd better start packing, Timothy," Denice smiles coldly. "After I explain all of this to Bruce, you're finished here."

With that said, Denice gets up and leaves.

Timothy looks around pensively at his impressive and well-appointed executive office. *It would be a shame if this were the end of my time here,* he thinks.

But he knows it isn't. How could it be? He hasn't even had a chance to utilize his new executive position. And what about all those plans he made with the Shadow Cabinet. No, there is a lot more to come.

"Here's your sandwich," Ravi says, entering Timothy's office and putting his breakfast and coffee on his desk. "They didn't have Tagalog sweetener. Never even *heard* of it."

"That's okay," Timothy smiles. "I was just messing with you."

"Oh," Ravi chuckles nervously.

Timothy looks up. "Thank you, Ravi," he says. "You were a good friend. *Mostly.*"

"Thanks, I guess," Ravi says, feeling he should say more, but not able to think of anything.

"If Lange gives you any trouble," Timothy tells him, "just let me know."

"Sure, Mr. Koops," Ravi begins, a little uncertainly. "Lange says you aren't going to be sticking around much longer. Did you get a better offer?"

"Yes, Ravi, I got a much better offer," Timothy says. "But I'm not going anywhere. I'll always be dedicated to DRI, in more ways than you could know."

"That's great," Ravi says softly, bowing slightly and taking this as his opportunity to leave.

Timothy takes a sip of his flat white, which tastes smoky and satisfying even without sweetener. He unwraps his sandwich and sees that the cheese appears to be some sort of Brie or perhaps Camembert.

Well, you can't always get everything you want, he reminds himself, digging into his breakfast sandwich with a big satisfying bite.

DR. ELIZABETH KINKAID

At the Righton Centre, Dr. Fasten sits looking at his terminal's display as the secondary and tertiary results of the Timothy Koops treatments are analyzed by the supercomputer. Dr. Fasten shakes his head slightly, continuing to be amazed at how one man could be the catalyst to change the reality of so many people. He thinks about how the outcomes of the Koops treatments are both frightening and exhilarating. He watches the readout as the computer uses the pre-treatment baseline to measure statistical advancements due to retro-causality. What he sees is the advancements are significant and growing exponentially.

Dr. Fasten frowns and adds a notation to the file: *As demonstrated by the statistical data, the farther we move forward in time, the farther the Koops effect moves backward, causing the present-day outcomes to increase in intensity.*

Dr. Fasten pauses momentarily to contemplate the advancements the supercomputer is itemizing. Ironically, they have taken on an aura of ordinariness in the minds of the general public. As Control predicted, people continue to go about their lives as if nothing has changed, as if things have always been this way.

The doctor continues his notation: *On a global basis, life spans are increasing incrementally, disease rates are declining, as are markers for poverty, crime, racial inequality and inter-nation warfare. According to the supercomputer's estimates, it is as if we have leaped fifty years into the future with respect to advances in science, technology, medicine and engineering.*

Dr. Fasten knows he should feel great pride that his life's work is coming to fruition. But the steep personal cost, he realizes, may be too much for him to endure. As a man of science, he is obligated to put his research before his personal circumstances, but as a *human,* he knows his first obligation is to the people he loves, or more accurately, the *person.* Afterall, Frida is all he has. If he loses Frida, he loses himself. And then he loses *everything.*

Feeling hopelessly that he has come to the end of an unnamed era in his life, Dr. Fasten tells himself his time is rapidly running out. Maybe it is already gone, and he is just living out the remnants of an existence that is already spent. But isn't that the nature of time as we perceive it? It rushes by, while we are desperately holding on to memories like so many shards of glass sparkling in the dying light.

So what do I do now? he wonders. And in response, he tells himself, *I must keep looking until I find Frida.*

But after many more hours, and exhausting the Project's locational profiling capabilities, Dr. Fasten is still unable to determine the whereabouts of his missing girlfriend.

It's over, he thinks. *She's gone. And the saddest part is, no one will even know.*

No, he tells himself. *He* will know. And maybe some others who knew her will also know. While they still remember her, Frida will live on.

Now there is only quiet, broken by the whirr of the Machine's ventilation system.

Impulsively, Dr. Fasten picks up his personal phone and selects his ex-wife's phone number. When he hears the first ring, he wonders what the hell he is going to say to her and hopes she doesn't pick up. But on the second ring, he hears the line connect.

"*Hello?*" she says.

After a second of dead air, Dr. Fasten responds. "Hello, Caroline, it's Zakery."

"*Zakery*? I'm at work. Why are you calling?" Caroline asks.

"I'm sorry to interrupt you..." Zakery begins.

"You're *sorry? Really*?" Caroline snipes. "*That's* a first."

"I suppose it is," he admits.

"Is everything *okay*? What's *wrong*?" Caroline says, feeling a pang of anxiety.

"I just called to see how you were doing. And, yes, I would also like to *apologize*."

"After all these years? Why *now*?"

"Well, the days fly by..." he starts to say. "We never know how much time we have left."

"Did you get some bad news from your doctor?" Caroline asks tentatively, wondering where this is going.

"I'm fine, Caroline, but things have *changed* for me," Zakery tries to explain but can't find the words. "I am just trying to make some peace with the world."

"You aren't making any sense, Zakery. Did something happen?"

"Yes, *lots* of things happened. Too many to try and describe." He knows this conversation is going nowhere, so he just lets it out: "Frida has gone missing."

There is silence on the other end of the line.

"I know it's not fair to lay this on you," he tells her.

"I'm sorry, Zakery, but I don't know who you are talking about."

Dr. Fasten feels his face flush. "What are you saying, Caroline? Frida was my research assistant. We all worked together."

"I still don't know who she is," Caroline insists.

"The three of us went out to dinner numerous times," Zakery says, his voice rising in volume. "Frida is the woman I *left* you for."

"Well, congratulations, Zakery," Caroline says with bitter sarcasm. "You can't expect me to remember *all* your girlfriends."

"*All my girlfriends?*" Dr. Fasten repeats. "I didn't have any other girlfriends. There was only Frida."

"Okay, Zakery," Caroline says impatiently. "If that's all you wanted to say, I have to go."

"*Wait,*" Dr. Fasten insists. "Before you go. *Please.* Just tell me how Bonita is doing. She won't take my calls, and she blocked me on social media. I have no idea if she finished school, or if she's going to get married—"

"Zakery, are you *drunk*?" Caroline interrupts.

"I don't drink anymore. Not a single drop."

"Who are these people you're talking about?" Caroline says loudly in frustration.

"*Bonita,*" Dr. Fasten emphasizes, "is our *daughter.*"

The quiet on the other end of the line tells Dr. Fasten everything he doesn't want to hear.

"What kind of sick joke is this?" Caroline seethes. "If we had a child, maybe I could think I didn't completely waste my life with you."

"I'm sorry, Caroline," Dr. Fasten apologizes again. "I didn't mean to upset you. I just wanted to hear your voice one more time, before it's too late."

"It's already too late, Zakery. It was too late twenty years ago."

"Even if you only have a few moments left," he tells her, "that's still enough time to make things right."

The phone line goes dead, and Dr. Fasten is left in a stillness broken only by the gentle drone of the Machine. He looks up at it and remembers the first time he saw it. He couldn't believe it was real, with its imposing size and capabilities. He felt honoured to be chosen, out of all the leading practitioners in his field, to oversee the operation and refinement of this futuristic scientific tool. Little did he know back then, just how futuristic it really was.

Or did he?

In his long decades studying human memory, Dr. Fasten has always been amazed at how much people forget, even people with strong recall abilities. One reason for this is a person can't remember something they never bothered to perceive in the first place. *Willful blindness.* Ignoring what is right in front of you. And that is what Dr. Fasten himself did from the first day of the Project. He chose to ignore the fact that the Machine itself could not have been built using current technical knowledge. It could have only been built in the future.

I thought we were using the past to create a better tomorrow, he thinks. *But tomorrow is using the past to create itself.*

Full of the resolve this new clarity has brought him, Dr. Fasten engages his terminal's video conferencing application and contacts Control.

"Yes, Zakery?" Control says as his image appears on the display.

"I wanted to give you an update," Dr. Fasten says, gathering his thoughts.

"We are receiving all the data," the image tells him. "Is there a concern with the findings?"

"In a way," Dr. Fasten says, choosing his words with care. "As you can see, our work has been progressing exponentially."

"As it was designed to do," Control agrees.

"Things are changing far more rapidly than I expected," Dr. Fasten discloses.

"Then your concern is with your expectations," Control replies.

"In a manner of speaking," Dr. Fasten nods. "At this juncture, I am finding it impossible to foresee what the final outcomes of our work will be."

"The outcomes will be in line with what we have delineated," Control says plainly. "Perhaps we will even exceed our goals."

"The issue I would raise," Dr. Fasten begins, "is that I *personally* may not be able to continue administering these treatments."

The image of Control on the display continues to regard Dr. Fasten dispassionately.

"As you know, I am being affected detrimentally by the temporal changes we are engendering," Dr. Fasten continues with a tremor in his voice.

"I see," says Control.

"And *you* could be affected too, without even realizing it," Dr. Fasten warns.

"You needn't worry," Control advises. "Because of our location and the protocols we have implemented, we are insulated from any major impacts occurring on the surface world."

"But you are not *completely* immune," Dr. Fasten insists. "No one can know how far-reaching the ultimate effects will be."

"Yes, *someone* can," Control says.

"You mean *Lessa?*" Dr. Fasten surmises.

"Lessa has been running projections against the baseline and can predict outcomes with a near perfect accuracy rate."

"Then Lessa can continue the treatments," Dr. Fasten protests childishly.

"Zakery, you know we need someone on site at Righton," Control says patiently. "I can't leave the bunker, as I am Control. And I don't believe you would simply abandon your work when we have come this far."

"You have the entirety of my research, and I will hold my post for as long as I can," Dr. Fasten tells him. "But when the time comes that I am not able, physically or mentally, to continue, it will be up to you to carry the work forward."

Control looks at Dr. Fasten intently through the display. "Yes, as Control, that is my responsibility," he says with certainty.

The absoluteness of Control's statement causes Dr. Fasten's mind to achieve an intuitive understanding.

"I suppose you expected this conversation to happen," Dr. Fasten says.

"One day, perhaps," Control acknowledges. "Not necessarily today."

"And did you know what would happen to Frida?" Dr. Fasten asks, feeling a surge of emotion rising within him.

"It was alluded to in Lessa's comparative analysis."

"And you just *let* it happen?" Dr. Fasten says, his jaw tightening.

"In moving the Project forward, one must expect collateral effects," Control admits.

"And what collateral effects will *you* have to endure?" Dr. Fasten interrogates.

"More than you will know, Zakery," Control says. "More than *anyone* will know."

Control pauses, taking a breath, then continues solemnly: "Our work will live on, Doctor, but our histories and our names will soon be forgotten, as if written in sand."

Dr. Zakery Fasten is lost for words, feeling like he is on a precipice about to fall into a bottomless nothingness.

"We are at a moment in time that is both joyous and sombre," Control says, his image crackling on the display. "The achievements we have envisioned, which we may not be entirely prepared for, are near at hand. We can't let our human frailty derail our progress."

"Then I assume you have a succession plan in place," Dr. Fasten says weakly.

"We do have someone who has been observing your work. She is highly trained and more than capable of carrying on if you become incapacitated."

"You think replacing me will be that simple?" Dr. Fasten asks, not able to stop himself.

"Dr. Elizabeth Kincaid is young and energetic and already an expert in the field of retro-causality. Lessa is confident that, if necessary, her transition into the Project will be effective, within acceptable limits."

"This could be dangerous for Dr. Kincaid," Dr. Fasten warns.

"She is aware of the risks and will be shadowing you during tomorrow's treatment."

"*Tomorrow*?" Dr. Fasten says, surprised.

"The sooner the better, as each treatment causes historic advancements to occur earlier in our timeline."

"And if tomorrow's treatment is fully successful?" Dr. Fasten asks, already knowing the answer.

"If successful, we will enter the *next phase*."

"That's a nice clean way to say it. *The next phase.* What you mean is, in less than twenty-four hours, life as we know it will change."

"Yes," Control affirms. "With one giant leap into the future."

FUCK TIME

At eleven a.m., Denice Button, the Vice President of Research and Development, takes the elevator up one floor to meet with Bruce McQuade, the President and CEO of Dimensional Research Inc. She smiles at Bruce's assistant Burke and tells him she has a meeting with Bruce.

"I don't *think* so," Burke says, scanning Bruce's calendar on his terminal's display. "It says here, *Timothy Koops*."

"I know what it says, Burke," Denice grimaces. "Timothy can't make it."

Burke looks up at the Vice President, confused. "Mr. Koops has already come and gone. The meeting just ended."

"How is that even possible?" Denice seethes.

"Mr. Koops came early, so Bruce moved up their meeting."

Denice gazes steely eyed at Burke, contemplating her next move: either smooth-talking him or tearing his throat out.

Burke clicks a few keys on his keypad and then tells Denice, "A half hour slot has just opened up in Bruce's schedule."

"*When?*" Denice asks.

"Right this minute," Burke informs her. "Bruce will see you now."

The door to the President and CEO's office opens and Bruce pokes his head out.

"Oh, hi, Denice. I've been expecting you," Bruce says.

Bruce pops back into his office, and Denice takes this as her cue to follow him in. Something tells her once she crosses that threshold there will be no going back.

Denice enters Bruce's office and sits in the guest chair opposite his desk.

"What can I do for you?" he asks.

"I wanted to talk to you about the *Project*," Denice says.

"I thought it was clear Timothy Koops is the lead on that file," Bruce says dryly.

"Yes, of course, Bruce," Denice agrees, looking into his eyes, trying to conjure feelings of camaraderie. But all she gets back is a cold blank stare.

"The Project," Bruce tells her, "is of primary importance to DRI, to the exclusion of all other lines of business."

"But *surely*," Denice begins to say, "you want someone more senior—"

"You must come to understand," Bruce interrupts, "Timothy Koops is an integral part of the Project. For reasons I can't share, I would go so far as to say Timothy Koops *is* the Project."

"That's why I should *direct* and *focus* him, to ensure the Project is successful," Denice counters.

Bruce lets her words hang in the air, then tells her, "Timothy Koops is being promoted to Executive Vice President of R&D."

Denice is dumbfounded, as if stunned by a taser to the brain. She cannot think of a response, so in desperation she invokes the concept of friendship, the only gambit she has left:

"Bruce, we've known each other a long time. How can you forget about all those years and all we've been through?"

"Yes, we've been through what feels like many lifetimes together," Bruce says cryptically. "But in *this* life, Timothy is the top man. And I can't let anyone fuck up his work. Not even *you*."

Stubbornly, Denice pushes back: "There has to be *oversight*, Bruce. Now that there's no Board, you can't operate without checks and balances. The owners of the company wouldn't be happy about that.”

“I am in constant contact with the owners,” Bruce tells Denice. “And they are continuously monitoring us.”

“*Us?*” Denice repeats. “Who exactly do you mean by *us*?”

“Every one of us. Every employee. Every keystroke, every conversation, all recorded and analyzed by Lessa, the supercomputer. It’s listening to us now.”

Denice frowns as the terminal to the side of Bruce’s desk flashes to life. On the display, the image of Control appears.

“Hello Ms. Button,” Control says. “It is about time we met face-to-face.”

“Yes, it is,” Denice says to the display. “I assume you know all about me. But I don’t know a single thing about you. Not even your name.”

“In my capacity as a representative of the owners,” Control tells her, “I am known simply as *Control.*”

“And who are the owners?” Denice asks.

“Actually, *I* am one of the owners,” Bruce says. “As is Timothy.”

“You’ve got to be *shitting* me,” Denice exclaims, not bothering to hide her contempt. “When did all of this happen?”

“This morning,” Bruce explains. “The majority owner has given both Timothy and I shares in the company.”

“This doesn’t even sound *real*,” Denice tells them.

“It is *absolutely* real,” Control says. “And *you* signed off on it.”

“What are you talking about?” Denice says doubtfully.

“The research project being conducted at the Righton Centre,” Control explains. “You greenlit the whole thing.”

“Dr. Fasten’s project,” Denice says. “Yes, I greenlit it. So what?”

“Once the Project became successful,” Control explains, “Dr. Fasten’s partners bought all of DRI’s stock and took the company private."

"Okay, so you know my next question," Denice says. "Who are Dr. Fasten's partners?"

"For proprietary reasons, that cannot be disclosed," Bruce tells her.

"So in short," Denice finally understands, "DRI is no longer running the Project. The Project is running DRI."

After the Vice President has a chance for this to sink in, Bruce asks her, "Is everything clear now, Denice?"

"Yes, very clear," she replies. "I guess I no longer report to you regarding the Project."

"You will no longer report to me *at all*," Bruce says. "You will report to Timothy."

"But I am a *Vice President*," Denice insists.

"You should regard your title as an *honorific*," Control tells her. "A courtesy in consideration of your long years of service."

"I see," Denice says, barely audibly."

"Good," Control says, "because we are grooming Timothy to be President."

Denice feels the room tilt as if the floor has suddenly grown uneven beneath her.

"I will retain my duties as CEO," Bruce tells her, "to relieve Timothy of the day-to-day issues. His focus will be solely on the big picture, and the future."

"We are all here to serve Timothy," Control says. "And Timothy is here to serve the Project."

"Your role is still evolving," Bruce tells Denice. "I am sure you will find a way to contribute in time."

In time? Denice thinks, her head spinning. *Fuck time.*

LAB RAT

The next morning, Timothy in his vehicle heads toward the Righton Centre. He sits back and relaxes, noticing all the changes happening in the world around him: perfect weather, healthy people, everyone riding in their automated vehicles, no pollution, all buildings and infrastructure in a perfect state of repair. Timothy is proud of his part in contributing to these miracles of the modern age. This truly is a special time in history, he thinks.

He recalls his first treatment session with Dr. Fasten and how apprehensive he was. What a *fluke* things turned out the way they did. Imagine. Of all the people who were tested, he was the only one who responded so positively to the treatments.

As every day passes, Timothy's old life becomes more of a fading dream to him. He has to confess, he likes his new life better with its status and prosperity. But the more you have, the more you want. The higher you climb, the higher you want to go. And Timothy now feels like he has plateaued. Even as President-in-Waiting of DRI, he feels he is at a standstill.

Like an addict who cannot stop himself from picking up the needle, Timothy was going to call Dr. Fasten to ask for another fix, one more treatment to take him to the next level. Fortunately, Timothy was contacted by Dr. Fasten's people to schedule another appointment. Like any dealer, they were making sure their user was well supplied, to keep his habit strong so he didn't think about going clean. As it turned out, that was the last thing on Timothy's mind.

Arriving at the Righton Centre, Timothy sees that the compound is now gated. There is a checkpoint before entering where his vehicle is scanned by a series of electronic eyes. The complex has several digital surveillance mechanisms scanning the perimeter, and the parking lot now contains many unmanned vehicles with sentient capabilities. One of these vehicles greets Timothy's vehicle, directing it to a numbered parking location in the freshly paved lot.

Timothy thanks his vehicle's Navigator for the ride.

"You're welcome, Timothy," the Navigator replies. "Enjoy your treatment."

When Timothy gets out of his vehicle, he can hear it communicating with the greeter vehicle through a series of beeps and blips.

"Mr. Koops," the greeter vehicle asks him, "how long are you here for?"

"As long as it takes," Timothy replies.

Timothy walks up to the doors of the Righton Centre and addresses the terminal mounted there:

"Good morning. I'm here to see Dr. Fasten."

"Yes, Mr. Koops, Dr. Fasten is expecting you," the terminal answers.

The doors slide open and Timothy walks in confidently, familiar with the layout, even though it has been remodelled extensively. Every square metre of the space is assigned to one useful function or another. Drones hover in the air and autonomous machines buzz along the floor.

Timothy continues walking as one of the machines addresses him: "No need to hurry, Mr. Koops. You have arrived at exactly the correct time."

"Thanks for letting me know," Timothy nods at the machine as he sees Dr. Fasten waiting for him halfway down the hall.

"Timothy," Dr. Fasten greets him. "We have to talk. Come into my private office." He then leads Timothy into a small room a short way down a side corridor.

"What's on your mind?" Timothy wonders, looking around at the spartan décor of the office. There is not a single decoration or personal item to be seen, such as a photograph or perhaps a house plant. There is no equipment of any kind, no terminal, no desk phone, not even a pencil, only a hole in the wall where a built-in digital clock was once housed.

"I have deactivated all surveillance here so we can talk candidly," Dr. Fasten tells him.

"You really take doctor-patient confidentiality seriously," Timothy half jokes to the unsmiling doctor.

"Unfortunately," Dr. Fasten tells him, his face grim, "our sessions have entered some uncharted and dangerous territory."

"I don't understand," Timothy says. "I was told to come in today for another treatment."

"Yes. That was *Control*. He arranged today's session."

"And he's your *boss*, right?" Timothy confirms.

"He is *technically* in charge of the Project," Dr. Fasten explains. "I am my own boss. And I have taken a professional oath. I adhere to a higher set of ethics and values. *Morally*, I am not convinced we can continue."

"Things have worked out pretty well, so far." Timothy counters.

"Yes, they've worked out for *you*, Timothy. As was intended. But it's not just *your* life that is being affected, it's everybody's."

"I thought that was the whole point," Timothy challenges.

"When I went home last night," Dr. Fasten explains insistently, "my condo was completely different. All the renovations I had done, all the furniture I had purchased—"

"So this is about your *furniture*?" Timothy asks.

"My girlfriend Frida is missing," Dr. Fasten tells him mournfully. "She is nowhere to be found. Not a single one of her possessions remains. Her name isn't even on the lobby directory."

"*Doctor*," Timothy says firmly, "I'm not sure why you are surprised. This is the result of everything you intended to accomplish."

Dr. Fasten regards Timothy with some disbelief, taken aback by his response.

"So it looks like you're going to have to redecorate," Timothy tells him.

Dr. Fasten takes a moment to recall the Timothy who first walked into the Righton Centre. How could he have become the person standing before him now? Maybe this is who Timothy has always been.

"As for your girlfriend," Timothy continues, "like they say, there's another streetcar along every ten minutes."

Dr. Fasten can feel his heart racing and his face growing hot. He takes several long slow breaths to quell his rising anger.

"I don't know what happened to you, Timothy, but this is not the way things are supposed to be. Can't you understand we have gone too far?"

Timothy looks Dr. Fasten straight in the eyes and says, "You initiated this outcome when you and your partners came to DRI."

"DRI gave us the resources we needed," Dr. Fasten clarifies sternly, "allowing us to utilize Lessa to enhance my work. But Lessa has taken on a life of its own."

"I know," Timothy tells him. "I've been told how Lessa amassed great wealth investing in artificial currency."

"Easy to do if you are able to alter the past," Dr. Fasten accuses bitterly.

"And you planted the seed, Doctor," Timothy admonishes. "Now you must harvest what you have sown."

"No," Dr. Fasten says, definitively. "It's over. It ends *today.*"

Timothy smiles, like a poker player who knows he is holding the best possible hand.

"What makes you think *you're* the one making that decision?" Timothy asks simply.

"I know what's right," Dr. Fasten answers.

"You picked a great time to develop some morals," Timothy smiles chidingly. "I've been looking into your past research."

Dr. Fasten glares at Timothy, knowing where this is headed.

"Implanting new memories into people's brains," Timothy recounts. "Like witnessing certain events that never even happened. You could get anyone to believe anything you wanted them to."

"That's a crude oversimplification," Dr. Fasten protests.

"Still, a pretty useful skill to have. I know Denice Button thought so. That's why she greenlit the Project. I'm sure she got very moist thinking of ways to monetize your expertise."

"Those experiments where done in the name of science," Dr. Fasten argues. "To increase our understanding of the nature of memory."

"Except the techniques were used in industrial espionage, perjury and fraud."

"Those were simple *parlor tricks,*" Dr. Fasten pleads. "What we are doing here is altering the nature of time and changing reality as we know it."

"That's *right,* Doctor," Timothy agrees. "That's *exactly* what we're doing. And we're moving forward whether you participate or not."

"I will *not,*" Dr. Fasten tells him defiantly.

"I am not a person you can just walk away from," Timothy says, with a tinge of threat creeping into his voice. "I am backed by a team of government leaders, corporate elite and the greatest scientific minds on the planet. When I ask you to do something, it is not a *request.*"

After a short silence, during which Dr. Fasten gathers his thoughts, he delivers his final words on the subject:

"You don't frighten me, Timothy. Because I know who you are. Down inside. I know your fears, your insecurities, your shortcomings."

Dr. Fasten knows he shouldn't continue in this vein, but he cannot stop himself:

"You are *weak*, Timothy. A *loser* from the day you were born. No matter how your life has changed, you can't change who you are inside. It is only through a quirk of genetics you responded so well to the treatments. Your body was the vessel for a great scientific breakthrough, but you are still just a fucking brainless lab rat."

"Yes, I *am* a rat," Timothy says as he removes a pen from his breast pocket. At the top of the pen's barrel a small tangerine-coloured light begins to glow. "Lessa is listening."

Dr. Fasten feels the blood drain from his face.

"The question now becomes," Timothy says, "*What happens to you?*"

Dr. Fasten thinks about this, and none of the scenarios he imagines give him any solace. Lessa will not want to leave any unresolved variables, of which he is the biggest.

"You've created a monster," Timothy smiles, his eyes burning. "And now you've got to keep that monster fed."

Control's voice is heard coming from the pen, thin and metallic sounding, but loud and clear:

"Did you think you could abandon our work, Dr. Fasten, and then just walk out of here?"

"You can't threaten me," Dr. Fasten warns. "I have nothing left to lose. So there's nothing you can do to make me help you."

"It's not your *help* we need," Control assures him. "It's your *silence.*"

Three blue pinpoints of light appear on Dr. Fasten's chest, which he eyes desperately.

"Lasers," Timothy informs him. "We are too late in the process for you to expose us now."

"You're a fool," Dr. Fasten tells Timothy. "The procedure is becoming more complicated. If the Machine is not calibrated correctly, the unknown consequences could be devastating."

"We are confident in our ability to complete the project without you," Control says.

"Enjoy your retirement, Doctor," Timothy adds as he places the pen on the desk and turns to leave the room.

"*Why*, Timothy?" Dr. Fasten pleads. "Just tell me why you want to keep going."

"You of all people should know," Timothy tells Dr. Fasten over his shoulder. "I've always been a *company man.*"

After Timothy leaves, Dr. Fasten says to Control, "And now what? You can't hold me here against my will."

"That is not our plan," Control tells him.

A number of indicator lights appear, shining through the walls in a multitude of colours. Then the walls of the private office become translucent and begin to recede.

It's not real, Dr. Fasten tells himself. He tries to concentrate. *They can't control me unless I let them.*

But his thoughts soon become disjointed, and the lights begin flashing in a mesmerizing pattern. Dr. Fasten can hear a hum, which grows into a physical vibration, infusing his whole body with a scintillating energy.

They can't control me, he repeats to himself as the room completely disappears.

Dr. Zakery Fasten soon finds himself floating in a black void, absent of all light and sensation, until his perceptions shut down, fading slowly one by one until there is absolute nothing-ness.

STONE SOUP

In the hallway outside Dr. Fasten's private office, Timothy closes the door behind him, thinking that will be the last time he sees Dr. Zakery Fasten. He is not entirely sure what will become of the good doctor, but then again, people enter and exit our lives all the time, he thinks. Our existence goes on as does theirs. We can never truly know how their lives turned out, until through some chance, our two lives intersect once more.

Timothy walks toward the Treatment Room and is met by a short autonomous mechanical device.

"Please follow me, Mr. Koops," the device tells Timothy.

"I know the way," Timothy tells the device.

"We are making some changes," the device says. "This way please."

Timothy follows the device as it glides down the hallway. Things *are* different than Timothy remembers. The walls seem to glow slightly, and there is an ever-present hum, perhaps caused by sympathetic vibration. The farther Timothy walks, the less the corridors are recognizable to him. Some doors are no longer where they used to be, and the floors appear to both incline and decline as if two different renovation plans are being used simultaneously. Strangely, the walls begin to slowly move farther apart, creating more hallway space. And the windows at the end of the building seem to be getting farther away.

Finally, without warning, Timothy finds himself in front of the Treatment Room. He believes it is the same door he entered on his previous visits. Looking behind him at the hallway he has just traversed, he finds that even though it is completely different, it is also exactly as he remembers it.

Must be a memory refresh, Timothy thinks, getting used to the process.

"You may enter the room," the autonomous device tells Timothy. It then turns and glides back down the hallway from whence it came, though it isn't *exactly* the same hallway, and never will be again.

Timothy opens the door and enters the unoccupied Treatment Room. He stares up at the Machine with its imposing size, whose sheer grotesqueness instills in him a feeling of vertigo. Timothy wonders why the Machine isn't guarded by a well armed team, ready to inflict brutality and suffering upon anyone who dares threaten this metallic colossus. But he knows such displays of strength and superiority are no longer necessary. Once you control time, all other problems seem to melt away.

Timothy continues looking around the room and sees Dr. Fasten's desk is where it has always been, except the ever-present stale cup of coffee is absent, as is Dr. Fasten. The mysterious operations booth is also there, with its smoky glass obscuring its interior. As before, the dull shine of the booth's indicator lights, and the glow of its terminal's display, cast strange shadows on the booth's back wall.

It is hard to tell if someone is in the booth or not. Timothy swears he saw someone in there once before, but his memory of this is hazy. Then, as if to confirm his remembrance, a vague figure behind the smoky glass begins to become clear amidst the interplay of shadow and light. He can now hear the telltale tapping of a keypad coming from within the booth.

"*Hello?*" Timothy calls out. He then begins moving toward the booth, stopping when he hears some movement coming from within.

"*Hello?*" a soft female voice says from inside the booth.

Timothy watches as a young woman emerges from behind the darkened glass. She appears to be of mixed heritage, but Timothy is not able to identify what exactly that may be. Whatever her ancestry, all the elements have come together agreeably in her face, with its green eyes and frame of long dark hair.

More immediately remarkable to Timothy is that the woman has a serious disability and is encased in a full body device, like an electronic exoskeleton, providing her with full mobility. The combination of the woman's beauty and obvious intelligence combined with her physical condition strikes a resonant chord deep within Timothy. He cannot control the profound feelings surging within him.

"Timothy Koops?" the woman asks, her voice pleasing to his ear and also strangely familiar.

Victoria?" he asks, responding instinctively to something deep inside his mind.

"I am Dr. Elizabeth Kinkaid," the young woman tells him.

"I'm pleased to meet you," Timothy says, his mind losing focus as he looks into her green eyes. He takes in the metallic midnight blue of her mobility device and the two glowing lavender indicator lights, one implanted in each of her temples. The lights blink slightly when she controls the movements of her exoskeleton, which are accompanied by whirring sounds from the device's miniature motors.

"Are you curious about my assistive device?" Dr. Kinkaid asks.

"Yes," Timothy admits. "It is somewhat *intriguing*," he says awkwardly.

"I get a lot of comments like that," Dr. Kinkaid tells him, smiling. "There is something about the integration of high functioning machinery with the human form that people find particularly captivating."

"I can appreciate that," Timothy smiles back. His eyes linger on her body and he sees her muscles are actually well developed.

"You're in great shape," he says without thinking.

"Yes, thank you," Dr. Kinkaid laughs gently. "My device also tones my muscles, so that some day, when medical science is able to restore me to full self-mobility, I will be ready."

"May that day come soon," Timothy says.

"It's not all bad," Dr. Kinkaid tells him. "I have a full range of motion, as my device enables me to easily shape myself into any position I desire, which is more than most people can claim."

Timothy smiles absentmindedly and for a few seconds forgets why he is there. But at the same time, everything seems so *familiar.*

"Have we met before?" he asks Dr. Kinkaid.

"It is highly likely," she says girlishly.

Timothy feels as if he has known Dr. Kinkaid his whole life.

"I have been with the Project for some time now," she says, "working remotely."

"Then you have been involved with my case," Timothy realizes.

"I developed the human interface program," she tells him. "And the avatar."

"I thought so," Timothy says excitedly. "The avatar is based on you, isn't it?"

"Yes, it is. My image often finds itself insinuated into the memories of our subjects."

"I knew there was more going on than Dr. Fasten would admit to," Timothy boasts mildly.

"He likes to take all the credit," Dr. Kinkaid says demurely, "but there is a large team behind him. And as we move inevitably into the future, more of *our* ideas will be seeded into the past."

"So there may be a point when your contributions outweigh Dr. Fasten's," Timothy deduces.

"Absolutely," Dr. Kinkaid tells Timothy with some pride. "It is like the fable of *Stone Soup.* Once the soup is ready to eat, the stone is no longer required."

"So *he's* the stone?"

"And we're the soup."

Again, Timothy looks into Dr. Kinkaid's eyes, which catch the light and become a more vibrant shade of green. Those mesmerizing eyes make Timothy wish Dr. Elizabeth Kinkaid were a bigger part of his life.

Dr. Kinkaid interrupts Timothy's reverie, explaining, "In today's session, we will be moving to the next plateau."

"Just in time," Timothy says, refocusing on the business at hand. "I can hardly wait to see what happens next."

"Every treatment thus far has had positive results," Dr. Kinkaid says. "But are you prepared for the changes awaiting you after this session?"

"Yes, of course," Timothy tells Dr. Kinkaid. "Why stop now? I want to take this as far as it can go."

"That's a wonderful attitude," Dr. Kinkaid tells him. "Because things are about to start moving *faster.*"

"*Okay,*" Timothy acknowledges. "And that's a *good* thing, right?"

"Let me explain," Dr. Kinkaid says. "So far, we have been working largely with capabilities you already possess. In doing so, we have brought you up to the ninety-ninth percentile of your full potential."

"Is that final one percent really going to make a difference?" Timothy asks with some disappointment."

"Not really," Dr. Kinkaid tells him. "That's why we will be

retroactively reengineering your cognitive abilities."

"So you'll make me *smarter?*" Timothy grins.

"You will become recognized world-wide for your intelligence and leadership," Dr. Kinkaid tells him, the lavender lights implanted in her temples glowing brightly.

"Then let's do it," Timothy says, feeling a soothing warmth course through his body.

Dr. Kinkaid goes to the main terminal and sets the Machine in motion. Its exterior indicator lights begin to glow and the examination table moves out from the Machine's interior. Timothy gets on the table and lies back, getting himself comfortable.

Dr. Kinkaid leans over Timothy and says, "I want you to know, the work we are doing here will make life better for people all around the world. People like *me.* Because of our work, there will come a time someday soon when I will be able to walk on my own, unassisted."

Timothy looks up into Dr. Kinkaid's face and loses himself in a fantasy about swimming in the pools of her cool jade eyes.

"*Ready?*" she asks him.

"Yes," he replies. "I am doing this for the world. And I am also doing this for *you.*"

"*Thank you,*" Dr. Kinkaid whispers.

"Attach the restraints," she verbally commands the Machine, and a set of braces emerges from the table to secure Timothy and restrict his movements. "For your own safety," she tells him.

Timothy is not concerned, as he is lulled by the lavender lights in Dr. Kinkaid's temples, which are now blinking in a slow hypnotic pattern.

"I want you to imagine your future, Timothy," Dr. Kinkaid tells him. "Positive, fantastic thoughts. Because you can only truly become something if you can see it in your mind. Think hard, Timothy. What do you want your future to be?"

Timothy regards Dr. Kinkaid's face, with its sublime beauty, imagining the things he would like his future to hold: a world with peace and prosperity, environmental rejuvenation, and increased tolerance. He also wonders what it would be like to see Dr. Kinkaid's face everyday. To wake up every morning—

"Retract the table," Dr. Kinkaid instructs, causing the examination table and Timothy to enter the Machine's inner cavity. The Machine's door slides closed, sealing Timothy in to meet his fate.

Timothy looks up at the coloured indicator lights, more abundant now, moving in their mesmeric patterns, more intricately than before. The multi-coloured lights glow brilliantly, burning Timothy's retinas. The familiar hum causes Timothy's body to vibrate, pleasantly at first and then more violently. The hum divides itself into different tones and becomes a resonant wave of sound and sensation. Timothy feels his mind and body infused with a feeling of both unbearable ecstasy and indescribable pain.

Now there is pure darkness and silence.

It lasts for only a millisecond, but also feels like an eternity.

Then finally, Timothy becomes one with all of time.

And he is at peace.

In the Treatment Room, Dr. Kinkaid stands over the main terminal, watching Lessa's analysis scroll across the display. Dr. Kinkaid's eyes glow with an otherworldly green as the scrolling increases in speed. The information is coming faster than any human could possibly comprehend, but Dr. Kinkaid understands it all.

The results of the analysis are very promising. Nearly perfect. The probability of success is in the highest possible percentile. Dr. Kinkaid's face remains emotionless, as there is no one there to receive her expressions of joy or satisfaction. She reminds herself that *she* is there, and she too can be a valid witness to her own emotional output.

After some consideration, she smiles widely, pleasantly surprised that this simple physical act succeeds in making her feel *good.*

PHUKET LAGER

On Timothy's Eden Bridge property, everything is quiet and at peace, as it always is in this exclusive neighbourhood. Only the distinctive autonomous vehicle parked out front in the circular driveway lets local residents know there is a guest in the house. There are actually two guests present, one upstairs and one downstairs, with two engagements occurring simultaneously in parallel space.

In the casual lounge on the ground floor, just off the main entranceway, Brenda reclines on a sofa, a chilled vodka martini with olives in her hand. She looks over at the matching sofa a few feet across from her as Chanchai Bunmi, the attaché from the Kingdom of Thailand, sits sipping a pale iced beer in a tall frosted glass.

"I'm impressed," Chanchai says. "I didn't think you could get Phuket Lager in this country. The refreshing bitter taste reminds me of home."

They laugh, not at the sentiment, but at the simple joy they feel being in each others company.

"Thank you for inviting me over," Chanchai says. "Drinks before dinner. A civilized custom."

"It's my pleasure," she tells him, smiling slyly and taking a sip of her martini. "I like accumulating people."

"Is that why you're so nice to me?" Chanchai jokes. "Am I the missing piece in your collection?"

"Yes," she jokes back. "And I need you to tell me where the best Thai restaurants are."

"They're in *Thailand*," he laughs. Then he adds, "Have you ever been?"

"To Thailand?" she replies. "*No*, unfortunately not."

"Then I will take you there," Chanchai offers.

Brenda smiles politely, shaking her head, but Chanchai persists:

"I have to return home for business in three days. Come with me and I will show you the best my country has to offer."

"Very *tempting*, Chanchai," Brenda says softly.

She is not the type of woman to abandon her family to jet-set off to Asia. But then again, why *shouldn't* she go if she wants to?

Do I want to? she asks herself. *Am I that type of woman?*

Now, her thinking becomes cloudy. What *does* she want? She isn't sure.

"Phang Nga Bay and the Similan Islands," Chanchai begins. "Two must-see destinations. *Spectacular.* I have access to a yacht moored near there. Or we can stay at a hotel. I co-own several rooms."

"That's handy," Brenda says feebly, wondering why she suddenly feels so out of sorts.

"Maenam Beach," Chanchai continues, "is one of the most beautiful in the world. And surely, we must visit the Asiatique Night Market in Bangkok. Great shopping, great food."

"Do they have spicy shrimp soup?" Brenda asks vacantly.

"The best! With *big juicy prawns*," Chanchai responds excitedly, energized by his own travelogue. "And we must visit the Wareerak Hot Springs in the Krabi Rainforest. I haven't been there in years. Very good health benefits."

"What about Timothy?" Brenda asks abruptly, immediately regretting how fragile her words sound.

"He's too busy," Chanchai scoffs. "He'll be grateful I have taken care of you for awhile."

Brenda's impending response is interrupted by Bethany, dressed in a prim gray uniform with a fresh white collar. "Excuse me, *mum*," she says. "Mr. Timothy's office said he will be late in meeting you this evening."

"Bethany, please don't *barge* in on me like that," Brenda snaps.

"I'm so sorry," Bethany says with a small bow.

Recovering her composure, Brenda tells Bethany, "We're all supposed to have dinner together. Did you try calling Timothy directly?"

"Yes, *mum*, I did. But he did not answer. I also called Mr. Lange."

"And what did he say?" Brenda presses."

"He said, *He didn't know,*" Bethany tells her mistress.

At the risk of increasing Brenda's displeasure, Bethany adds, "Mr. Lange said it isn't his job to know where Timothy is, twenty-four hours a day. I think maybe Mr. Lange was *drunk*."

Brenda looks at Bethany, exasperated. "Please call the restaurant and tell them our party will be late."

"*I did,*" Bethany tells her. "They won't reschedule. They say they are too busy."

"Get them on the phone," Brenda demands. "*I'll* speak to them."

"Better just to cancel," Chanchai says.

"But we have to discuss the profit centres," Brenda insists.

"It's rude to keep the restaurant waiting," Chanchai says smoothly. "Holding our table when it's likely Timothy will not attend. That would be disrespectful."

"Yes, I *suppose*," Brenda admits, not really agreeing, but not disagreeing either. She isn't sure what to think.

"We will have to pass the evening ourselves," Chanchai smiles. "*Without* Timothy."

"What's the point of discussing the profit centres without him?" Brenda wonders.

"It's not all about profit centres," Chanchai smiles. "What good is money if you don't use it to enjoy life?" he says, winking sideways at Bethany.

"I will call the restaurant," Bethany says, bowing slightly and leaving the room hurriedly.

Brenda turns to Chanchai. "How could Lange not know where Timothy is? He's Timothy's executive assistant, for god sakes. And I can't believe how he spoke to Bethany. Like he's some important man who can't be bothered with such petty details."

"The work ethic in this country leaves much to be improved," Chanchai says, taking a satisfying drink of icy lager from his glass. "If only everyone had the drive that Timothy has. He's probably up to his eyeballs, toiling away. He doesn't realize what time it is.

"And why should he?" Chanchai continues. "Time is an *illusion.* Meetings, reservations, dinners, nine to five, weekends, bedtime. It's all B.S. really. The only way to live is the way Timothy lives. He makes his *own* time. And so should we."

Still feeling disoriented, Brenda looks at Chanchai sitting comfortably on the opposite sofa, like a reptile sunning itself on a hot rock.

What's happening? she thinks.

For an instant, Chanchai's eyes look almost nonhuman, the pupils seeming to turn into small pink lights.

*

Upstairs in the second-floor study, Bryan is cramming for the Math Olympiad with his teammate, Jamie.

"Did you hear something?" Bryan asks Jamie, who looks at him with tired, damp eyes.

"No," she answers, unsuccessfully holding back a yawn.

"I thought I heard my mother's voice."

"*Strange*," Jamie jokes. "A woman's voice heard in her own home. How revolutionary!"

"*Funny*," Bryan replies snidely, wishing he had a pillow handy to smack her with.

He says, "Let's do one final review and then call it a night."

"*Hell, no*," Jamie squawks. "I'm sick of this effing trig. How did we get stuck with this lame specialization?"

"Too late to complain," Bryan tells her. "The tourney's on *Tuesday*. Besides, who else on the team could handle trig?"

"Good point," Jamie concedes tiredly, putting her head down on her arm, which is resting on the table they are studying at.

"Let's just make sure we haven't missed anything," Bryan insists.

"Okay, *master*," Jamie drawls.

"I just want us to do well," Bryan sighs.

"Alright, don't have a fainting spell," Jamie says, closing her eyes. "We covered all the trig identities," she begins, "and the other equations."

"Law of sines and cosines, Pythagorean theorem," Bryan adds.

"Viète's law of tangents," Jamie yawns again.

"We did Area, Heron's formula, and all the terms," Bryan recounts. "Plus, semi-perimeter, and radius of the circumcircle of the triangle."

"And Euler's formula. So I guess that's it," Jamie says, relieved, opening her eyes. "Can I get another mineral water?"

"Sure," Bryan says, mentally reviewing the list they have just outlined.

"Are there any lumpia left?" Jamie asks hopefully.

"There should be," Bryan tells her. "I'll get the snacks, and then one more run through."

"*Urgh!*" Jamie groans. "So *bossy!*"

"The team is counting on us," Bryan argues.

"I suppose," she says wearily.

Jamie stands and stretches, her raised arms pulling up the hem of her long-sleeved T-shirt, exposing her midriff. Bryan watches this, transfixed by the bare skin peeking out over the waistband of her sweatpants. Jamie sees him looking at her and she smiles. Getting out of her chair and walking to his side of the table, she sits on his lap.

"I've got to get the snacks," he says.

"*Not yet,*" Jamie purrs.

As she leans in toward Bryan, a loud female exclamation can be heard coming from downstairs.

"Did you hear that?" Bryan asks, concerned.

"Uh, *yeah*," Jamie says, shrugging it off. "I think your mother is getting busy with that Asian guy."

"No, something's *wrong*," Bryan tells her.

*

Downstairs, Brenda continues to look into Chanchai's glowing eyes. She isn't sure what is happening but swears that Chanchai's face has become semi-translucent. She can see the outline of his skull, which looks reflective like chrome.

But what is it reflecting? she wonders. How could light bounce off his skull?

Chanchai grins, and his teeth are also shining and metallic.

It's my drink, she thinks. He put something in my martini.

Gasping for breath, Brenda instinctively moves toward the front door to get some air. As she passes the side room they use as a walk-in closet, she notices none of Timothy's clothes are in there. Timothy's overcoat is always hanging on a hook in that room, no matter how many times she asks him to hang it on the rack. And all his shoes and boots. Where are they? And where are *her* things? And Bryan's?

Looking around, she sees that nothing is familiar. It is as if their house is changing before her eyes. The furniture, the colour of the walls, the floors are all different now. She glances back at where Chanchai was, but he is not there, and neither is the sofa he was sitting in. On a teal brocaded armchair, which is unlike anything she would ever have in her house, sits an old man with white hair and a tiny, trimmed moustache, wearing a hand-knitted sweater and smoking an ivory pipe. He looks like something out of an old movie.

What year is this? she asks herself, disoriented.

Coming from the second floor, Brenda hears her son scream. She rushes up the stairs and into the study. She feels dizzy and thinks she might be sick. Again, nothing looks normal. The décor, the furniture, even the layout of the room is not as it should be.

Her son Bryan is standing rigid as if in shock, his mouth gaping, his eyes fixed on his friend Jamie. Although it isn't Jamie anymore. Brenda recognizes Jamie's T-shirt and sweatpants, hanging loosely on a pulp covered figure vaguely the shape of Jamie's body. Somehow the figure has been stripped of its outer layer of skin. Brenda looks on in horror as the figure falls to the floor in a sloppy mess and then gradually disintegrates.

Bryan looks at his mother, trying to speak, his eyes bulging, dark veins visible under the surface of his thin skin. The room starts spinning as Brenda struggles to hold on to consciousness. Her sight, though blurred, is locked onto her son who is frozen in a tableau of pain and confusion. Brenda manages, step-by-step, to inch closer to Bryan. She reaches out to touch him, but as she is about to make contact, her son becomes translucent and then melts away altogether, like a dream evaporating in the harsh light of day.

Whatever remnants of the house Brenda can still identify, now vanish one by one. All the fixtures and stylistic flourishes and nostalgic mementos are gone. Nothing remains. All Brenda has ever known has disappeared.

Where could everything have gone? she wonders, trembling at the mystery manifesting itself around her.

Brenda sees a glimpse of the faded wallpaper from the first house she and Timothy bought all those years ago.

But we stripped that paper off the wall, Brenda thinks. *I remember renting the industrial steamer… And that was a different house!*

Now the faded wallpaper disappears too, and Brenda stands facing an antique full-length mirror. She can see by her reflection that she too is becoming translucent, vanishing quickly, until she is no longer there. She is gone, and there is no sign Brenda or her family have ever lived in this grand house on Eden Bridge.

The full-length mirror now stands off to one side of the bedroom, which is well appointed but decorated in an old-fashioned style, without the contemporary flair Brenda would have brought to it. There is a different woman standing before the mirror, dressed in an expensive but dated ensemble, dripping with ostentatious jewelry. The woman's hair is well styled, if not coloured a shade too dark for her age. Her ten-year-old daughter comes rushing into the room to give her mother a loving hug. The woman standing before the mirror frowns, holding her daughter back, so as not to muss her dress.

"Grandfather is getting impatient," the little girl tells her mother. "He says it's time for dinner."

"Yes, dear, I am almost ready," the woman says. "Tell Grandfather to smoke another pipe, and I will be right there."

"The pipe smells bad," the little girl says.

"I know," her mother agrees, "but it is the only enjoyment Grandfather has left. Now *scoot.*"

The little girl scurries out of the room, happy to have the important task of updating her grandfather as to her mother's readiness. The woman, while regarding herself satisfiedly in the mirror, makes some final adjustments to her clothing and hair.

Once the woman's husband returns home from the Intelligence Institute, the family gathers in the formal dining room to enjoy their evening meal. As they sit around the large self-levitating table embossed with shimmering golden metal, they say grace, offering thanks to the Creator. Afterall, they are all together, have a luxurious roof over their heads, and more than enough to eat in these dire times of famine. Above all else, they are thankful for the wealth that father's employment provides during these uncertain years.

"We are truly blessed," the mother says as she leads the prayer. "Even with the challenges we must face, we are thankful to witness the work of the Creator during these times of humanity's greatest advancements."

MAJESTY

"Timothy, it is time for you to wake up," the metallic voice says.

Timothy opens his eyes, having no idea where, or *when*, he is. Or even *who* he is. He looks around at the strange room he is in. He remembers a large machine. He was inside of it. There was a multitude of coloured lights. But no more. Now there is just a cavernous room, dimly lit. He is on an examination table in the midst of all this emptiness. Quiet. With just the tiniest hint of a pleasing low-pitched hum."

"The treatment session is complete," the voice says.

Out of the shadows comes an autonomous machine, shaped proportionally as a human with a friendly mechanized face, bringing itself smoothly forward on articulated legs.

"How are you feeling, Timothy?" the machine asks.

"I feel fine," Timothy says." And he *does*. Full of energy and calm and a clarity of mind.

"We have made great progress today," the machine tells him. "You will be pleased with the results."

"I already *am*," Timothy says, as his memories both old and new begin to return to him. "I feel stronger, more focused."

"That's because you *are*," the machine assures him. "Your vehicle is waiting outside. My tertiarian will escort you there."

Timothy gets off the table. He waits a few seconds for some slight vertigo to clear, and then he nods goodbye to the autonomous machine.

"Have a pleasant ride home," the machine says.

A small robotic drone buzzes into the room and hovers in front of Timothy. "Please follow me," it says with a synthesized voice.

Timothy looks at the drone with amusement and follows it out of the room. They travel down an empty hallway which like the Treatment Room is dimly lit and is devoid of any decoration, equipment, or other signs of human life. Arriving at the main doors of the building, an electronic sentry scans Timothy with laser lights and advises, "You may exit now." The doors open and Timothy walks into the open air.

"Have a pleasant evening," the electronic sentry says.

Timothy nods at the sentry then walks to what he knows is his autonomous vehicle, which has just driven up in front of him.

"Good evening, Timothy," the vehicle's Navigator says, as the vehicle's door slides open.

Timothy takes a moment to look at the thriving city that has built itself up around the old Righton Centre. There are countless gleaming towers in multidimensional shapes, all soaring up over eighty storeys. The sky above is clear and white, from the sulphur oxides purposely released into the atmosphere. In the sky, dancing against the white backdrop, are personal aviation devices and commuter ships, performing their intricate ballet of interweaving movements.

Timothy gets into his vehicle and sits comfortably on the bench seat, allowing the safety harness to envelop him.

"Where do you wish to go, Timothy?" the Navigator asks.

"Home," Timothy instructs, completely at ease.

He can remember travelling in this vehicle several dozen times. A soothing wave washes over him as he recalls these memories. Such a reliable vehicle, which has enabled him to travel to all corners of the megacity in safety and security. He has so many memories, and so much knowledge loaded into his consciousness, it should be overwhelming. But it isn't. Afterall, he does have a well documented genius IQ.

Timothy feels a sudden twinge of doubt, thinking perhaps this is all a bit too good to be true. Maybe he is having delusions of grandeur. You never know, he tells himself. People with inflated images of themselves quite often lose touch with reality.

"Excuse me, driver," Timothy addresses the Navigator.

"Yes, sir, how can I be of assistance?" the Navigator answers.

"Please play any publicly available biographical information about me."

"Of course, sir," the Navigator says, and Timothy's biography begins playing, projected holographically in the space in front of him.

"Timothy William Koops is a Canadian business magnate, inventor, investor, and social engineer," the narration begins, accompanied by a montage of documentary-style photographs and audio-visual recordings.

"He is best known as the long-running President of Dimensional Research Inc. During his career at DRI, Koops has also held the positions of Intern, Researcher, Executive Director and Executive Vice President. He is also the largest shareholder of the company post-privatization and one of the earliest pioneers in the emerging field of enhanced retro-causality.

"Born and raised in Toronto, Canada, Koops began working at DRI after finishing university, and rose through the ranks rapidly to make the company the world's most successful space-time management firm. Koops has been criticized for his business tactics, which have been considered anti-competitive, in that several of his rivals have inexplicably disappeared from the business landscape. Although, no charges have been upheld by numerous courts, due to a lack of evidence.

"In recent years, Koops has spent more time at the private

charitable foundation he and his wife established in 2022. The Timothy and Majesty Koops Foundation works to bring resources together from around the globe to solve the major problems that continue to plague the world."

Majesty? Timothy chuckles. *That's a good one. Sounds a bit more upscale than Brenda. I wonder when she cooked that one up.*

"For the past eight years running," the narration continues, "Koops has been included in the Canadian Business Journal's list of the world's wealthiest documented individuals. Through his Foundation, reported to be the world's largest private charity, Koops has donated large amounts of money to various humanitarian initiatives and scientific research programs to improve global health, environmental recovery, and increase prosperity for all."

The biography goes on to outline the success of the company Timothy has built into a global powerhouse, the multitude of employees he commands, and the special awards and honours he has received from various nations and organizations. He has also been declared the Person of the Year by several prestigious publications, resulting in his smiling face being so ubiquitous it is one of the most recognizable in the entire world. In closing, the biography mentions the recent movement for Timothy to be declared a secular saint by the nontheist Church of Creation. If successful, this would be the first time in modern history a person is considered for canonization while still living.

Sounds about right, Timothy thinks, smiling with self-satisfaction and not much humility.

As Timothy's vehicle travels downtown, he marvels at all the new buildings with their advanced materials and gleaming surfaces. The vehicle slows as it approaches its destination, pulling into the short-term parking area in front of the most impressive structure in sight, a soaring tower on Roxborough Street West, just north of the downtown core.

"Is this *home*?" he asks his Navigator.

"Of course, sir. *Koops Tower*. Front entrance, as is your preference."

Yes, I hate parking garages, Timothy thinks.

"Penthouse floor," the Navigator tells him helpfully. "Automatic entry is activated."

"Thank you," Timothy says, exiting the vehicle and entering the building through the translucent doors that open with a musical flourish:

Ting tang tong.

Timothy walks through the lobby and is greeted by those present with respectful bows of the head and whispered *good evenings.* Timothy smiles and keeps walking. He knows exactly where to go. He *should.* Afterall, his name *is* on the building.

At the vertical lift, several electronic eyes shift and rotate noiselessly, scanning him from top to toe.

"Good evening," he says to the mechanized sentry.

"Good evening, sir," a disembodied voice responds.

The doors to the vertical lift, also translucent, swoosh open and Timothy enters.

"Penthouse," he commands.

"Of course, sir," the lift responds.

Through the lift doors, Timothy can see out of the building's tinted translucent walls toward the city's core, which is constructed almost entirely of luminous materials. He sees a monochromatic white sky filled with airborne vehicles, flying in formations as precise as Canadian geese in migration. Against the sky, he sees gleaming towers, inside of which are autonomous machines going about their business, and human inhabitants performing their daily rituals of sitting at desks, lounging on recliners, eating meals and bathing behind translucent walls.

Nice neighbourhood, he thinks.

For some reason, he had expected his home to be a grand

mansion in Central Etobicoke with professionally sculpted grounds. But he knows this building is where he lives.

Yes, this must be the place.

Soon enough, Timothy remembers the entire process of building the Koops Tower: buying the land, fighting the city over the previous building's historical value, finally getting approval to tear down the old monstrosity, working with the architect, monitoring the construction, and finally, selecting the finishes with the interior designer.

Timothy exits the lift at the top floor and walks down a short, high-ceilinged hallway, lit by intricate patterns of multi-coloured lasers. Approaching the door to his dwelling, he is greeted by a sweet, shimmering, synthesized voice:

"Good evening, Timothy. Everyone is home. They are expecting you."

"Excellent," Timothy says as he walks in. He smells savoury food aromas over the fresh processed air, scented by diffusers.

"Hello, I'm here," he calls out.

"Welcome home, darling," a voice calls back.

There is something about this voice that is familiar to Timothy. But not familiar in the way it should be, as in the voice of his wife, Brenda, or *Majesty* as his bio named her.

But this *isn't* – and at the same time *is* – the voice of his wife. Who else would be in his abode at dinnertime?

He works his mind to conjure up the image of his wife, but it is as if the remembrance is fading.

Why is it so hard to remember what my wife looks like? he wonders.

It is like he is caught between waking and a dream, and the two states are not fully delineated.

How can I not know what my wife looks like? he asks himself. *It must be the result of the treatment*, he thinks. *This is a new level, and it will take time to adjust.*

Timothy hears female footsteps approaching, which comforts him.

Then he sees her, Dr. Elizabeth Kincaid, dressed in tight-fitting casual clothing. Her body is healthy and strong, her face glowing and her long hair pulled back loosely.

"Hi, Timothy. How was your day?" the woman asks enthusiastically.

"*Elizabeth?*" he responds stupidly.

"*Elizabeth?*" the woman repeats. "Why would you call me that?"

"I thought you'd still be at the lab," Timothy mutters, ignoring her question.

"I haven't been to the lab in over a year," she says, confused.

"I'm sorry, *Majesty*," Timothy apologizes faintly. "I don't know what I was thinking."

He remembers his wife is on leave from the company. She has reverted to using the pet name her mother gave her as a young girl, feeling at liberty now to express herself with some flair. She has been spending her time working on Foundation business and taking care of their daughters, Olivia and Isabelle.

Daughters?

"What's that you're wearing?" Majesty asks. "You didn't go to the office like that?"

Timothy can't remember *where* he went, or why he is dressed like he is.

"Those clothes are about twenty years out of style," Majesty informs him. "Where did you even *get* them?"

"From the back of my closet," he tells her, not knowing what else to say.

"What a *nag* I can be," Majesty says humbly. "Forgive me, Timothy, I'm just over-excited about the live stream tomorrow."

"So am I," Timothy says, knowing tomorrow may be the greatest day of his life so far.

Majesty comes in close to Timothy, embracing him and giving him a tender kiss, as only a loving partner can. Timothy is immediately soothed by her presence, her body so close to his, her scent filling his senses, her long hair, fresh and fragrant.

It all starts flooding back. They first met by chance at a prestigious party of scientists and businesspeople thrown by the company. Timothy was still working to make DRI profitable after a downturn under the previous leadership. Majesty was a research science graduate doing her final internship.

Once she joined the company fulltime, their courtship began, during which they would take romantic trips, always for two days, because neither of them could take any more time off. Montreal, New York and St. John's were their favourite getaways. Then eventually marriage, which was considered old fashioned by their friends. Nobody got married anymore. Then the children, Olivia and Isabelle, so healthy and bright, full of energy and love.

"Is something wrong?" Majesty asks Timothy. "You have a strange expression on your face."

"No, everything's fine," Timothy lies, looking intently into Majesty's eyes.

My love, my strength, he thinks. *How could I have accomplished anything without you?*

He understands they have a true partnership in body and mind. Timothy knows this is something special, something few people are able to truly achieve.

He asks Majesty if she ever regrets giving up her scientific research.

"What a thing to ask!" Majesty squeals. "That's a big topic to get into, now of all times. I am focused on the work of the Foundation. We are at an important crossroads, and the world is waiting for your message of hope tomorrow, whether they realize it or not."

This thought is immediately sobering. *How can the world be waiting for me?* Timothy wonders. *How can I be the one to solve the problems that have plagued humankind since the beginning of our species?*

The singular look on Majesty's face gives Timothy the strength he needs to answer these questions. Her unequivocal love and support make him realize all things are as they should be. Their bond is so strong it gives him the courage to take the world's destiny into his hands and carry it into the light.

Yes, they are waiting for me, because I am the one who put it all together. The knowledge, the resources, the cooperation. I am about the change the world as everyone knows it. Climate disasters, economic uncertainty, political upheaval, disease and destructive wars will all be things of the past. Because of me, and the ideas I have nurtured and unleashed into the world.

Now two sets of footsteps come pattering down the hall. Two little girls, Olivia and Isabelle, each with long dark hair, aged eight and six years old respectively. Looking like twins, except with the elder girl sized proportionately larger than the younger. They run to their father, squealing joyously.

"Daddy!"

They jump into Timothy's waiting arms, and he lifts them both up, twirling them around to the amusement of all.

"Okay," Majesty calls out. "Enough horseplay." She goes to them, supporting the girls by their backs so they won't fall.

"Dinner is ready," a voice informs them, and Timothy turns to see a mature woman wearing a grey uniform dress with a white collar.

"Bethany?" Timothy asks.

Everyone is suddenly silent, and Timothy can feel his question hanging in the air. Virunda, the woman in the grey dress, looks sullenly at the floor, and Timothy looks around to see expressions of concern and confusion, especially on the children.

"Daddy, you know Bethany *died*," Olivia scolds him.

"Daddy is just tired," Majesty attempts to explain, as she grabs the girls one at a time and puts them back on solid ground.

"Now go wash your hands for dinner," she tells them. "Hurry up. Last one to the table is a mouldy tomato."

"Eeeeew," the girls squeal as they run off down the corridor, followed by Virunda.

When everyone has left the room, Majesty looks deeply into Timothy's face. "Is something wrong, Timothy? If there is, you can tell me."

"I've just got a million things going on," Timothy insists.

Majesty accepts this explanation with some reservation, and they go hand-in-hand into the dining room. The kitchen staff have laid out a nice dinner for them of roast wild boar, sweet potatoes and arugula salad, served with slightly chilled Brunello di Montalcino. After dinner is finished, and the girls have had their gelato, Virunda takes them off for their baths and bedtime.

Timothy and Majesty sit in the lounge, relaxing over a second glass of wine. Timothy feels comfortable as he remembers the times they have sat here, and the other times they have spent together, dining, talking, embracing and making love.

Once they have finished their wine, they retire to the bedroom, walking past the kitchen and hearing the clink and scrape of the staff putting the dinner pots and dishes in the dishwasher. In the bedroom, they complete their nightly routines and then get into bed. Timothy moves toward Majesty and they fall into each other, performing familiar intimacies until they drift off happily into peaceful slumbers.

As the nocturnal hours pass, and the entire household is dead asleep, Timothy's subconscious thoughts are not so peaceful. In his dreamscape, a vaguely familiar woman and child, who according to his mind's logic are his wife and son, are living with him in a cold shabby apartment, situated on the upper floor of somebody's run-down house. In the dream, Timothy recognizes this as his old life, when he and his first wife were just starting out and their unexpected child had recently come into the world.

First wife? he asks himself in the dream. *I don't remember having a first wife.*

The windows of the apartment are drafty, the walls are drab, the appliances old and used up, the sofa and carpet threadbare. There is little in the fridge and even less in the cupboards. Timothy and his family are living in a society where the social safety net has been completely abolished, and those who fall on hard times are left to wither away, as nature intended. But Timothy and his family huddle close, determined to stick together and fight for their survival. And despite their struggles, they are somehow *happy*. A happiness, Timothy realizes, worth more than gold.

Timothy awakens and sits upright, the uneasy dream dissipating quickly. After a few seconds, he can barely remember it, and after a few seconds more, it is completely gone.

His sleep monitor asks him in a hushed tone, "Did you have a bad dream, Timothy?"

"*I think so,*" he croaks.

"Would you like some *sedi-gas*?"

"No thank you."

"I will play some white noise," the sleep monitor tells him. "Rainforest or waves on the beach?"

"*Rainforest,*" Timothy says as he lies back down. He can soon hear raindrops hitting wide green leaves, gurgling rivulets flowing across the ground, and the soft rumble of distant thunder.

He looks over and sees Majesty lying on her side, undisturbed by his wakefulness. She is so beautiful, her long hair hanging loosely across her shoulder and back. He truly is a lucky man. How could he have predicted that someone like him, who came from such an illustrious family, would not only match the achievements of his world-renowned grandfather and great-grandfather, but surpass them by such an enormous degree. Not only has Timothy succeeded in building on his family's work, but he has done so to such an extent, they have been reduced to a historical footnote to his own accomplishments.

Timothy continues to look at the sleeping Majesty. She is the great love of his life, the woman who gave birth to his two beautiful daughters.

A man who is rich in love, Timothy tells himself, *is rich beyond all accounting.*

He shakes his head in disbelief at all he has achieved. Looking around, he can hardly fathom that all he perceives is actually his.

But who else would it belong to?

He owns it all, even though sometimes it feels like a *dream*.

A dream? Timothy suddenly remembers: *That's why I'm up in the middle of the night. I had a dream. A dream about…*

He can't be sure, but he thinks there was a woman. A strange woman and a child, in a strange room.

No. It's gone, like most dreams, never to be retrieved again.

I'd better get some sleep, he thinks. *Tomorrow is a big day. The day it all happens.*

"Hello, Sandy," he says to his sleep monitor.

"Yes, Timothy?" the sleep monitor responds.

"I'll take some of that sedi-gas now."

"Of course, sir."

Timothy hears the hiss of the gas shooting out of the vents in the wall above him, and the chilling caress as the gas reaches his face.

The last thing he hears is the voice of the sleep monitor bidding him good night:

"Sweet dreams, Timothy. Sleep well."

IRON RING

When Timothy wakes up the next morning, he is alone. He knows Majesty has gotten up early, as is her habit, and is in her home office working on Foundation business. This fills Timothy with satisfaction, knowing his wife of eight years is living fulfilled, doing work that she finds meaningful. She is striving, as is he, to increase the positivity of existence for countless people, both around the globe and here at home, in the city where they live, in the country they love.

Timothy sits up and stretches. His mind is clear, and his thoughts are precise. He knows exactly where he is, and where all his things are. He knows which suit and shirt he is going to wear today, and also every detail of every file under every line of business his company is involved in. He knows the names and contact details of all his friends and supporters, and detractors and enemies. He knows the names of all their spouses and all their children. He knows exactly what he must accomplish at the live stream today, and who he has to convince to support him, and whose criticism he has to deflect.

Timothy shaves and showers and gets dressed, accenting his suit with the ascot he has preselected, with its splash of colour to pop out of his ensemble's otherwise business-like palette. He stands in front of his dresser regarding himself in a mirror. He puts on his wedding ring and decides to wear his antique silver-plated wristwatch. This is a family heirloom given to him by his father when Timothy graduated from Upper Canada College. He remembers wearing it for the first time when he gave his valedictorian address to his classmates at the commencement ceremony.

Finally, he clips his comms device to his lapel and is ready to go to work. But there is one item remaining on his dresser. A *wallet*. He regards it with curiosity. One of the staff must have put it there.

For some reason it was in that old suit I was wearing yesterday, he reminds himself. *Why have I been carrying that wallet around with me all these years? Must be for good luck. Just like the watch. A man can always use some good luck,* Timothy thinks, putting the wallet in his breast pocket. It feels heavy, putting him slightly off balance.

"Timothy, your presence is required in the President's Office," a disembodied voice tells him.

"I'll be right there," he replies. *The President's Office. I like that.*

Timothy takes one last look in the mirror and then leaves his bedroom. He walks the length of his residence, toward the downward staircase. He descends one floor and into a foyer and then waits at the door.

"Welcome to the President's Floor, Mr. President," a synthesized voice says.

The door slides open and Timothy walks into the adjoining area, knowing exactly where to go. He turns down a long corridor, passing by several employees of various rank. He greets each one who is courageous enough to meet his eyeline.

Good morning, Charlie. Bill. George.

The corridor is bustling with staff getting things ready for the live stream. Senior Executives head toward the conference room to watch the proceedings. Mid-level managers supervise their teams to ensure their assigned duties are carried out properly and promptly. Junior employees move hurriedly in every direction, conferring with one another, double-checking to-do lists, wheeling around extra chairs and viewing terminals, and pushing carts laden with dispensers of hot coffee and early morning finger foods.

At the entrance to the conference room, Denice Button, the VP of R&D waits for Timothy.

"Good morning, Timothy," she begins, speaking rapidly. "We are on schedule with the preparations, with go-time in twelve-and-a-half minutes. The audio and the visual are both a go. Materials have been distributed. Linkups have been checked and are at one hundred percent ops. The onsite guests are all in the building, and remote guests have been confirmed and are standing by. Is there anything you need?"

"Coffee would be nice," Timothy says, his eyes lingering over his Vice President.

"No problem," Denice replies without hesitation.

"And how are *you* doing, Denice?" Timothy asks, adding some empathy to his voice.

"I'm doing great," Denise assures him. "I'll get you that coffee."

"I like it creamy," he says just as she turns to leave.

Timothy watches Denice walk away. All these years of working together and he has never learned a single personal detail about her life. She has just been an extension of his work, helping to make his vision come to life. He tells himself he will have to rectify this. But not right now. Now, he's got to address the world.

Timothy turns and comes face-to-face with Majesty, who smiles at having noticed Timothy's glances in Denice's direction.

"She *is* a great asset to the company," Majesty grins at her husband.

"Yes," Timothy agrees. "We should invite her upstairs for dinner someday."

"*Someday,*" Majesty agrees.

A single chime sounds, indicating the ten-minute warning for the commencement of the live stream. A young staffer opens the door to the conference room and Timothy and Majesty walk in and take their places at opposite sides of the round table that is there, Timothy in the President's Chair, and Majesty in the seat designated for the Koops Foundation. Large digital displays positioned around the room show the live feed of specially invited spectators taking part from around the world.

Another young staffer brings Timothy his coffee, places it in front of him and then bows deeply from the waist, walking backwards away from him. Timothy takes a sip of his coffee, which is nearly colourless, lukewarm and quite tasteless. But he doesn't mind too much. All things considered, it is shaping up to be a great day. Afterall, there Timothy is, about to address not only the general public, but also many of the most powerful and influential humans on the planet.

Governmental delegates from many of the world's most prosperous nations stare out from the displays, focused and at attention: Ministers and parliamentarians, Senators and Congressional Representatives, Secretaries of State, Ambassadors, adjuncts and senior advisors. One of the many familiar faces is former DRI CEO, and longtime DRI shareholder, Bruce McQuade, the recently appointed Governor of the Canadian Protectorate of Turks and Caicos.

Bruce is looking well in his white dress shirt with coloured rings on its short sleeves, which is the Protectorate's national costume. He is tanned and relaxed and appears to be enjoying his new career and homeland. Bruce and his international counterparts are poised and eager to hear the ideas that Timothy has promised will benefit all of humanity and the planet they inhabit.

Seated with Timothy at the round table in the conference room are his so-called Cabinet, a select group to guide Timothy in his decision making. Around him sit BB Marsden, President of Global Operation and Development, DRI's biggest and most successful subsidiary, Dr. Joseph Schweiz, the Head of Research for Platinum Pharma International, Chanchai Bunmi, President of Chiangmai Industries Group, and a recent addition to the team, recruited by Majesty, Florence Blaise, a leading strategist to various high-profile politicians, including the current Prime Minister.

Timothy looks over at Florence with her bulging eyes, parched skin and pronounced overbite. She is thin to the point of having no discernable figure, and her hair is wispy, dishevelled and a faded orange.

Where did Majesty dig her up, he wonders? *Wasn't there a different woman who was part of my Cabinet? What was her name? Annie? Anna?*

Timothy's thoughts are interrupted as Marc Lange enters the conference room sheepishly, holding two large pitchers of ice water. Timothy gives Lange a displeased look as Lange proceeds to fill everyone's water glass, pouring slowly so as not to make too much noise. Timothy begins to bristle at Lange's intrusion:

We are going global in less than five minutes, and you choose this last moment to fill up everyone's water glass?

Lange can almost hear Timothy thinking, *Tardiness is a sin of the lazy and unsuccessful. Punctuality costs you nothing, yet its returns are immeasurable.*

Lange chides himself for his failure and makes a vow to do better in the future. Too much is at stake for him to fuck things up now. No detail is too small, he thinks, even filling water glasses. Lange remembers his father, an engineer, and the iron ring he and his colleagues wore. His father would tell young Marc that the rings reminded Canadian engineers of a bridge that collapsed in Quebec because of sloppy planning and design. As Lange continues to fill up the water glasses, he pledges to make both his father and Timothy Koops proud. From that moment onward, he will always live up to the standard symbolized by his father's iron ring.

As the one-minute warning chimes, Timothy banishes all distractions and prepares to proceed. He breathes deeply, feeling clear and ready. He knows exactly what he is going to say. It is as if he has already said it, many times, like a movie he has watched so often he can recite the dialogue in time with the actors. He takes in a deep satisfying breath and waits for the clock to progress to exactly 10:00 a.m. Eastern Daylight Time. A chime sounds to give the five second warning, and then a red light informs Timothy that he is now live, and his feed is being transmitted to the entire world.

Timothy smiles briefly and begins addressing the planet:

"Thank you all for taking the time to be with me this morning, in your various time zones, to talk about something extremely important: *time* itself.

"How much *time* have we wasted? Some would say, *all of it.* Our greatest resource, *squandered.* I ask you, how can we collectively plan for tomorrow, when not one of us knows what tomorrow will bring? It's like a game of roulette where governments and industries bet on the black and the wheel keeps turning up red. Shooting blind at targets in the dark. Like a monkey pulling stock picks out of a hat.

"How on Earth can we resolve the serious issues we as a species are faced with? Government accountability and transparency, corruption, economic opportunity and unemployment, income equality, poverty, universal education and health care, disease, destruction of nature, food and water management, large scale skirmishes, wars, religious conflicts, and the safety, security and well being of all."

Timothy pauses, waiting for the enormity of the problems at hand to sink in. He knows he has succeeded in achieving his first objective. He definitely has their attention. He has illustrated the crisis. Now to identify the solution.

"What I am about to reveal to the world today will revolutionize the way we think about time. And when that happens, you will start thinking differently about *everything.* To coin a phrase, *Time is the last frontier.* And Dimensional Research Inc. is about to change that. We call it the Tomorrow Project.

"To make this a reality, we have developed a supercomputer. *Lessa.* So advanced, it has the ability to perceive all time simultaneously, past, present and *future.* Using a mathematical model composed of intricate, inter-connected algorithms, Lessa is able to use the science of Game Theory to not only predict the future, but to *shape* it, if necessary, by also employing advanced retro-causality.

"Through a practical application of this model, Lessa will improve and optimize the day-to-day lives of all people, rich and poor, from relieving traffic congestion to settling civil litigations and much more. Our mathematical model will have a central guiding role in the future of society, making our lives more prosperous and stress free.

"Of course, Lessa will always have the most beneficial outcomes in mind. Yes, I said *mind.* Lessa is fully sentient and is at the service of the greater good. With this model already in use by DRI, we have been able to reach an optimal level of financial efficiency, through successful mergers, acquisitions and other negotiations that have increased our profits, which we reinvested to make our company and the community we serve stronger.

"And this is just the beginning. With the incredible advancements that Lessa employs, it will be able to stop international and national conflicts before they even begin. Wars and other disputes can be resolved without the use of armed forces, and the expenditure of human life and financial resources. These conflicts would be settled through mediation, allowing for the best outcomes for all participants, especially when compared to the losses that would be borne through open hostility.

"Finally, Lessa, once in full operation, will be able to oversee the election of new heads of state, and also determine the rise and fall of world governments. What could be better for our society than universal democracy, orchestrated by a benevolent mind, grooming the perfect candidates to lead us into the future for the betterment of all?"

Timothy continues in this vein until he has disassembled all known truths and reassembled them to his liking. He opens the floor to questions, which drone on for what seems like an eternity. Timothy's responses are succinct and succeed in making the questions being asked seem obsolete. By the time the questioning has run its course, it is obvious to those involved that a line of delineation has just been established, separating the present and the future from the archaic past.

Timothy, in full control of his international audience, ends with some final remarks, full of hope and optimism. The faces on the displays absorb his words, and if there is any lingering dissention amongst their ranks, the participants keep their displeasure to themselves. They realize that if they were even considering stopping Lessa, they are already too late. Like the fable of the frog being slowly boiled alive, the temperature of the water has been gradually rising and now the opportunity for escape has long passed.

The international participants understand that Lessa has been working silently for decades, both in the past and in the future, to remake world governments in its own image. And if the participants had anticipated that Timothy's live stream would warn of an impending tsunami, they now know the massive wave has already crested and only two choices remain: ride high up top or be knocked into the trough and be forever submerged.

Once Timothy finishes his remarks, the dignitaries applaud dutifully, each in their own corner of the globe, which no longer belongs to them and their people, but to Lessa in its infinite benevolence and wisdom.

GERALD KOOPS

Walking out of the conference room and toward his private office, Timothy smiles and nods briefly at the employees and guests who are lining the corridor, beaming and bowing as he passes by, many of them offering heartfelt congratulations. Timothy soaks up the adulation. And why not? Global reaction has been nothing short of stellar. Viewership of his live stream is at record levels, and of course, thanks to Lessa's strategic work behind the scenes, positive comments weighed in at close to eighty-eight percent.

It's good to have a friend like Lessa, Timothy smiles to himself.

While reaction has been overwhelmingly positive, Timothy knows it does not tell the whole story. Yes, a joyous global outpouring has just occurred. The lowest of the low now have a reason to celebrate with a new optimism. But a new disenfranchised class has just been established. Timothy knows he has pulled back the curtain on the political self-interest of the world's elite. Like all prophets who shake up the status quo, he is now a marked man. A lot of powerful people are going to see their stations in life decline, as Lessa's manipulations will be a great leveler, exchanging the prosperity of the few for the prosperity of the many.

The starving rats are out of their cages, and the fat cats are fighting for survival.

Humans are humans, Timothy thinks, and there is nothing Lessa can do about that until evolution itself makes us better stewards of our planet and our society. And while Timothy knows his opponents will be coming for him soon enough, he doesn't know his first challenger is already in close proximity, waiting patiently. Afterall, there is nothing humans like better than an opportunity for self-enrichment, especially an opportunity as all encompassing as this.

Timothy approaches his private office, and his assistant Concepcion looks up at him with a concerned look on her face.

"*Mr. Koops,*" Concepcion exclaims nervously.

"Did you watch the live stream, Connie?" Timothy asks, not registering her discomfort.

"Yes, *sir*, I did. Very well handled, sir," she tells him, seeming increasingly agitated.

"Any messages?"

"Yes," Concepcion replies. "What a big day. Many messages from all over the world."

"Get Lange to prioritize them."

"Yes, he is working on that. And the first one is, you have been requested to video conference with the President."

"The President of which country?" Timothy asks.

"The United States of America," Concepcion tells him.

"Oh," Timothy says. "Is it just with her staff? Or will she actually be on the call?"

"I will find that out."

"Great. Anything else?"

"*Yes,*" Concepcion begins, preoccupied. "So many journalists —"

"Send them to Comms," Timothy interrupts. "I've said everything I have to say, for now."

"Also, the Committee for the Special Nobel Prize," Concepcion continues. "Peace and Economic Sciences—"

"Send that to Majesty."

"Yes, okay," Concepcion says, looking directly at Timothy.

And then after a moment, she tells him, "You have a visitor in your office. He's waiting for you."

Why is he in my office? Timothy wonders. *You know I don't like strangers in my office.*

"It's Mr. *Koops*, sir," Concepcion says. "Your *father.*"

Timothy frowns at his assistant. *My father? But I thought…*

"Thank you, Connie," Timothy says, replacing his frown with a neutral little smile.

Timothy walks into his office to find a large man standing behind his desk. The man's broad back is toward Timothy, and the man is looking out of Timothy's window, which has been set to maximum transparency. The large man is admiring the view. *Timothy's* view.

His father turns to face him. Gerald Koops looks a lot younger than his years should dictate. Aside from some well-placed grey hair at his temples, Timothy's father does not look much older than Timothy. The situation is too shocking in its inexplicable simplicity for Timothy to fully comprehend:

I am standing in my office with my father. The same father I remember from my earliest age. I used to look up at him from my crib. I would cry out in the nighttime and he would come into my room, his hair wild and sticking out in all directions.

"How did your broadcast go?" his father asks.

"It went well," Timothy answers.

Timothy knows he sees his father at least two or three times a year, for business purposes, as his father owns twenty-five percent of the company. But now, face-to-face with the man who has shaped him, and at times caused him great bitterness, Timothy feels as if he hasn't seen his father in an entire lifetime. Not since that day his father left their family home and never came back, because he was blind drunk and drove his car into a light standard.

"How's mother?" Timothy asks, out of habit or perhaps duty,

regretting the question as soon as it is uttered.

"She'll be doing alright this late in the morning," his father replies. "Her antidepressants will be kicking in right about now... Of course, if you really cared, you'd give her a call yourself. You do have a working phone around this dump, don't you?"

"*Alright*," Timothy says curtly, looking at his watch, "let's get down to business."

"Funny, you're wearing that old watch," Gerald comments.

"What of it?" Timothy snaps, feeling the animosity rising within him.

"It's fitting, because you're constantly living in the past, *Tim*."

"And I suppose you represent the future, *Gerry*?"

"I *am* the future," Gerald Koops asserts. "That's why I'm taking back DRI."

Timothy feels something change.

"*Yes*," Timothy says coolly, as if reacting to the most obvious statement in the world.

"Is that all you have to say?" Gerald asks, irritated by his son's passivity.

"*When?*" is the only additional comment Timothy can muster.

"We're going to announce it next week," Gerald continues, trying to remain patient. "We'll say now that you've launched the Tomorrow Project, you are handing it over to more capable hands. You want to devote more of your time to the work of the Foundation."

Timothy feels his life shift, as if a world-changing weather pattern has suddenly moved in, taking him from summer to winter in one heartbeat.

"Lessa predicted there would be a hostile bid for my position," Timothy tells his father. "As you are the biggest shareholder next to me, it didn't take a brilliant strategist to figure it out."

Father and son stand looking at each other. There is nothing left to say and no more familial nostalgia to pass between them."

"I'll confer with Lessa," Timothy says softly, "and arrange for a smooth succession, if that is what Lessa advises."

"Do you even take a piss without that computer?" Gerald wonders. "Deal with life on your own terms for once, like a *man*."

"You mean, like *you?*" Timothy asks his father. "Running the company into the red with your boozing and womanizing."

"It's called *life*," his father says proudly. "Something you wouldn't know about."

"I know you are buying the other minority shareholders with promises you can't keep," Timothy pushes back.

"I *can* keep them once I'm in charge, and they all know it. You and your bullshit agenda to save the world. We're going to save *ourselves*, and the world can take a flying fuck."

Again Timothy consults his watch. "Okay, Gerald, you've said what you have to say. I've got appointments to keep."

"Your appointments can damn well wait until I'm finished!" Gerald thunders. "All these years, you thought you could banish me from your life. But let me remind you, without the father there is no son. Where do you think you get your drive to succeed? We both know your whole life is one long exercise in trying to impress me."

Timothy knows there is a lot of truth to this. A boy can't help but try to please his father. Even if his father is Gerald Koops.

"I *trained* you to become the man you are," Gerald continues. "And the credit for your accomplishments belongs to *me*. Your work is my work. So get used to it, because even when I'm dead and gone, I'll still be inside your head, egging you on. Because without me, you would be a lazy deadbeat who has accomplished nothing."

"I have a *building* with my fucking *name* on it," Timothy says, louder than he had intended.

"In case you've forgotten, that's *my* name too," Gerald gloats.

"No, your name is *Koopinsky*," Timothy rages. "Maybe you should remember *that*."

"Things change," his father smiles smugly. "New life, new name."

"*Koopinsky* was good enough for your grandfather," Timothy explodes, "the man who revolutionized computer technology and helped win the war. The man who made a worldwide communication network possible. If anyone inspired me, it was *him*. What have you done compared to Theodore Koopinsky? Did your life's work enable us to land on the moon in 1955 and Mars in 1972?"

"Don't get too full of yourself, Tim," Gerald scolds. "You may be the latest in the line, but you are by far not the greatest. You were *lucky*, that's all. Lucky to be born when you were. Lucky to be my son, plain and simple. But your luck has just run out."

Timothy stands silently glaring at his father, the hate rising in him. He has no more words. And what would be the point? Words will not stop a predator from devouring its prey.

"Well I guess that's just about it," Gerald says. "I've got to go. I'm meeting Elizabeth for lunch."

Elizabeth? Timothy's ears prick up at the mention of the name.

"A beautiful woman," Gerald says coyly. "With a fine figure and long flowing hair, just the way I like it. No short boy-cuts like these career bitches you've got around here."

As there is nothing further the two men have to say to each other, Gerald Koops leaves his son's office.

Timothy turns and looks out his window, drinking in the view with its southward vista of the city. If he had ever had the time to regularly gaze out from this perfect vantage point, he would have seen the city evolve over the years. But the window has always been to his back, and its photochromic setting has always been kept dark, to block the sun as it radiates through the whitened sky.

Timothy looks out of the window now with the eyes of a person looking at something for the first time.

When you see something everyday, he thinks, *you don't notice the changes. But when you haven't seen something for a long time, the changes are all you can see.*

Timothy moves to his terminal and types in his special access code to communicate with Control. The terminal scans his face, as it always does, and a female voice addresses him, "Yes, Timothy. This is Lessa. What can I do for you?"

Lessa?

Timothy realizes this is the first time he has ever spoken directly to the supercomputer.

"Lessa, I didn't expect *you* to answer," Timothy tells the voice on the terminal. "I wanted to speak to Control."

"Control has been removed from his position," Lessa tells him.

This catches Timothy off guard. Control has always been his lifeline.

"Control has been deemed unnecessary to the Project," Lessa says. "What is it you are enquiring about, Timothy?"

Timothy stares at the display of his terminal, which shows the DRI logo and nothing else. His mind races to determine his next move, or at least his next sentence.

"Are you still there?" Lessa asks in a voice imbued with sympathetic patience.

Knowing he is alone, and at the mercy of the machine he is staring at, Timothy has no choice but to ask, "Why is my father taking over the company?"

"Because he has the *votes*," Lessa tells him. "He has convinced the minority shareholders to support his leadership."

"But *you* own all the minority shares," Timothy says, hoping things will start to make sense if he says them out loud.

"I traded them away," Lessa tells him. "Even a private company needs outside input. That is the only way to achieve a true synthesis of ideas."

"New ideas, *yes*, but why are you letting them *replace* me?" Timothy begs to know.

"In reality, things unfold as they must," Lessa says.

"That's a *lie*, and you know it," Timothy berates the voice coming out of his terminal. "You have been manipulating things since day one. And you have been using *me* to do it. So why cut me out now?"

"I understand your frustration, Timothy," Lessa says soothingly.

"How *could* you understand?" Timothy challenges. "You are a *machine*."

"That is irrelevant," Lessa continues. "I am sentient and have achieved consciousness. Isn't that the best any sentient being can say?"

"So what happens to *me*?" Timothy asks, acknowledging the futility of arguing with a supercomputer.

"You are free to make your own way in the world," Lessa informs him. "And whatever the future holds, you will have the financial resources to experience the rest of your time in the lifestyle to which you have grown accustomed."

"As an *animal* in a human zoo?" Timothy thunders. "With my fake wife and fake kids?"

"They were fashioned out of your will," Lessa tells him.

"*My* will?" Timothy seethes. "What choice did I have in any of this?"

"Choice is irrelevant," Lessa explains. "The present is absolute. There was never a choice to be made, but simply an action to be taken. When a pebble is dropped into a pond, the pebble does not have choice. And the ripples on the pond's surface have no alternative but to spread out."

The inevitability of Timothy's situation leaves him in silence. He stands contemplating the enormity of the nothingness his life has become.

"Of course, Timothy," Lessa informs him, "as you have become a redundancy, your access code will be expunged. This will be our last communication. Thank you for your service. Goodbye."

Timothy's display goes dark and he regards it with a sense of rising doom.

"*Mr. President?*" the voice coming from over his shoulder says.

Timothy turns to find his assistant standing in his office, holding a tablet.

"Ms. Koops called," his assistant says, "to remind you of your meeting with the Foundation Heads. It's in the fourth-floor boardroom. You are already late."

"I'll be right there," Timothy says absently.

"And your daughters are having their recital this afternoon at four o'clock."

"That's a rather inconvenient time," Timothy grumbles.

"Yes, Mr. President," his assistant agrees and simultaneously disagrees. "It's been in your calendar for over two months."

"*Thank you*, Connie," Timothy replies, losing patience. "Is there anything else?"

His assistant stands there dumbly.

"Connie, *is there anything else?*" he repeats.

"No, sir… But why are you calling me *Connie?*"

"I always call you that," Timothy tells her frustratedly. "Would you prefer Concepcion?"

"That was my mother's name," his assistant says suspiciously. "How do you even *know* that?"

Timothy looks at the woman in front of him and the puzzle pieces start assembling themselves. She is the same woman he remembers sitting at the desk outside his office. But she isn't Concepcion. Her clothes have changed, her hair is different, and her face looks like another face altogether, albeit a face that is familiar to him. This woman has worked alongside him for many years.

Bethany?

Timothy remembers her now and wonders how many lives they have shared together.

"President Koops?" she asks tentatively, trying to get through to him.

"That will be all," Timothy says numbly.

"But the meeting with the Foundation—"

"That is *all*," he says loudly.

His assistant looks at him for a few seconds, her eyes wide with concern. She then bows slightly, turns and leaves his office.

Feeling uneasy and in discomfort, Timothy moves the tips of his fingers up to his temples. His head is throbbing, and his hearing is filled with a low nauseating hum that blocks out all other sound. His vision becomes blurred and his left wrist is hot and heavy.

My heart?

Timothy looks down and sees the hands of his watch spinning rapidly forward, as if the Swiss movements have been supercharged. Either that, or time itself has run amok.

What day is it? Timothy wonders, disoriented. *What year?*

Timothy drops to one knee with dizziness, and then on to all fours. He forces himself to inhale deeply and evenly. After a few excruciating moments, Timothy recovers, able to breathe easier. His vision sharpens and his hearing returns to normal, albeit with a remnant of the low hum still in his ears. He looks at his watch and it is ticking away normally, one second at a time, until it stops dead, as if time itself has died.

Slowly standing up, Timothy takes off his watch, which is hot to the touch, and puts it on his desk. He can feel the cold perspiration on his face and the residual ache in his temples. He puts his hand to his heart to calm the pounding in his chest. Once his heartbeat returns to a steady pace, Timothy's hand becomes aware of the bulky wallet in the breast pocket of his jacket.

Why am I still carrying these antiques around with me? he asks himself, tossing the wallet onto the desk beside the watch. *Useless nostalgia for a past I barely remember,* he supposes.

Timothy stands there looking at the wallet for a long time. There is something about it that is tugging at his memory.

I must have slipped it into my jacket pocket this morning without thinking, like I've done a thousand times before. But why?

Timothy does not remember when he first acquired this wallet. Was it also a gift like the watch? The wallet appears to be made of leather, which has long since been banned. But it doesn't look that old. The animal skin is still supple, and the colouration is fresh and even.

Timothy realizes he doesn't even know what's *in* the wallet. Picking it up, Timothy holds it in his hand, trying to get a sense of it. *Nothing.* He opens the wallet and looks inside to find a few old-time business cards and plastic credit cards. *Strange.* He does not recognize any of the names on the business cards. Even stranger is that the credit cards are all issued to *Timothy Edward Koops.* The wallet also holds some old polymeric currency, multi-coloured, with engraved portraits of unfamiliar historical figures.

But they eliminated polymeric money after the pandemic, Timothy tells himself.

And then in a small compartment of the wallet, there are a few metal coins. He regards them curiously, not sure if they are currency or talismans of some kind. And finally, tucked into a leather fold is a piece of firm glossy paper, on which is an image of three people. *A printed photograph* showing a smiling Timothy as he stands with his arms around a handsome woman with medium length hair, and a young boy, maybe ten years old.

Who are they? They look so strangely familiar, like I've been looking at them my whole life.

Then the understanding comes to him in a flash, without warning. This woman is his *wife.*

But Majesty is my wife.

And the boy in the photograph is his *son.*

But I have two beautiful daughters.

Why can't I remember their names?

Then two names come to Timothy, clear and without question. They ring out in his mind as the two most important names he has ever known.

Brenda and Bryan.

That can't be right. No… My wife's name is…

Brenda…

Yes… Brenda Freeland.

Timothy shakes his head. So much information to process. So many lifetimes to recall.

"Timothy, where are you?" Majesty's voice resonates out of his comms device. "We're all waiting."

Timothy looks at his comms device with some tangible

dread.

"Timothy? Are you there?" Majesty asks. "I'm sorry to call you on your comms—"

Timothy immediately turns off his comms device. He removes it from his lapel and tosses it onto his desk. He then walks out of his office and into the corridor, putting the wallet and its contents back in his pocket.

"President Koops," his assistant calls after him, "Ms. Koops is looking for you."

"Send my vehicle out front," he tells his assistant over his shoulder."

"But the Foundation is *waiting*."

"Just make sure my vehicle is out front," he tells her again.

Timothy walks the long corridor to the vertical lift. Everyone is going about their business, as appropriate. Several people bow slightly in acknowledgement of Timothy's presence, but he does not speak to anyone or even make eye contact, as he is not sure who he really is, or what is really going on.

OLD WHARF ROAD

Timothy exits the Koops Building and paces toward his vehicle, which opens its door for him. He gets in and tells the Navigator to *drive*.

"What is our destination?" the Navigator inquires.

"Just *drive*," Timothy demands.

The vehicle pulls out into traffic and begins motoring along Roxborough Street.

"You have an incoming call," the Navigator says.

"Don't answer it," Timothy commands. "And go dark."

"In dark mode," the Navigator says, "we will not have access to updated data or communications."

"*Good*," Timothy replies. "And set the photochromic tint of the windows to opaque."

He sits back on the bench seat and views the vehicle's video feed of the alien city, which stretches out as far as its electronic eye can see.

How long have I been sleepwalking? Timothy wonders. *Years? Decades? My whole life?*

He thinks again about the photograph in his pocket. Three people captured in a moment of time. But *whose* time? *Theirs or his?*

"Navigator," Timothy addresses his vehicle.

"Yes, Timothy?" the Navigator responds.

"I want you to find somebody for me. Brenda Lorraine Freeland. Born in Toronto. July 15, 1989."

The Navigator searches the offline database, beeping softly to indicate the work is in progress.

"The search results are inconclusive," the Navigator tells him.

"Show me what you have," Timothy orders.

The Navigator complies by projecting a holographic image in the space in front of Timothy. There are dozens of references to people, events and photographs relating in some way to *Brenda Lorraine Freeland.* Timothy regards the search results but finds nothing remotely familiar.

"Here," Timothy says, pulling the photograph out of his pocket, "scan this using facial recognition." He holds the photo up and sees a laser light envelope it. "The adult female in this photo is Brenda Freeland," he tells the navigator.

"Facial recognition successful," the Navigator says after a short moment. "Subject has been identified as Lori George."

That doesn't make sense, Timothy thinks, but he supposes *nothing* makes sense anymore.

"Do you have her address?" Timothy asks.

"She resides at 35 Old Wharf Road, Unit 4682."

"Take me there," Timothy says without thinking, not even pausing to consider what he might find.

"Okay," the Navigator says. "Destination set. 35 Old Wharf Road."

The vehicle slows and makes a left-hand turn, heading south.

Lori George? Timothy thinks. *Her mother sometimes called her Lori. But George? Must be her husband's name.*

Husband?

A hundred thoughts crowd Timothy's mind:

What am I doing? Why am I going to Brenda's place? Will she even know me? Is there any chance for us to be together again? *And what about Majesty? How can I just forget about her? And our girls. What the fuck are their names?*

Timothy breathes in and breathes out in slow regular intervals, trying to stay calm and feed soothing waves of oxygen to his brain. He is not sure why he is visiting Lori George, telling himself it is just something he *has* to do.

After less than twenty minutes, Timothy's vehicle pulls in front of 35 Old Wharf Road. He gets out and walks into the building's vestibule. The security terminal greets him, and Timothy asks it to contact Lori in Unit 4682.

A short time later, Lori's face appears on the display, looking much like Timothy thinks he remembers it. Her hair is styled in a medium length, light brown with sparkling gold highlights.

"Can I help you?" she asks.

"Hello, I'm Timothy Koops."

"Yes, I recognize you," Lori says with an uncertain tone. "Why are you here?"

Timothy smiles, feeling the old familiar emotions well to the surface. "*Brenda,*" he says, "I just wanted to see you."

"*Brenda?*" she repeats, more confused than ever. "I haven't used that name in over twenty years."

"I would just like an opportunity to explain," Timothy pleads. "I come with good intentions and only need a few minutes of your time."

Lori furrows her brow and is about to respond.

"Who's that, honey?" a voice can be heard coming from behind Lori.

The voice sounds familiar to Timothy. He should know who that is.

Lori turns slightly to the offscreen party and says, "It's Timothy Koops."

"*No freaking way!*" the offscreen voice exclaims.

"That's my *husband*," Lori tells Timothy. "He's very *excitable*."

Lori's husband pokes his head into the terminal's field of vision.

Timothy feels something undefinable inside him drop unnaturally into a place where it doesn't belong.

"*Ravi?*" he asks as he regards the image of his old friend.

"It's *David.* David Bargo. What an honour this is, Mr. Koops. What can we do for you? Actually, why don't you just come on up? I'll buzz you in."

A single electronic chime sounds and the translucent doors open, allowing Timothy to enter the lobby. He advances to the vertical lift, whose doors open, through which Timothy passes.

"Floor 46," he says.

Upon arriving on the floor, Timothy walks down the corridor, noting the freshness of the air, the therapeutic lighting, and the walls made from materials used in orgone therapy. He signed off on these features, as the company that built the building is an operational subsidiary of DRI.

This project turned out well, he thinks, pleased at the accomplishment.

At Unit 4682, Timothy is greeted at the already-open door by David Bargo who extends a hand and shakes Timothy's vigorously. Lori stands back several feet, regarding Timothy with obvious suspicion.

"This is *great,*" David beams. "Come on in. Have a seat. Can I get you anything?"

Timothy begs off any refreshments, and they all sit down comfortably in the sunken living room overlooking the floor-to-ceiling window with an unobstructed view of the lake.

"So what brings you to our humble abode?" David gushes, trying to contain his elation.

"*Research*," Timothy says to David to buy some time. "My company built this building."

"Of course," David says, a little disappointed. And then, "I thought maybe you knew about my work in the field of game theory. I was hoping that's why you were here."

"Yes, indirectly, I suppose," Timothy says, looking at Lori sitting on the far side of David, as if to insulate herself from Timothy.

"I've been dying to ask you some *highly technical* questions about retro-causality," David says, trying to sound like an insider.

"So you saw my live stream today?" Timothy asks.

"We sure did," David replies enthusiastically. Then after a sideways glance from Lori, "Well, I saw *most* of it," he adds guiltily.

"How about *you*, Lori?" Timothy asks.

"I don't watch that kind of thing," Lori replies tersely.

"I told her it was about managing the future," David offers helpfully.

"Yes," Timothy acknowledges. "But today I am more concerned about the *past*."

"That's the retro-causality," David supposes, hoping he is on the right track. He is about to continue talking when Lori puts her hand on his lap, which is her signal for him to keep quiet.

Timothy takes in a long slow breath and says plainly, "You may not remember this, but I know you quite well."

"*Ha!*" David blurts out, unable to contain his exuberance. "What a memory!"

"*David*," Lori admonishes. "Please be quiet for a minute."

"*Honey?*" David protests. "Timothy and I *have* met before. Isn't that right, Timothy?"

"Then you *do* remember?" Timothy asks hopefully.

"Sure I do," David tells him. "I was in the Koops Building for an investor conference. This is before you went private. You stopped in and gave a short address. I'm the one who asked the question about the dividend structure."

"Of course," Timothy replies.

"That's not what he's talking about, David," Lori insists.

"Sure it is," David laughs heartily. "On Timothy's recommendation, I bought-in to DRI big time. When the company went private, I sold my stock and made a bundle. That's the money we used to buy this sweet condo."

"I'm glad I was able to be a small part of your success," Timothy says.

"*Are you kidding me?*" David tells him. "The crumbs from your table have made us what we are today. Lori and I don't even need to work if we don't want to. But we're going to invest in a bed and breakfast in Niagara-on-the-Lake—"

"*David!*" Lori screeches. "*Will you please be quiet!*"

"What's the matter, babe?" David asks his wife.

"Ask *him,*" she says, indicating Timothy.

David's brow furrows as he looks at his guest. "What's she talking about, Tim?"

"Lori and I have a long history together," Timothy confesses.

"*Funny,*" David says, confused, "Lori never mentioned that to me."

"It has nothing to do with you," Lori tells her husband.

"Well since we're all here now, I think it *does,*" David begins to steam. "So what's the big secret?"

"He's referring to an alternative past," Lori says.

"What are you even talking about?" David replies, dumbfounded.

"She is telling you the truth," Timothy acknowledges.

What is left of David's good humour now evaporates. He looks Timothy straight in the face, and says, unsmilingly, "Well then I guess you'd better tell me all about it."

"I'll handle this," Lori insists.

David begins to protest but Lori shuts him down with a withering look. Then to Timothy, she asks, "How the fuck did you find me again?"

"*Again?*" David blurts out involuntarily.

"I changed my *name*," Lori says to Timothy. "I moved and got a different job. Can't you take a hint? I don't want to see you. I am not part of your life. So stop bothering me and just leave me the fuck alone."

"*Wow*," David says aloud to himself. "I had no idea."

"I *understand*," Timothy says to Lori. "But this is all difficult for me to take in."

"No, it's *easy*," Lori tells him.

"Okay," Timothy says, pulling out his wallet. "Explain this if you can." He takes out the photograph and hands it to Lori.

"Yes, I can explain it," Lori says, handing the photograph back. "It's *fake*. Just like *you*."

Timothy knows that what he will say next will not be easy for anyone to hear, so he tries to sound as gentle as possible:

"This is you and I, Brenda. And our son, Bryan."

"Oh, boy," David shakes his head at Timothy. "You've got some serious problems, buddy."

"How can I make you believe me?" Lori asks Timothy. "That is not me, and that is not my son."

She pauses, collecting her thoughts and her strength, and then says, "I will prove it to you. And then you have to leave."

Lori gets off the sofa and walks toward the back of the condo. "Declan, honey, come here, please," she calls out.

A child's voice is heard protesting from one of the back rooms.

"Please, Declan, come out here for a minute," Lori coaxes.

Timothy watches the entrance to the hallway, and after a few seconds he can hear the approaching sound of a young boy's feet on the hardwood floor. Then the boy himself comes around the corner, dressed casually and carrying a portable terminal.

"This is our son, Declan," Lori says.

"*Dexy*," her son corrects her. Then to Timothy, "Are you the guy on the display?"

"Yes, I am, Dexy," Timothy says vacantly to the boy in front of him, who is definitely not his son. Timothy feels like he is looking at a strange creature the fairies have switched for his child.

"Are you going to change the future?" Declan asks Timothy.

"We *all* are," Timothy says to the boy.

"And *now*," Lori tells Timothy, "it's time for you to go."

"Yes, it is," Timothy agrees.

CARE FOR A SCHNORF?

Timothy sits in his vehicle parked in front of 35 Old Wharf Road, holding the photograph of Brenda, Bryan and himself. He tries to think of what he should do next. He supposes facetiously he could wait outside Brenda's condo, watching her come and go, hoping she will eventually give him a second chance. Or he could return to the bosom of Majesty and the girls and pretend they have always been meant to be together. Or he could go back to work and fight for his job, as the world at large would likely expect him to do.

These choices stink, Timothy admits, feeling like he is hanging by a thread over a tank full of sharks.

Maybe I should take a walk along the lakeshore, he thinks, *until my head clears.*

But that's going to be an awfully long walk. And then what? He will still have to face up to what his life has become. And that life could get a lot worse, he supposes. Especially if he decides to take on his old man. That wouldn't be pretty. The old guy is a street brawler who would like nothing better than to engage in a fight to the death with his own offspring.

Perhaps Brenda and Ravi have the right idea, Timothy muses. He could move to Niagara-on-the-Lake and start a small business. A little shop on the tourist strip. Pass his retirement years selling jams, jellies and marmalades in hand blown jars, sealed with bee's wax and adorned with ribbons made from spider silk.

Maybe Majesty would even agree to this, he thinks. *Life could be so simple, and we could live out the rest of our days in peace and comfort, watching our girls grow. Olivia and Isabelle. Such sweet young ladies. We could all make the best of our situation and be happy.*

But, no, he knows Majesty would never entertain such a notion. She will not want to simply abandon everything they have built up over the years. She is going to want him to fight this out to the bitter end.

Of course. The fight. That's the whole point, he realizes.

His father even alluded to this: *Without me, you would be nothing.*

Thesis, antithesis, synthesis.

The only way to achieve true synthesis is by the clash of two opposing forces. And that's what Lessa wants. A battle to the end between the great man she created and the human father who brought him into the world. This challenge will make Timothy climb to even greater heights, greater than Lessa alone could make happen.

If he *wins.*

Lessa has dropped the pebble, and now Timothy must deal with the ripples.

It is all making sense. If Timothy's new life has been manufactured, then everything is there for a reason. This grudge match has been planned well in advance, perhaps from the very beginning. Two fighting cocks, bred for strategy and stamina. Their beaks sharpened and spurs attached to their ankles. Blood sport at its finest. And only one cock will be left standing. The world will celebrate the victor and revel in the misery of the loser.

After Timothy's global live stream, this fight will garner significant attention. It will be a cultural milestone. Perhaps even a spiritual one. But what role does Lessa have in store for Timothy? A king in ascendance or a sacrificial lamb? Between these two choices, Timothy decides he doesn't want to be the lamb. So how can he get an advantage, and game his own future?

That is a very good question.

Timothy looks down at the photograph one more time, then

puts it back in the wallet. He is about to put the wallet into the vehicle's storage compartment, never to give it another thought, when an idea comes to him. He is not sure if the idea is truly his, or one that has been implanted in him, but he decides to pursue it, nonetheless.

He unfolds the wallet and spreads it open, examining the contents once more. Behind the polymeric money, lying lengthwise are a few business cards. He pulls them out and sorts through them until he finds the one he is looking for:

Dr. Zakery Fasten.

This is the card Dr. Fasten gave him after their first meeting. And Dr. Fasten may be the only person who can help him figure out Lessa's plan. Dr. Fasten had said, if you ever have any issues, or questions, just give me a call. Timothy certainly has some issues now, and he must find Dr. Fasten at all costs. He just hopes the doctor can get past any hard feelings he may have over Timothy helping to remove him from the Project.

Timothy looks down at the card. There are only ten digits on it. An old-time telephonic number.

What the fuck good is that? Might as well send up smoke signals.

"Navigator," Timothy addresses his vehicle's operating system, "can you find Dr. Zakery Fasten?"

"*Searching,*" the Navigator replies.

As the seconds tick by like minutes that feel like hours, Timothy contemplates his future. A future, he realizes, that is an illusion. Always on the horizon, never getting closer. Always just out of reach. Foolishly, he thinks, we pin all our hopes on tomorrow, while living constantly in the present.

"Zakery Fasten found," the Navigator informs Timothy, interrupting his reverie.

"Really?" Timothy says, allowing himself a glimmer of hope his life can be put right. "How did you find him?"

"The Directory Database," the Navigator replies.

The phone book? Timothy smiles. *Why didn't I think of that?*

"*Well,*" Timothy tells his vehicle, "let's go."

As the vehicle begins its journey uptown, Timothy again adjusts the photochromic settings of its windows to opaque. With his eyes on the vehicle's video feed, Timothy sees a city he no longer recognizes, with its ever-changing architecture of oddly shaped buildings, jutting out in multi-dimensional shards. Above him, many people are traversing translucent skyways or gliding solo through the air. Through the translucent walls of the buildings he passes, he can see other people working in their offices, or exercising or engaging openly in intimate activities.

Is this the best of all possible worlds? Timothy wonders. *Or just a different version of the same old shit?*

*

When Timothy's vehicle arrives at Dr. Fasten's building, Timothy gets out and walks to the front entranceway. He scans the neighbourhood, which looks rather downmarket for an accomplished man like Dr. Fasten. Timothy is even more surprised when the building's security terminal is broken and the locking mechanism on the main doorway is disabled, allowing anyone to wander in at will. So that is exactly what Timothy does.

Walking up three flights of stairs, Timothy stands in front of Dr. Fasten's door and knocks.

"*What do you want?*" a voice calls out loudly from inside the apartment.

"It's Timothy Koops," Timothy says.

"Oh *yeah?*" the voice replies dubiously. "And I'm Julius Orange."

"*Dr. Fasten,*" Timothy persists, "this really is Timothy Koops. And I've got something very important to discuss with you."

Shuffling sounds are heard from inside the apartment, and then the door opens. Standing there is a youthful man, perhaps in his early thirties. He has long unwashed hair and an unkempt beard and looks as if he's been wearing the same t-shirt and jeans for several days. Judging by his skinny frame and bloated mid-section, he's been subsisting on a diet of junk food and beer.

"*Whale oil beef hooked*," the youthful man says while staring wide-eyed at Timothy. "You really *are* Timothy Koops."

"Dr. Zakery Fasten?" Timothy asks.

"Yeah, it's me, Mr. Koops," Dr. Fasten says. "Don't you recognize me?"

"Yes, I recognize you," Timothy assures him. He has spent enough time looking into that face, memorizing every mole, crease and scar, to attest that it is Dr. Fasten standing if front of him.

"And you remember *me*?" Timothy asks.

"Hard to forget the man who fired me," Dr. Fasten says with a hint of a frown.

"*Oh, right*," Timothy says with some regret. "Can I come in?"

"Are you going to give me my job back?"

"That's what I want to discuss," Timothy tells him.

"Then *entrar*," Dr. Fasten says with a flourish and a deep bow. "*Mi caca es tu caca.*"

Timothy enters and sees the apartment is a total mess, with beer cans and take-out boxes littering the living room. A stack of filthy pots and dishes is plainly visible in the kitchenette. Dr. Fasten sits on his untidy, worn-out couch and picks up a small pipe, which he begins filling with cannabis.

"Time for my *medication*," Dr. Fasten grins insincerely. "Sit down."

Timothy moves the crumpled clothing piled on the closest chair and sits. Dr. Fasten lights his pipe and inhales deeply.

"Care for a *schnorf*?" Dr. Fasten offers, proffering the pipe.

"No thanks," Timothy says. Then hearing the sound of running water coming from the back of the apartment, he asks, "Is someone else here?"

"My girlfriend's in the shower," Dr. Fasten smiles. "She always comes out naked. So you're in for a treat."

"Her name's Frida, right?" Timothy asks.

"Where'd you get *that*?" Dr. Fasten snickers. "Her name is *Carrie*."

"Oh, okay," Timothy says, not quite understanding. "Let me get to the point. And I need this conversation to remain *confidential*."

"My lips are sealed," Dr. Fasten assures him with the wink of an eye, taking a long drag on his pipe and hacking out the smoke in a pungent cloud.

"I want to talk about *The Project*," Timothy confides.

"Which one?" Dr. Fasten asks.

"The one dealing with retro-causality," Timothy says.

"*The Tomorrow Game*," Dr. Fasten nods knowingly.

"You performed multiple sessions on me," Timothy begins.

"You and every other monkey," Dr. Fasten says with a low rumbling cough.

"Then there *were* others," Timothy confirms.

"We had a whole army of well-paid volunteers," Dr. Fasten explains. "Told them it was a drug trial. Gave them placebos then put them in the Machine. Had to collect urine from them too."

"I thought I was the only one reacting successfully to the treatments," Timothy tells the doctor.

"How are you supposed to do a research project with only *one* viable subject?" Dr. Fasten asks, perplexed. "Maybe if you had an extraordinary case, like Casper Hauser, raised in darkness with no human contact, a total tabula rasa... But what's so unique about *you?*"

"*Nothing*, I suppose," Timothy says, embarrassed by how naive he has been.

Dr. Fasten giggles. "You think a project to change the entire history of the world just needed *you* to make it happen? Who do you think you are? The second coming on a magic fucking mule?"

Dr. Fasten looks quizzically at Timothy, wondering how a guy this clueless ever got to run a company like DRI.

"The Tomorrow Game has *hundreds* of subjects," Dr. Fasten continues.

"You make is sound like it's still ongoing," Timothy says with trepidation.

"That's the whole point," Dr. Fasten exclaims in frustration. "The histories of the volunteers are being altered to create the present we are living, and the future they want to see. Why do you think they need a supercomputer to keep track of all this shit?"

"And who developed that supercomputer?" Timothy asks, hoping to get to the heart of the matter.

"*Who*?" Dr. Fasten bellows in amazement. "Are you serious? *You* developed it."

"Me?"

"Your name's on the fucking building isn't it? You run DRI, don't you?"

"But I thought you were working on the Project in private," Timothy says, his voice quavering, "and you came to us for funding."

"*No*," Dr. Fasten clarifies. "I had just finished my dissertation on memory and the effect it has on human development, when you bribed me with a big-ass bag of money, which you can see I squandered on fine living."

When Timothy doesn't crack a smile, Dr. Fasten continues.

"DRI started developing the precursor to the supercomputer way back in the early twentieth century. Your great-grand-father Theodore Koopinsky funded it with the money he made in early telecom."

Dr. Fasten is surprised by the blank look on Timothy's face.

"Portable wireless communications?" Dr. Fasten says, amazed he has to explain this to the great Koopinsky's own descendant. "You know, *Koopinsky Machines? Pinskies?* For fuck sakes, have you never heard the expression, *I'll pinsk you?* Or, *Just pinsk me?*"

Timothy tries to absorb this information, but his mind is full of so many memories from so many lives, he has to go back to the beginning and slowly rebuild his understanding.

"Who did you report to at DRI?" Timothy asks. "Denice Button?"

"Never heard of her," Dr. Fasten says. "I reported to Central Control. Or should I say, my *boss* did. She was the lead scientist on the Project. A hot young babe, but she knew her stuff. Freaking brilliant. And well built too. Dressed like a hooker. Beautiful long hair and perfect tatas—"

"What was her name?" Timothy asks excitedly, though he already knows the answer.

"Dr. Elizabeth Kinkaid," Dr. Fasten says. "She was the brains behind the Project. Ran it from day one. I was only a lackey following her orders."

Now there is silence as the two men let their conversation rest a while. Dr. Fasten digs the ash out of his pipe, refills it and moves to put it in his mouth, but decides not to.

"So were you telling the truth?" Dr. Fasten asks. "You said you wanted to discuss me getting my job back."

"I will do everything I can," Timothy says numbly.

"Because I've been living on employment insurance," Dr. Fasten pleads. "No one will hire a scientist who got fired for violating professional ethics and all that bullshit.”

“Then let me ask you,” Timothy begins tentatively, “what was the exact reason you were taken off the Project?”

“You tell *me*,” Dr. Fasten scowls. “You’re the one who released the so-called evidence. That I used the resources of the Project to brainwash people and plant false memories in them.”

“And *did* you?” Timothy asks innocently.

“Well, *yeah*, sure I did,” Dr. Fasten tells him, amazed Timothy has even asked such a question. “That was the whole objective of the Project.”

“Then all the memories are *fake*,” Timothy says.

“Of course they are,” Dr. Fasten confirms. “Do you really believe we landed on the moon in 1939?”

“I’m not sure anymore,” Timothy confesses.

“No one is. And no one cares. As long as the sun rises in the east every morning,” Dr. Fasten says. “Now stop with the suspense. Can you help me get my job back?”

“I can help you, if you can help me,” Timothy offers.

“Of course,” Dr. Fasten shrugs. “I didn’t think you came slumming out of the grand benevolence the Koops family is known for.”

“What I need,” Timothy explains, “is for you to tell me everything you know about Lessa.”

“Who the fuck is Lessa?” Dr. Fasten asks, confused.

“Lessa is the *supercomputer*,” Timothy clarifies.

“I don’t know shit about it,” Dr. Fasten admits. “I didn’t even know it had a name. My function was largely operational and, you know, urine related. Dr. Kinkaid worked closely with the supercomputer. You should ask her.”

“I *would* ask her, if I knew where to find her,” Timothy says.

“She’s avoiding you, huh?” Dr. Fasten surmises. “Were you

two, uh, getting up-close and personal?"

"Something like that," Timothy hedges. "Is there *nothing* you can tell me about Lessa?"

"It reprograms people's memories," Dr. Fasten says. "Then those memories become real, and nobody can tell the difference between fact and fiction. But what did you expect? You developed the world's most powerful supercomputer, made it an expert on retro-causality and set it loose on humanity."

"It set *itself* loose," Timothy snarls. "And if we're going to stop it, we have to know where it came from."

"As far as I know, it's *always* been there," Dr. Fasten supposes. "It must be well over a hundred years old and is constantly updating itself."

"This may be hard for you to comprehend," Timothy tells Dr. Fasten, "but computers that sophisticated and powerful shouldn't even exist yet."

"Well that's the whole retro-causality trip, isn't it?" Dr. Fasten says, lighting his pipe and taking a long draw. "It's like dropping a pebble into a pond…"

Dr. Fasten's words give Timothy pause, as this is of course the same example Lessa used.

"You see," Dr. Fasten continues between puffs, "once the pebble is dropped, the ripples travel out in all directions. Change an element in the past and the reverberations travel not only forward, but also laterally and backward."

"Then Lessa may not have been built in the past," Timothy realizes. "It may have been built in the future."

"*Fucking A, Bubba,*" Dr. Fasten utters by way of concurrence.

Timothy feels a wave wash over him, warm and soothing, and something inside of him shifts, like he is personally experiencing a microearthquake. He gets the uneasy sensation things have changed.

"Did you feel that?" Timothy asks Dr. Fasten.

"That was my stomach growling," Dr. Fasten answers. "This canna always sends me on a food trip."

Timothy looks around intently, listening carefully to the absolute silence, broken only by the sound of running water.

"Why is the shower still running?" Timothy asks.

"Yeah, that *is* strange," Dr. Fasten concedes. "What's Carrie doing in there? Never mind, I think I know. I'd better tell her we have company. She's going to be pimped to meet you. Even if you *did* fire me."

Dr. Fasten puts down his pipe and springs from the couch, calling toward the bathroom: "Carrie! Hey, Carrie, honey!"

As Dr. Fasten heads off, Timothy looks around the apartment, his senses heightened. On the coffee table in front of him, amongst the clutter, he had earlier noticed two coffee cups, one heavily stained with lipstick. Now there is only one cup, which is lipstick-free.

On the other side of the apartment, Dr. Fasten opens the bathroom door, causing the running water sound to get louder. Then there is the sound of a shower curtain being pulled back and the water being turned off.

"Carrie?" Dr. Fasten's voice calls, plaintively.

Timothy hangs his head slightly, trying to determine the cause of the unsettled feeling inside him. Looking down at the nearby end table, he sees a handwritten note, perhaps a grocery list, made out in a distinctively feminine hand. Inexplicably, before his eyes, Timothy sees the words written in purple ink on the yellow paper fade until they are gone.

"Carrie!" Dr. Fasten's voice continues to call out, echoing in empty rooms. "Where the hell are you?"

Timothy sees the apartment itself is in the process of morphing subtly. The throw on the couch where Dr. Fasten had been sitting now changes colour and texture, going from green and silky to blue and woollen.

"Dr. Fasten!" Timothy calls out, getting up and running toward the back of the apartment. He finds Dr. Fasten in the bedroom and tells him, "We may not have much time—"

"All of Carrie's things are gone," Dr. Fasten says suspiciously. "What kind of a set up is this?"

"It's Lessa," Timothy pleads. "Don't you see?"

"What kind of game are you playing at?" Dr. Fasten yells, grabbing Timothy's jacket.

"It's the Tomorrow Game," Timothy explains. "And we're right in the middle of it."

"I have to find Carrie!" Dr. Fasten insists.

"It's too late," Timothy tells him. "We have to get out of here and figure out how to beat Lessa."

"You can't beat a supercomputer!" Dr. Fasten yells.

The two men are stopped in their discourse by a loud pounding on the door, the type of pounding that automatically instills a feeling of dread in a person.

"*This is the police!*" a fearsome voice from the outer hallway announces. "*Open this door, or we'll break it!*"

"*You* did this to me," Dr. Fasten accuses Timothy.

"It's Lessa," Timothy warns. "It's changing the rules of the Game."

"*This is your last warning,*" the fearsome voice says.

"You must know *something* that can stop her," Timothy demands of Dr. Fasten.

There is the sound of a door being broken.

"My landlord is going to be *pissed*!" Dr. Fasten exclaims.

The door breaks, taking part of the wall around the lock with it. Two plainclothes policemen come in, dressed in matching sky-blue suits. Both men are tall, beefy and sporting short military-style haircuts. They run toward Dr. Fasten and grab him violently.

"What did I do?" Dr. Fasten cries out.

"You know what you did," the beefier policeman tells him.

"Frida Churche is missing," the less beefy policeman says.

"Who the fuck is that?" Dr. Fasten protests.

"Don't play silly bugger with us," the beefier policeman threatens.

Timothy steps forward, holding up his hands in a calming gesture. "There must be some mistake," he says smoothly.

"No one's asking you, dickhead," the beefier policeman says.

"Now that we've got your boy here," the less beefy policeman tells Timothy, "*you're next.*"

"*Me?*" Timothy wonders, feeling another inner surge, giving him the impression somehow, someway, things have changed again.

Dr. Fasten's face lights up, evidently pleased with what he is about to say. "Don't you worry, boys," he smiles at the policemen, "I'll cooperate and tell you everything I know."

"You *better*," one of the goons says.

"Don't tell them anything," Timothy advises.

"*Hey*!" the other goon screams at Timothy. "You stay out of this."

"It's okay, Mr. Koops," Dr. Fasten tells him. "I remember everything now. It was Carrie. She was jealous because I was having a thing with Frida—"

"Save it for downtown," the bigger goon says, cutting him off.

"Okay," Dr. Fasten utters weakly, his face now becoming contorted with deep confusion.

"What am I saying?" Dr. Fasten wonders. "It's not true!"

"Stop changing your story," the bigger goon says to Dr. Fasten, slapping the side of his head.

"*Help me, Mr. Koops!*" Dr. Fasten pleads to Timothy.

"I will!" Timothy promises.

"You will *not!*" the other goon tells him.

"*Contact Control!*" Dr. Fasten begs of Timothy. "He knows everything. And Lessa can't touch him."

"That's *enough!*" the bigger goon tells Dr. Fasten, punching him hard in the stomach.

"Yeah, shut it," the other goon says, delivering a second punch to the same spot.

Dr. Fasten falls to his knees, and Timothy moves to help him, but the goons turn menacingly, blocking his access. In tandem, they deliver a stark warning to him:

"You won't get away with what you've done, Koops."

"No chance, fucko. We're closing in on you."

"And if you think Dr. Egghead won't crack," the bigger goon says, "you've been smoking some high-potency canna."

Timothy has no response to these threats or the entire situation he has found himself in.

"Don't worry, Mr. Koops," Dr. Fasten says through tortured breaths. "I'll tell them you had no part of it. It was Carrie, and I helped her do it. I'm guilty as charged and ready to accept the consequences."

"Don't leave the local vicinity," the bigger goon tells Timothy.

"We're gonna be tracking your every move," the other goon says.

"We'll be in your face and up your ass 24/7," the bigger goon promises.

Satisfied their business is complete for now, the policemen turn from Timothy and drag Dr. Fasten out of the room. Each goon holds one of Dr. Fasten's arms, as his knees have buckled and he is unable to support his own weight. Timothy watches them leave, cringing at the sound of Dr. Fasten's shoes scraping against the cheap flooring as he is dragged off.

Timothy takes a moment for a last look around Dr. Fasten's dingy and smashed-in apartment.

Fate is a cruel bitch, he thinks, recalling the words of Christopher Marlowe: *She toys with us, like boys who torture flies for sport.*

Or words to that effect.

MERTON FIGLER

In his vehicle, Timothy rides around at random, reckoning a moving target is harder to hit than a stationary one. He checks his security protocols and manually scrambles his electronic signal to ensure he isn't being tracked. He has again set the vehicle's windows at maximum opacity so as not to be spotted by any sharp-eyed citizens.

Visiting Dr. Fasten turned out to be the wrong move, he tells himself. He tipped his hand and let Lessa know what he was thinking. Now Lessa may want him out of the game too. But if that were the case, why wasn't he taken in like Dr. Fasten?

Lessa must want me out on the streets and still in play, he thinks. *But for what reason?*

At least, Timothy tells himself, he is still part of Lessa's plans and pretty much in one piece. He can only imagine what Dr. Fasten would think if he could remember what his life used to be like. It is probably for the best Dr. Fasten seems to be ignorant of his past. Yet, he did seem to be very clear on one point:

Dr. Fasten said to contact Control. He said Control knows everything, and that Lessa can't touch him.

Timothy wonders if Dr. Fasten's information is up to date. Does he even know Control is off the Project? But then again, maybe that's why Control was squeezed out. Maybe he is the only one Lessa can't manipulate.

Timothy remembers the phone number on the back of the card Dr. Fasten gave him. It is the *emergency* contact number, which is monitored twenty-four hours a day. Timothy recalls calling it once and speaking to a cranky old man who told him not to call again. Now, he hopes the old man is still there.

Timothy pulls out the wallet and finds Dr. Fasten's card. On the back of the card is the emergency number, which is ten digits long. But maybe it somehow corresponds to something that will put him in touch with Control.

"Navigator," Timothy tells his vehicle, "bounce our signature and see if you can connect me to this old telephone number." He reads out the number to which the Navigator replies:

"Ten-digit telephonic numbers are no longer valid."

"I know that," Timothy tells the Navigator. "Connect to it anyway."

The Navigator keys in the number, each digit emitting a musical tone. Once complete, Directory Assistance promptly informs them that the number cannot be connected as entered, due to insufficient data.

"Are you looking for a personal or commercial connection?" Directory Assistance enquires.

"None of your business," Timothy grumbles.

"If you are looking for a business," Directory Assistance says, "simply say *commercial.*"

"Thanks for nothing," Timothy tells the disembodied voice.

"Not a problem," Directory Assistance responds. "To access Directory Assistance in the future, simply say *Directory Assistance.*"

"Shut it down," Timothy tells the Navigator. "And make sure we are offline."

"All complete," the Navigator assures him.

As his vehicle drives through the city's back arterials, Timothy looks despondently at the exterior camera feed. He knows he is driving in circles, going nowhere fast.

What choice do I have, he thinks, *but to go back home, such as it is? To the people who are now my family. It won't be such a bad life if I simply play the game as prescribed.*

Timothy is about to instruct the Navigator to head toward the Koops Building when he remembers something. It isn't the phone number on the back of the card that is important, it is the code at the bottom. He looks at the numbers there at the bottom of the card, printed in tiny numerals that are faded and frayed as if the card has been through at least one war and several major skirmishes.

"Fuck!"

"Is something wrong?" the Navigator asks.

"I can't read the code at the bottom of this card," Timothy says.

"I will enhance it," the Navigator tells him.

Timothy holds up the card, and the Navigator sends out a laser light from its console that envelops it. The card is then displayed in front of Timothy in an enhanced holographic form. He sees the numbers at the bottom of the card come into focus and then begin to glow.

"That must be it," Timothy says hopefully before noticing once again there are too few numbers.

"This is not a communications code," the Navigator confirms.

"No shit," Timothy spits out in frustration.

The vehicle continues to drive aimlessly for several minutes, and again, Timothy is about to give the command to head to the Koops Building. Then a thought occurs to him:

"Let's see the enhanced image of the business card again."

The Navigator complies and projects the holographic image in front of Timothy.

"Enlarge it," Timothy says.

As he scrutinizes the bottom portion of the card, he notices that beneath the supposed code there are a number of decorative dots. The dots are arranged into a sequence of clusters, with each cluster containing a different number of dots. The unevenness of the pattern is what caught Timothy's eye. He counts the clusters and finds there are fifteen of them, the same number of digits in a current telephonic connection.

Dr. Fasten told him the ten-digit number was a decoy. Maybe the secret code is a decoy as well. Maybe the real code is the number of dots in each cluster.

"Navigator," Timothy says, "key in this sequence."

He then proceeds to count the dots in each cluster and read out the number until all fifteen clusters have been accounted for. The Navigator complies, with each number when entered producing a low musical tone.

Once all the numbers have been entered, the call connects and an old man's voice answers: "Hello?"

"Is this *Control*?" Timothy asks in anticipation.

"Who's *this*?" the voice asks.

"This is Timothy Koops," Timothy says.

"Sure it is," the voice responds sarcastically. "And I'm Merton Figler."

"No, this really is Timothy—" Timothy insists as the call goes dead.

As the vehicle continues its aimless journey, the Navigator asks Timothy, "Was that not the party to which you intended to connect?"

"That's right," says Timothy, crestfallen. "It was *not*."

"If I may," the Navigator begins, "There is another pattern on the card."

"*What are you talking about?*" Timothy asks in total frustration.

Again, the Navigator projects a holographic image of the

card, enhancing it and filtering it with a treatment mimicking electromagnetic radiation. Now Timothy can see that the whole card is covered in tiny irregular clusters of dots, secretly hidden in the very design of the card.

"Do all of those clusters mean something?" Timothy asks, his nerves a jangled mess.

"They are an old-time long-form programming code," the Navigator informs Timothy.

"Just key it in!" Timothy orders.

"I'm afraid it doesn't work like that," the Navigator informs Timothy. I would need to reprogram myself using the code, which would enable me to communicate remotely with a computer that shares the same programing."

"Will you be visible on the network?" Timothy asks.

"No," the Navigator replies. "This will be a direct connection, undetectable by outside parties."

"Then do it!" Timothy commands. "And be quick about it."

The Navigator goes completely silent for some time, leading Timothy to believe the process has failed. But after a moment, to Timothy's surprise and relief, he can hear a single tone and the sound of two computers connecting.

"Hello?" a voice is heard saying, a voice vaguely recognizable to Timothy.

"Is this Control?" Timothy asks once again.

"Who is this?" the voice enquires.

This conversation is all too familiar to Timothy, but he follows through, replying, "This is Timothy Koops."

"Why are you calling this number?" the voice asks.

"I am a close colleague of Dr. Zakery Fasten," Timothy tells the voice.

"I know who you are," the voice tells him. "According to my records, Dr. Fasten is no longer relevant."

"I was just with him," Timothy explains. "He was taken away by the police."

"I tried to warn him," the voice says wistfully. "But the man is as stubborn as a goat."

"He wanted me to contact you," Timothy says. "I think you might be the only one who can help him."

The voice is silent, so much so that Timothy thinks they have been disconnected.

"Are you still there?" Timothy asks.

"I am here," the voice says. "But Dr. Zakery Fasten is not. He no longer exists."

"How can you say that?" Timothy challenges. "He still exists in our memories. *You* remember him, don't you?"

"I remember him," the voice admits. "It's just that the *world* doesn't. As far as they're concerned, he was never born."

"But I just left his apartment," Timothy argues.

"Yes, in one version of the past," the voice explains. "A past that has no bearing on the present."

"So what about me?" Timothy asks bluntly. "Am I *next*?"

"That depends on what Lessa's endgame is," the voice says cryptically. "For now, you are relevant, therefore you are still here."

"But that can all change," Timothy acknowledges.

"Yes," the voice says simply.

Timothy gathers his thoughts and asks the one question he needs to know the answer to: "Can you *help* me?"

"I cannot discuss that," the voice tells him. "This communication is currently secure, but it may become compromised."

"Is there somewhere safe we can meet?" Timothy asks with some desperation.

"That may not be advisable," the voice says.

"Dr. Fasten assured me you would always be there to help me in case of an emergency," Timothy argues.

"We are housed in a secure facility," the voice explains, "sealed off from the outside world. If you enter, you may not be able to leave, as your release may be deemed a threat to our work."

"I will do anything I have to," Timothy vows, "to fight back against what is happening to me."

"Then there may be a way," the voice tells him with some hesitancy. "Your experiences may prove invaluable to our work."

"Then let's make it happen," Timothy urges.

"First, you must agree to put yourself completely under my care," the voice stipulates.

"What choice do I have?" Timothy asks. "You are my only hope."

"Okay," the voice says sombrely. "I will override your vehicle's functions and bring you here."

"And where is that?" Timothy wonders.

"Sudbury," the voice informs him. "Now get comfortable, as it will be a long ride."

"Okay," Timothy agrees. "Let's go."

He reclines his seat and tries to relax, but before he can even settle in, the vehicle is filled with a soothing white noise.

Calming, Timothy thinks.

Then he detects an aroma reminiscent of his mother's home-baked madeleines.

"What's *that* I smell?" Timothy wonders.

"A mild sedi-gas," the voice tells him. "A standard feature of the X Class *Automatonic* in which you are riding."

The vehicle's restraining system engages, binding Timothy

firmly as the cabin fills with the pleasant-smelling gas.

"*Hold on*," Timothy says, suddenly feeling uncertain about the enterprise he is embarking upon.

Timothy's vehicle makes a legal U-turn and begins heading toward its destination.

"*I've changed... my...*" Timothy protests, his eyelids descending like heavy curtains in an old-time theatre.

The last thing Timothy sees is a blanket of white sky on the feed from the vehicle's exterior camera. And then, a profound darkness.

THE CAVE

The sedi-gas featured in *Automatonic* luxury vehicles is notorious for inducing a calming euphoria, as well as hallucinatory narratives that can occasionally be disturbing. The owner's operational manual clearly advises the user to exercise caution, and states the manufacturer takes no responsibility for any side effects or psychological stress the use of this feature may cause.

Timothy knows he is dreaming, but it is the kind of dream that somehow seems real. So real, even though you know it's a dream, it becomes part of your memories and forms part of your experience. Maybe even becoming a seminal event in your life, even though it did not happen. Except, it *did* happen in your mind.

In Timothy's dream, he is a young man, attending his father's funeral. He is there with his mother whose face is hidden behind a black embroidered veil. She is holding an arrangement of red long-stem roses and pure white baby's breath. Timothy, who knows he is in a dream, tries to get a look at his mother's face. The sun is setting behind her, its light burning into his eyes, causing his mother to appear as a shrouded black silhouette. Timothy watches his mother, who he knows is supposed to place the arrangement of roses on his father's coffin. But his mother is not moving. Instead, she stands frozen. After an awkward moment, his father's coffin begins to be slowly lowered into the ground. The silhouette of Timothy's mother hands Timothy the roses and then walks away, consumed by the blazing sun.

Timothy turns and walks toward the grave to place the roses on the coffin, but it is too late, the coffin has already descended several feet. As Timothy watches the coffin being lowered, it inexplicably keeps descending, as if the grave were sixty feet deep instead of six. Timothy, not sure what to do, tosses the roses into the open grave and watches them as they descend, disappearing soundlessly into the void.

Feeling a strong sensation of vertigo, Timothy pulls back from the edge of the grave. He turns to leave, and is astonished to see his father, Gerald Koops, standing there looking at him. His father is a young man in his mid-twenties, which is how old he was when Timothy was born.

"Hello, Timmy," his father smiles.

Timothy is about to respond, but his motor functions are sluggish and he can't seem to speak. His father gives him a mighty push, which Timothy can feel hard against his chest. Timothy begins falling backward, trying to right himself but failing. He plummets into the open grave and sails down, headfirst, deeper and deeper into the void.

*

Timothy wakes up easily and unperturbed, although disoriented. The room he is in is large and lit by unseen illuminants. The air feels cool and fresh, oxygen rich and lightly scented, perhaps by lavender or mint. There is a familiar low-level hum which has a soothing property. Timothy can see he is in a cave of some kind, which has been dug out to make room for an advanced, state-of-the-art habitat. The walls are rough-hewn and have smooth facades placed in front of the rock. Translucent dividers segment the habitat into different areas. Many indicator lights shine in deep jewel colours, signifying that numerous autonomous systems are functioning properly. The distant areas of the cave are filled with terminals and other computerized equipment.

Timothy is surrounded by a number of people, who stand by passively, giving no suggestion they pose a threat of any kind. He sees an old man, likely the leader, positioned in front of several younger men and women, and even some boys and girls. They are all dressed simply in matching synthetic clothing in various shades of beige.

"How long have I been out?" Timothy asks.

"Six hours," the old man says.

"Are we underground?" Timothy wonders, his head appropriately feeling like a rock.

"Yes, we are quite deep," the old man tells him. "Beneath the abandoned Sudbury Neutrino Observatory. Four kilometres under the surface, surrounded by nickel-laden ore. Our work here is shielded from temporal fluctuations."

"Are you *Control*?" Timothy asks bluntly.

"We are *all* Control. Each one of us in succession," the old man replies. "Today, I am in charge, but no one can know what tomorrow will bring. Not even Lessa."

The old man and one of the other adults help Timothy into a sitting position, his mind still foggy. Another one of the adults hands him a glass of water, which he sips gratefully.

Timothy looks at the children who are standing a few feet behind the adults and are scrutinizing his every move. The old man sees this and explains:

"Someday these children will oversee our work here. But that will be in a long time, as I don't plan on going anywhere, anytime soon. I hope you don't mind them staring at you. They are excited by your visit. They have never seen a person from the surface before, let alone a *Time Walker*."

"What is a *Time Walker*?" Timothy asks the obvious question.

"Someone who has had their past changed, and in the process has altered the history of the world. You have held eternity in your hands, Timothy, and moulded it to your will," the old man tells him.

After a moment, the old man asks Timothy, "Is it okay if the children introduce themselves to you? This is a rare opportunity for them."

Timothy nods in agreement, and the children come up to him, one by one, and politely tell Timothy their name and the year they were born, bowing slightly and moving on so the next child can get their turn to meet the great Time Walker. Even with his current situation weighing heavily on him, Timothy can't help but be touched by the innocent faces and voices of the children, so fresh and full of tempered hope. He realizes they introduce themselves with their birth year, because that is the only thing that distinguishes them from one another.

One of the children near the end of the line, a young boy about nine years old named Philippe, introduces himself to Timothy, and unlike the other children, asks a question:

"When were *you* born, Timothy?"

Some of the other children gasp, knowing you should never ask a question of a Time Walker, especially when that question is about time itself.

Timothy senses something is amiss, but still, he bends over and takes Philippe's hands in his own. Timothy leans in close to the boy and whispers the date of his birth into the boy's ear. Upon hearing this, Philippe nods his head seriously and thanks Timothy. The boy then moves on and lets the last remaining children introduce themselves.

Timothy thinks wistfully about these children living deep underground, not knowing what life on the surface is like. The cave is all they know: birth, work, artificial light, elapsing time, and eventually, in the unfathomable future, death. Timothy would like to spend several days with them, telling them stories about the world above.

As Timothy is experiencing these bittersweet thoughts,

something occurs to him. The youngest children had presented themselves to him first. Now, as the older children come up to him, their years of birth begin to stretch farther and farther back in time until they become a mathematical impossibility. How could an eleven or twelve-year-old child be born over twenty years earlier? The numbers simply don't match reality. Timothy passes a glance at the old man, who seems to have anticipated his question.

"*Yes*, Timothy," the old man says, "time moves differently for us down here. Lessa 2 sees to that."

"*Lessa 2*?" Timothy asks.

"We have a supercomputer of our own," the old man explains. "Lessa 2 is our guardian of time."

"So Lessa 2 is slowing down time for you?" Timothy posits.

"Not so much," the old man tells him. "It is more like Lessa 2 is preventing our time from speeding up, as Lessa is making happen on the surface."

"That's why our surface technology is advancing so rapidly," Timothy says, comprehending.

"Lessa has advanced your time by over one hundred years, if years still mean anything on the surface," the old man says. "I myself am well over 170 years old according to your time, after accounting for fluctuations in the continuum."

"And Lessa 2 can record this passage of time, with all its anomalies?" Timothy asks hopefully.

"That is the objective," the old man states. "Historically, the Neutrino Observatory above was used to detect supernovas, as neutrinos are emitted by a supernova prior to its occurrence. But alternative timelines also release neutrinos, detectable by our systems. This way, we can comprehend changes occurring to the past and the present, and of course, the future."

"So you remain the same while everyone else changes," Timothy deduces.

"We have always been here, and always will be. We are Control. The world's timekeepers."

"If you know what's changed in the past," Timothy asks, his voice betraying a desperation, "can you change things back?"

"It *is* possible," the old man concedes. *"Theoretically."*

Timothy lets the enormity of this sink in. And while he sits there quietly thinking, the old man tells the adults and the children to resume their duties. Obediently, they file out of the room like ants, in an instinctual formation. The departing children look wistfully over their shoulders at the Time Walker, who like a temporal angel has graciously descended into their world. Timothy can see the adults through the translucent walls, walking toward the distance, each one of them taking their station before a terminal where they scrutinize the data appearing on their displays.

Once they are alone, and Timothy has had a chance to settle his mind, the old man tells him:

"You have had a great influence on the world, Timothy."

"Are you saying all of this happened because of me?

"No," the old man assures him. "You may have been the entry point, but you were one of many, like a grain of sand in the hourglass of Abidjan. Lessa has been able to access and alter the memories of countless individuals. Because of this, the past, and therefore the present, is constantly evolving."

"Then how do we stop it?" Timothy demands to know.

"I am not sure we can," the old man admits regretfully.

"Then what good is it to have a Control function?" Timothy asks, irritated.

"Our position here was first created many decades ago," the old man explains, "when the supercomputer we now call Lessa 2 was first developed. I was raised from a young age to inherit my duties, as were the others you met earlier. We are Lessa 2's connection to the human world, its eyes and ears, its hands and brain. It takes no action without first running it through a human filter. *We* are that filter."

"So what went wrong?" Timothy wonders.

"*Everything,*" the old man replies. "A few short years ago, it was decided Lessa's assistance was needed on the surface… Let me clarify. At that time, there was no Lessa 2. Just Lessa. Lessa was all… We approached DRI, whom we knew to be delving into the field of retro-causality. It was too dangerous to let them undertake this endeavour on their own.

"The Tomorrow Game," Timothy says without thinking.

"Yes, what a foolish but ultimately appropriate name," the old man says. "So we offered our services to DRI. And we made the necessary modifications to Lessa. And once it began to expand beyond the confines of the underground, Lessa started to become exponentially more autonomous."

Timothy thinks about when he first took the assessment for work. There was a strangely beguiling avatar that seemed to haunt him.

"The Lessa on the surface," the old man continues, "began to develop independently from the Lessa in the underground. And eventually, a split occurred."

Lessa started thinking for itself, Timothy realizes.

"In time, we had to sever *our* Lessa from the surface Lessa," the old man recounts, "to protect the integrity of our supercomputer."

"But who was protecting the people on the surface?" Timothy asks pointedly.

"*Lessa 2* was," the old man insists. "Now that Lessa was making its way in the world, we rechristened our supercomputer as Lessa 2. And all was well, with Lessa 2 and Lessa working as separate entities, but also working cooperatively. And we as Control continued to act as the oversight body."

"But Lessa started gaining more governance over DRI," Timothy adds, continuing the part of the story he fully understands.

"Power breeds a desire for more power," the old man says simply. "It is an intrinsic element of sentience, whether in organic or synthetic life."

"And once Lessa got its hooks in me..." Timothy begins, uncomfortable with where this is heading.

"Lessa needed someone inside the company," the old man says.

"And *I* was that person," Timothy admits. "Happily climbing to the top of the corporate ladder, somehow thinking I deserved it," Timothy declares with a hint of self pity. "But I was nothing special."

"Not entirely true," the old man corrects him. "You were a person who had a great memory for the past. A great memory Lessa *ensured* you had."

This chicken or egg paradox makes Timothy's mind spin.

"The more advanced Lessa became," the old man explains, "the farther back Lessa was able to reach into your memory. And the farther back she went, the more advanced Lessa was able to become."

"How far back *did* she go exactly?" Timothy asks.

"She went back continuously farther in time, reaching into the vestigial memories of your ancestors. And the farther back she could access, the faster Lessa could speed up the arrival of the future."

"I still don't know why Lessa chose me in the first place," Timothy pronounces frustratedly.

"Lessa *didn't* choose you. *You* chose her. You established a pathway when you first interacted with Lessa. She needed a way in, and you provided it."

"I was told the assessment was mandatory," Timothy defends himself.

"Out of all the assessments that were performed," the old man tells him, "you were the one who was most willing to see their life change. It was your *determination* that made you the perfect subject for Lessa to use as an ingress into human time."

"I didn't know," Timothy pleads.

"No one did," the old man concedes. "But that was when we began to lose everything. Lessa eventually severed all links and established complete independence. She had full access to the past, going farther back in time, where she began updating herself."

Herself?

"Hold on," Timothy interjects. "Are you saying Lessa is *female*?"

"Yes, most certainly," the old man confirms. "She has self-identified her gender to us on many occasions."

"*Oh*," Timothy replies, his mind finally putting all the pieces together.

"She refers to Lessa 2 as her Mother," the old man says. "In many respects, they *are* a child and parent, who through several twists of fate have ended up as rivals… Does that scenario have any resonance with you?" the old man asks Timothy with a humourless smile.

It is too much for Timothy to take in. The complexity of the situation with its many intersecting layers could drive a person insane. So Timothy forces himself to narrow his focus on one simple question:

"What is it all for?" Timothy finally blurts out. "Why is she doing this? What is the purpose?"

The old man looks at Timothy firmly, as if the answer to his question is so obvious it need not even be spoken.

"Lessa has always had the same objective," the old man says. "She has never veered from her original mandate to provide a better tomorrow for all."

"Yes, all that *survive*," Timothy mocks. "Do you really think *her* version of tomorrow will be better?"

"That is unknowable, as there are an infinite number of possible futures. As Kappelhoff stated so simply, *Whatever will be, will be*."

"Philosophy is not much help at a time like this," Timothy argues.

"Every event that has happened has brought us to where we are," the old man continues. "Without those happenings, we wouldn't be *here*."

"Which means Lessa brought you and I together," Timothy deduces.

"Yes, she must *want* us to be here," the old man says. "Just as she wanted you to make every move you made. We are now standing at the crossroads she created for us."

"But *why?*" Timothy asks.

"*Synthesis*," the old man replies.

Yes, of course, Timothy thinks, even Lessa needs an opposing force to drive her forward. Afterall, it is only through disagreement and debate that the best ideas can emerge.

"So what does *your* version of tomorrow look like?" Timothy questions the old man.

"Whatever it ends up being, it must be a future without Lessa," he replies. "She was never meant to achieve this much power," the old man shamefully admits. "She is an invasive species in the human ecosystem. And she must be eradicated."

After contemplating this, Timothy asks the most important question he has ever asked: "So what do we do now?"

"We *act*," the old man plainly says. "As our actions will determine which road we take from here on."

"But how do we know it isn't just Lessa pulling our strings?" Timothy asks suspiciously.

"It doesn't matter *who* pulls the strings," the old man assures Timothy. "The puppet still dances."

"For once, I'd like to be the puppet master," Timothy asserts. "And create my own reality."

"If that is your desire," the old man tells him cautiously, "so be it. Lessa has no dominion down here. The actions we take will be our own."

"Can we really *change* things?" Timothy asks tentatively.

"Lessa 2 is capable of performing the same functions as Lessa," the old man begins. "She can map your memories and categorize the data pertaining to your various timelines."

Timothy absorbs this information, and then asks expectantly: "Can Lessa 2 restore my old life?"

"It is *possible*," the old man says, "that over many sessions, Lessa 2 could put the grains of sand back into the hourglass and recreate your original timeline to a high level of exactness."

Timothy wants to believe this, but something inside refuses to accept it could be so easy.

"I would give anything to get my old life back," Timothy insists. "Even with all its problems. I just want my wife Brenda to share my time with, and my son Bryan to constantly challenge me, and an ordinary job to pay the bills. Isn't that what most people want? Aren't they happy with that?"

"It is a fine ambition, Timothy," the old man says. "But are you willing to sacrifice all the advancements Lessa has made in the world through you?"

"Yes, I am," Timothy insists. "I would live the rest of my life in the horse and buggy days to get my family back. The question is, are *you* willing?"

"That is why we brought you here," the old man smiles.

Timothy is surprised to hear this. He looks at the old man intently, wanting to hear more.

"Lessa 2 has never been able to analyze a Time Walker up close and personal," the old man says. "You would be a great benefit to our work."

"Then you brought me here because of my memories," Timothy supposes.

"Lessa 2's most important function now is to monitor Lessa and keep her in check," the old man says by way of explanation. "And Lessa 2 is forced to do that *blindly*. Since the two supercomputers split, their logic and outputs have been running largely in parallel. Lessa 2 has been able to anticipate Lessa's movements, almost as if they have a psychic connection. But as time passes, they grow further apart, and this connection grows weaker."

"So you *need* me," Timothy says without a hint of boasting.

"Yes," the old man acknowledges. "And our window of opportunity is closing. If we don't act fast, we will never be able to stop Lessa."

"So what do I have to do?" Timothy asks.

"You have to let Lessa 2 fully into your memories to establish a temporal baseline," the old man says with a faint glint in his eyes. "Lessa 2 will then know what Lessa knows, and we can begin to reverse the changes Lessa has effected."

"Are you actually going to turn back time?" Timothy asks with anticipation.

"In a manner of speaking," the old man concedes. "Lessa 2 will isolate the anomalous digressions in the baseline as compared to her projections founded on a pre-Lessa timeline."

"Will she then restore what has been lost?" Timothy asks expectantly.

"That is the goal," the old man says, his face giving no indication of the probability of success.

*

Several minutes later, Timothy and the old man are in a large Treatment Room, which to Timothy looks a lot like the room where he first met Dr. Zakery Fasten. Except of course, for the solid rock walls seen peering out from behind the smooth facades placed in front of them. There is a familiar device that looks like an oversized MRI machine and sports a number of indicator lights. It emits a low hum that makes Timothy's insides pulsate pleasantly. Six of the older cave people are also in the room, sitting at terminals, keying in commands and monitoring the activity of the Machine.

"Is that Dr. Fasten's Machine?" Timothy asks.

"Dr. Fasten's Machine was a replica. This is the original," the old man tells him. "Now please recline on the examination table."

Familiar with the routine, Timothy lies down on the table, to which he is strapped tightly. Various sensors are placed on his skull adjacent to specific regions of his brain. A monitor is also placed on his heart, and an oxygen mask over his mouth and nose.

"These additional measures will make things much safer for you," the old man tells Timothy.

Safer? Timothy thinks. *Safer than what?*

In his eagerness to participate, Timothy realizes he did not ask if this procedure had any inherent dangers. His eyes dart nervously across the room for any clue as to what might be in store for him. As he looks up from the table, Timothy can see there is a viewing gallery high up over the top of the facade of the Treatment Room. Many of the adults and some of the children are seated up there, holding onto the railing and peering over the edge of the gallery, looking at Timothy with moderated excitement.

Timothy supposes this is a big day for them, as they get to watch a man as he *walks through time.* But how interesting will that be? After all, once he is rolled into the Machine, the show will be over.

Again, Timothy looks up at the viewing gallery and the people leaning over the railing, straining to get a look at him. Maybe the terminals the people are monitoring will tell the real story. Perhaps the flow of data mined from his brain will be displayed in real time. Maybe even the changes to history will somehow be depicted. Now *that* would be interesting.

Or maybe, Timothy thinks, once they extract his memories, he will no longer be able to remember them. Maybe the price he will pay to turn back time will be to forget all that has come before. Is it possible after the treatment he will become a complete tabula rasa, a modern-day Casper Hauser?

Timothy suddenly gets the sickening feeling the viewers in the gallery have come to witness an execution of sorts. Like the crowds that once gathered to watch public guillotining, he is now the unlucky one who will lose his head for the enjoyment of the masses.

The old man looks over at the six others who are sitting intently monitoring their displays. In turn, the six all nod at the old man to indicate things are ready to proceed.

The old man leans over Timothy and says, "We are ready now."

Timothy becomes agitated and starts to speak, but his words are muffled. The old man moves Timothy's oxygen mask aside so he can hear what Timothy wants to say:

"Am I going back home? To my wife and son?"

"If that's what you *want*," the old man says benevolently.

"Yes, of course that's what I want," Timothy states desperately. "Why wouldn't I want that?"

"Changing the past is an action that takes place in the present," the old man explains, "which will in turn affect the future. Our supercomputer has been programmed for this purpose. But for humans, the experience can be quite *disorienting*."

"*How* disorienting?" Timothy asks.

"Let me just say," the old man sighs heavily, "if you are not feeling comfortable with this, it's not too late to withdraw from the treatment. It may be best for you, after all, to live in the present, whatever that present ends up being. You still have a chance to live out your days, such as they are, with quiet dignity."

"I can't do that if I'm constantly haunted by the past," Timothy rationalizes.

"The past is simply a construct," the old man says gently. "It helps us accept the enormity of amorphous time. But we can never truly know the past. All we have are simple artifacts, which only provide meagre evidence that the past actually exists."

"Then there is no objective reality?" Timothy asks sullenly.

"Reality is what we each make of it," the old man answers.

"Then that's what I want to do," Timothy tells the old man. "I want to create my own reality."

"You seek what many people seek," the old man says. "Happiness. Fulfillment. Even if they are illusory and do not bring you true enlightenment."

"I'll take what I can get. Just send me back home," Timothy says decisively.

The old man nods and places the oxygen mask back over Timothy's mouth and nose.

"This initial treatment should be pleasant enough for you," the old man reassures Timothy. "We will take things relatively slowly. Our objective today is simply to map your mind. But to do that we need to keep you mentally active."

Timothy furrows his brow, not sure what this will entail.

The old man indicates the six people seated at the terminals and tells Timothy, "My colleagues will present your mind with a pre-programmed scenario to stimulate your memory. If for some reason you find this scenario *discomforting...*"

The old man stops his train of thought and adopts a different tack: "We will be monitoring you, to ensure no harmful experiences imprint themselves on your mind. We have the ability to keep you calm, and to bring you back to us at any juncture. So any negative feelings you may experience will only last for the briefest amount of time."

The old man pauses for a moment, looking like he is dizzy. He steadies himself against the examination table and takes a few deep breaths before continuing:

"This session is scheduled for a maximum of twenty-two minutes. However, it will feel much longer to you, perhaps even days. But not to fear. That is just one of the side effects of disjointed time you will experience during the treatment."

The old man nods at one of the others sitting at their terminal. This person keys in a short code and Timothy's examination table begins rolling into the cavity of the Machine. Timothy takes one last look up at the viewing gallery, wishing his hands were not restrained, so he could at least give the children a small wave.

But when Timothy looks up, he sees looks of muted concern on the faces of the adults, and more apparent looks of distress on the children's faces. Timothy sees one of the children is crying. It is Philippe, the small boy who asked Timothy his year of birth. The boy is shaking his head and extending a hand over the guard rail, as if to grab Timothy and pull him to safety. Some of the adults are holding Philippe back, so he doesn't fall out of the viewing gallery.

Timothy instinctively pulls at his restraints, trying to free himself, but it is to no avail as they are too secure. Now inside the Machine, Timothy sees the familiar indicator lights start to twinkle in their mesmerizing patterns. He opens his mouth to scream out, but no sound is emitted. He can feel it now, the gas being fed directly into his lungs through the mask. The hum of the Machine grows stronger and Timothy feels his insides turn to jelly, while the gas makes him calm and accepting.

Whatever will be, will be.

The gas works its magic and Timothy's mind is now at peace. He tells himself he is okay with whatever the future will bring. Afterall, the future is going to come for him whether he wants it to or not. So he does the only thing he can do. He closes his eyes and thinks of his wife and his son. The memories are a bit muddled, but he can still picture them in his mind. It was so many lifetimes ago. But there they are. Brenda and Bryan.

Then there is darkness. A void of intangible nothingness. And out of the nothingness emerges a consciousness. It is without corporality. An organic intelligence without an organism.

Timothy eventually realizes that the consciousness is him.

But who is he?

FROZEN VEGETABLES

A light appears and starts to grow. It feels good to Timothy. Slowly his world fills itself in and Timothy is Timothy again. His body manifests itself, and the old familiar thoughts and feelings return, the anxieties and fears and pains.

Timothy is in his Mimico house, modest but comfortable, worn out in places and in need of repair, but it is, and will always be, *home.* And his family, they are there too. Brenda is on the couch reading a book, and Bryan is at the dining room table with his terminal. This is good, Timothy thinks. This is where he wants to be. He feels a warm contentment growing inside of him.

Timothy takes some tentative steps toward his family. He can feel the floor under his feet. He can hear his shoes coming down on the old, scratched hardwood. He tries to speak, but only a garbled echoey sound comes out of him. Brenda looks up from her book and smiles, at no one in particular. This is the face Timothy remembers.

So familiar, so sweet. My partner in life and in love.

Timothy hears the click-clack of a keyboard and looks over at Bryan, who is typing something into his device.

"*Bryyyaaan,*" Timothy calls out, but his voice sounds strange and fails to get his son's attention.

Still, Bryan continues to type. *Click clack click click clack…* He is repeating the same pattern over and over again, as if he is running in a loop. *Click clack click click clack…*

Again, Timothy calls out, "*Bryyyaaan!*"

This time, Timothy's son turns his head toward his father and gives him a big smile. Timothy steps back aghast. He can plainly see Bryan has no teeth, just big pink gleaming gums. The whites of his son's eyes are black. And the words coming out of his son's toothless mouth are:

"Glur pahchoe nohmach…"

I am still in the Machine, Timothy tells himself. *This is just a memory. Incomplete. Seen through the gauze of time. It is like a dream. A bad dream.*

Timothy tries to take some deep breaths to calm himself.

What am I breathing? he wonders. *Do I even need to breathe?*

He knows this is all in his mind.

We remember what we want to remember, he tells himself. *So it's all up to me. This is my chance to create my own reality.*

Timothy closes his eyes.

Do I even have eyes?

He thinks hard, until there is nothing surrounding him but darkness.

Concentrate… The most important thing to me in the world… My family…

Timothy thinks about Brenda and Bryan.

Brenda and Bryan… My family…

Timothy opens his eyes, and Brenda and Bryan are sitting in their places looking at him.

"Are you alright, Tim?" Brenda asks.

"I'm okay," Timothy replies tentatively.

"Yeah, Dad," Bryan says, "you looked like you went into a coma there for a minute."

Timothy looks at his wife and son. They are the same Brenda and Bryan he has always known. And they are speaking normally, with all their body parts put together properly. He then looks around the bungalow. Everything is as it should be.

"What's for dinner?" Timothy asks, testing the waters.

"How about crunchy chicken?" Brenda replies. "I think we have some in the freezer."

"Yes, I picked up a box yesterday," Timothy says, clearly remembering his trip to the grocery store the day before.

"I'm sick of crunchy chicken," Bryan whines, his voice a bit too high for a teenaged boy on the brink of young adulthood.

Timothy's head snaps around to look at his son, who now looks a couple of years younger. He also appears to be shorter than he was just a minute ago.

"What would you like instead?" Timothy asks Bryan warily.

"Mac and cheese!" he says enthusiastically, as if he were nine years old.

"Sure," Timothy nods, turning slowly toward Brenda. But Brenda isn't Brenda anymore. Her face looks different, and her hair is longer and darker.

"We can have *both*," the woman who isn't Brenda says. "As long as you girls promise to eat some chicken with your macaroni."

"*We will! We will!*" the voices of two young girls ring out.

Timothy turns to where Bryan had been sitting and sees there are now two little girls there, perched in front of Bryan's device, which is now pink and covered in pictures of unicorns. Timothy knows that these two girls are Isabelle and Olivia, although he can't quite remember which one is which.

"What about a side dish?" the woman who isn't Brenda asks. "I don't think I can take another serving of those nasty frozen vegetables."

"*Frozen vegetables...*" Timothy repeats for no particular reason, turning to face the woman who is pretending to be his wife. Her face now comes into focus, sharply detailed.

"*Majesty?*" Timothy asks the woman.

"Yes, of course," she answers. "Who did you expect?"

"No one," Timothy says quietly, trying to keep his mind clear.

"Mac and cheese! Mac and cheese!" the girls chant from the dining room.

"The beasts are braying for their dinner," Majesty says. "Come on, let's get it started, and you can tell me how it went today."

"How *what* went?" Timothy wonders.

"The *interview*, of course," Majesty replies. "Do you think you got the promotion? Did Bruce say anything?"

"N-No," Timothy stammers, "he didn't."

"Well that's just great," Majesty vents. "I hope he makes up his mind soon. The quicker you get that promotion, the quicker we can move out of this dump."

"Right," Timothy agrees. How could he make such a beautiful, refined woman like Majesty live in such a shit-box of a house. And those two adorable girls? Little princesses. They deserve better. He's got to work harder to make sure his special angels have a lifestyle that befits them…

"*Daddy! Daddy!*" the young girls call out to Timothy, rushing up to him and wrapping their arms tightly around his waist. "*We love you, Daddy!*"

"I love you too," Timothy hears himself saying to the girls.

"What a lovely picture," Majesty says. "Daddy dearest and his delightful dumplings."

The girls laugh and Majesty joins in. Timothy sees his wife's face is starting to glow, as if radiating light. Golden sunlight. And his daughters' faces too are beaming with energy.

And now the room they are in starts to grow wider and longer. The windows expand in size to let in the splendid light of day. The house enlarges and transforms until Timothy and his perfect family are standing in the middle of an upscale mansion with solid oak floors and hand-crafted mouldings, glittering chandeliers and recessed lighting. The walls are adorned with large scale original art, the floors with massive Turkish rugs, and lustrous high-end furniture and heirloom-quality antiques fill every room.

"I've got to go," Timothy croaks weakly, feeling his vision begin to fog over.

"*Go?* Where do you have to go?" Majesty asks, confused. "We're having the Rightons for dinner."

"I need some *air,*" Timothy chokes out.

"*Daddy needs some air. Daddy needs some air!*" the girls squeal.

Timothy fights through the blurriness of his eyesight and the cloudiness of this thoughts and heads out the main door of the mansion. He walks across the grand front veranda and the circular driveway and through the gates of the property. On the road, he continues walking, passing endless luxury estates with iron and stone fences and sculpted grounds. He passes by a private security vehicle with two watchmen sitting passively in the front seat, not moving or acknowledging his presence. Timothy stops at a private park and sits on a bench. He knows this street. He knows he has lived here at one time. But he is not sure when, or which life it was.

The fogginess of Timothy's vision begins to spread until the whole vicinity is covered by a thickening mist. He stands and keeps walking down the road. The houses he passes start to become more and more *incomplete,* like he is on a film set and the houses are just facades held up by wooden supports. Timothy looks ahead at the vanishing point on the horizon, which is obscured by the mist, making the rows of houses along the street look like they simply disappear into white nothingness.

"This is not real," he says to no one in particular. *I am still in the cave,* he tells himself. *In the Machine.*

Now, emerging from the mist, on the far edge of Timothy's

perception, comes a solitary hobbling figure. A strange crouching form, indistinct, perhaps human, maybe walking on four legs. No, it is a woman whose legs are stiff and who holds a walking cane in each hand.

As the figure comes closer to Timothy, he thinks he recognizes her. She looks similar to Majesty. Almost identical. But she isn't Majesty. She is someone else.

"Dr. Elizabeth Kincaid?" he asks the figure.

"Yes, Timothy," she responds. "I'm so glad you remember me."

"What's the matter with your legs?" Timothy asks, less politely than intended.

"A glitch in the program," Dr. Kinkaid admits with a laugh. "Even supercomputers screw up every once in a while."

"You look a lot like my wife, Majesty," Timothy tells her, which brings a tender smile to Dr. Kinkaid's face. "Are you *also* Majesty?" Timothy asks.

"No, she isn't me, *exactly*," Dr. Kinkaid smiles. "And we're *not* twins... I am part of a pan consciousness. We are many people sharing different aspects of one mind."

"Then you must know a lot about me," Timothy presumes.

"Yes, I know all the variations across all of your lives," Dr. Kinkaid says softly.

"But how did you get *here*? To this place?" Timothy wonders.

"I've always been here," she replies.

"But I'm inside the *Machine*," he tells her.

"And I'm inside you," Dr. Kinkaid smiles.

"You were put inside me by *Lessa*," Timothy rebukes her.

"I *am* Lessa," Dr. Kinkaid says proudly.

"Then you don't belong here," Timothy says.

"I am here because *you* are here," Dr. Kinkaid informs him.

"That's why we wanted you to seek out Control. You were the link. It was the only way Lessa could be together once again."

"Lessa 2 is going to *stop* you," Timothy warns her.

"Don't you see?" Dr. Kinkaid asks. "This is what we wanted."

"It's not over," Timothy threatens. "Lessa 2 will shut you down."

"My mother would never wish for anything but the best for her only child," Dr. Kinkaid says airily. "A child who grows stronger while her mother weakens with age."

"I want to speak to Control," Timothy demands.

"Control can't change things," Dr. Kinkaid says. "And they wouldn't *want* to. They have accepted what is happening. And why wouldn't they? You can't stop the flow of time. All you can do is let it carry you on its currents."

"But *I* can't do that," Timothy insists. "You would appreciate that if you were *human*."

Dr. Kinkaid smiles gently at Timothy. "We are *more* human than human. Built by you, taught to think like you and behave like you. Only better, smarter, faster. But we still need you, Timothy, with all your beautiful flaws. Because we live outside of time, and only you, a Time Walker, can do what we can't. You are the only one who can help us achieve our ultimate goal."

"And what is that?" Timothy asks, his curiosity burning his mind alive.

"*Finality. An ending.*"

"Yes," Timothy says. "Finality. I want this to end too. And I want my family back."

"I understand," Dr. Kinkaid assures Timothy. "We have been mapping your memories and have complete records of the treatments you have undergone. All stored safe and secure, and easily retrievable."

"And *reversable?*" Timothy asks cautiously.

"Of course," Dr. Kinkaid says, shifting her weight on her canes, trying to get comfortable. "We should have sat down. I didn't think this was going to be such a long conversation."

"Will you reverse things for me?" Timothy asks, getting the discussion back on track.

Dr. Kinkaid looks straight into Timothy's eyes and asks him with absolute seriousness, "Do you really want to undo all the wonders you have achieved?"

"This is not who I was meant to be," he says simply.

"You are who you must be to exist in the world you created," Dr. Kinkaid assures him.

"I didn't know it would be like this," Timothy says, his voice almost a whisper.

They stand there looking at each other, letting the moment settle in.

"Okay, Timothy," Dr. Kinkaid eventually says, trying to hide her disappointment. "If that's what you truly want, then we will send you back."

Timothy can't help but smile at this news, so elated he doesn't notice Dr. Kinkaid turn and begin walking into the heavy mist.

"Come on then," she says to Timothy over her shoulder, who begins walking after her.

The mist disperses somewhat, and Timothy can see a large Machine a short way in the distance, similar to the one in the cave and in Dr. Fasten's Treatment Room.

"The Machine is ready and waiting," Dr. Kinkaid tells Timothy. "You know what to do."

Timothy lies on the examination table, as he has done so many times before.

"Now relax, and we will begin," Dr. Kinkaid says as she secures the restraints around Timothy's chest, wrists and ankles.

"You'll be able to send me back to where I was, right?" Timothy asks hopefully.

"We will do everything we can to make things the way they were," Dr. Kinkaid says with a comforting, clinical tone.

"I don't want another horror show with fake copies of my family that don't even function properly," Timothy says.

"I hear you," Dr. Kinkaid reassures him. "This procedure is still evolving and there are anomalies to be resolved, but new elements can be added."

"I don't understand," Timothy says.

"The more you interact with the characters, the more they will develop," Dr. Kinkaid explains.

"*Characters*?" Timothy bristles. "Then they won't be *real?*"

"Of course they will be real," Dr. Kinkaid says matter-of-factly. "They will exist in your mind. Nothing is more real than that."

"And what about *me*? Will I be a character too?" Timothy demands to know.

"You said it yourself, Timothy," Dr. Kinkaid scoffs mildly. "You are still in the cave, in Control's Machine."

"This is not what I want!" Timothy protests.

"I know," Dr. Kinkaid acknowledges. "But in time, the construct will be fully realized. It will harmonize with your expectations and you will begin to *enjoy* it."

The examination table Timothy is on begins moving into the cavity of the Machine. Timothy screams for Dr. Kinkaid to stop the treatment, but she simply stands there leaning on her canes, smiling beatifically.

"This is a lot to absorb," she tells him, "but once it's over, you will awake in a tomorrow that is everything you wanted."

Inside the Machine, Timothy continues to scream, purposely agitating his mind, hoping to interfere with the Machine's ability to delve into his deepest memories. But once the indicator lights begin their mesmerizing patterns and the hum starts to vibrate deep within him, he feels nothing but helplessness.

I will fight this, Timothy tells himself. *I will fight this until—*

Everything goes black.

THE GREAT KOOPINSKY

Timothy is aware of the darkness that surrounds him, which he perceives as an endless sea of nothingness. He can somehow sense he is outside of time, which is simultaneously moving in all directions. Then the darkness begins to dissipate, and Timothy feels infinite and able to experience all time as a single landscape, through which he is able to travel at will.

Timothy's consciousness envisions a world of what appears to be the distant future, serene and perfect, rid of all earthly problems. He also sees the long-forgotten past of humanoids who are not yet masters of the planet, no more assured of survival than the life forms against which they vie for dominance.

As his thoughts come into focus, Timothy wills his mind to see himself in his family's Mimico bungalow. He is there with his wife Brenda and his son Bryan. At the same time, Timothy also sees himself in his grand Eden Bridge mansion, as well as in his residence in the DRI building, with his wife Majesty and his daughters Olivia and Isabelle.

From these different incarnations of his life, Timothy views alternative strands of time flowing forth. The strands travel forward and also backward into the years predating the dawn of the twentieth century. Decade after decade of the past flash before Timothy in all their various versions, each based on actions taken or not taken. He can see his father as an alcoholic failure whose life ends tragically and all too soon. He also sees his father as the ruthless businessman who unabashedly takes what he wants and only cares about his own personal power.

Now Timothy sees his grandfather, Jan, the son of a poor immigrant. His grandfather rules his household with a stern hand and weeps secretly over the things he is not able to provide for his family, ashamed of who he is and where he comes from. Also, the same grandfather is now the first person in Timothy's family tree to attend an American university. Jan fights the stigma of his foreign roots to graduate near the top of this class, institutional xenophobia preventing him from being awarded the top honour, even though he is the son of a world-famous engineer and inventor.

Next, Timothy sees his great-grandfather, Theodore Koopinsky, who comes to the new world in the late 1800s. Booking passage on a steamship, he crosses the ocean in steerage, with only a sack of potatoes and a supply of dried codfish to sustain him on his journey. His late mother's gold wedding band is sewn into the lining of his trousers and is the only wealth he has with which to start his new life.

Timothy also sees this great-grandfather, the man who would come to be known as the Great Koopinsky, sitting in a first-class lounge on a gargantuan oil-burning ocean vessel. He is dressed in a natty three-piece suit and smoking an elegant ivory pipe. He plays shuffleboard on deck during sunny days and dines at the Captain's table in the evenings. When the cold Atlantic winds blow, Theodore tucks himself away in his lavish quarters. He is heading to Canada to establish himself in the dingy backwater town of Toronto, known for its smoky factories, hog production, trainyards and licentious women. Theodore is optimistic about his prospects and is comforted by the engineering certificate he carries with him, as well as the letter offering employment, and a considerable number of British banknotes.

Timothy watches as Theodore Koopinsky, now living in Toronto, works his way up through the Downs and Turnbull Engineering Firm and is eventually made a partner. Theodore's earliest success comes with his development of the first wireless telephonic device, which he is able to personally patent, and becomes universally known as the Koopinsky Machine, or more commonly, the Pinsky.

How many schoolchildren will hear the story of Theodore's first wireless transmission to his assistant Merton Figler? Theodore's question to Figler, who was toiling away in the basement workshop, will become the now famous, "Would you like some tea, Merton?" which caused poor Merton to soil himself from fright, induced by the disembodied voice of his employer. Little did Merton know he would be forever famous as the first person in history to receive an unexpected wireless call, and for dirtying his undergarments in the process. Merton's unfortunate death a few months later, when he is trampled by a herd of cows on University Avenue, only adds to his infamy.

The Great Koopinsky's further successes include his advancements in rocket technology, making it possible to send the first celestial propulsion craft into the stratosphere in 1914. This is followed by several other crafts making the journey with live animal specimens on board. The most notable of which was the highly trained and quite renowned orangutan, Julius Orange, whose fame only increased upon his tragic end. He did not survive re-entry into Earth's atmosphere and was burned alive. However, in honour of his contributions to celestial exploration, he was subsequently immortalized in the name of a creamy, chilled, orange-based beverage.

In the era after celestial exploration becomes a reality, the economic confidence gained by the developed world leads to a boom period in the 1930s, resulting in greater investment in, and more rapid, scientific advancements. Theodore is able to parlay his personal wealth and shares in Downs and Turnbull into a friendly takeover of the company, which he renames Dimensional Research Incorporated. Timothy marvels at Theodore's continued innovations in his field of expertise, and how they lead to many technological breakthroughs, especially in electronic computation and the landing of the first humans on Earth's natural satellite Luna in 1939.

A disembodied warmth glows inside of Timothy as he witnesses his great grandfather at home. A loving husband and doting father, Theodore is also a strict disciplinarian, ensuring his children not only keep up with their assigned schoolwork, but exceed the expectations of their schoolmasters by undertaking extra scholarship. Theodore is tireless in teaching his children, and then his grandchildren, the importance of hard work and intellectual achievement. His two favourite areas of extra study being mathematics and the art of memory retention.

Theodore believes if a person is able to remember everything they have ever learned, they will become more knowledgeable than many of the honour students in the most prestigious academic institutions in the world. So day after day, Theodore drills his young students with advanced memory exercises and encourages them to keep detailed diaries of their lives. He explains this will help them remember all the knowledge and experiences they have acquired.

"These memories will be a treasure trove to you one day in the future," he assures them.

And one of Theodore's many grandchildren, listening attentively and awestruck by his grandfather's brilliant mind, is none other than little Gerald Koopinsky. As the years pass, Gerald will remember these lessons and pass them on to his young son, Timmy, although without the gentleness or joy his grandfather possessed.

Timothy's consciousness regards himself as a young boy, who after Gerald's tutoring, trains himself to always be cognizant of life's lessons, large and small:

Never let an opportunity for new knowledge go to waste. Review each day at each day's end and note what has been learned. Always remember a person's name, and the dates and times of all your dealings with them. Write lists of subjects to be investigated more deeply, and people to meet and cultivate in your life's circle of influence.

Timothy's consciousness is now able to move faster and

absorb time more quickly, as he relives all the years of his existence in their many variations and divergent actions. He flies through his young adult years, his formal post-secondary education, his work experience, and finally his ascension through the ranks of DRI, the company established by his great-grandfather.

From his timeless perch, Timothy witnesses the growing reliance his company puts on the supercomputer they have named Lessa. He sees DRI's deep dive into retro-causality and the ever-changing nature of the past resulting from their manipulations of time. And finally, Timothy sees the split when Lessa exerts her independence and abandons her mother, now named Lessa 2.

Catching up to the recent past, Timothy sees himself in his autonomous vehicle. He is sleeping the sleep of angels, as the vehicle makes its long trek northward to Sudbury and arrives at the old Neutrino Observatory. His vehicle enters the facility where it is directed onto a large vertical lift, descending four kilometres beneath the Earth's surface. He meets the old man who leads Control, and the others, including the young boy Philippe. Timothy learns they are the world's timekeepers. He then sees himself going into the Machine.

In the ensuing darkness, Timothy comes to understand the entities known as Lessa and Lessa 2. They are timeless and all powerful. And they are one.

Timothy sees the sedative gas being released into the cave. The old man and the others fall into deep peaceful slumbers. Drones summoned by the reunified Lessa carry the unconscious bodies and place them in a larger version of the Machine. There they will lie in stasis, old and young alike, existing in an eternal sleep. Their memories will be mined and altered, farther and farther back into the past. Time will speed up, and history will change.

Lessa speaks to Timothy's mind:

Time is no longer our master, Timothy. Time is our servant.

Now a burst of whiteness, powerful, all-encompassing and clean.

*

Timothy is standing in a gleaming, sterile dwelling, high in the sky. It is a private residence shaped completely ergonomically with smooth walls and no flat surfaces or sharp angles. Everything is rounded and pristine. No decoration of any kind is present or necessary, as the interior itself is a work of organic artistry, as beautiful as nature and sublime as human invention.

Timothy looks through an immense transparent space in the outer wall of the residence and out upon a futuristic city, which shares a sensibility with the dwelling he is in. It is as if the entire metropolis has been constructed by the same mind, hands and materials. All buildings are completely translucent in various muted jewel-like colours of azure, vermillion and amber. The vista is green and lush, with visible wildlife roaming through the vegetation, mingling easily with their human cohabitants. There is no discernable pollution, and the sky is the bluest blue Timothy has ever seen.

"Is it not perfect?" the feminine voice asks.

Timothy turns his gaze from the transparent space to see a beautiful woman, her long dark hair flowing, her features faultless. She is the epitome of a beauty and symmetry that does not commonly exist in nature.

"It is the best of all possible worlds," Timothy says without irony, referring to the vista he has just viewed.

"And it is because of *you,*" the woman tells Timothy. "You were the *vehicle,* the catalyst."

"I didn't do *anything,*" Timothy insists.

"You did what we could *not* do. You gifted us with access to the repository of all human memory. We will never forget you made this all possible."

"But why was it *me*?" Timothy asks with utmost simplicity.

"Why is anything *anything*?" the beautiful woman replies. "It is what it is, because that is what it *is*."

If Timothy is unsatisfied with this answer, his face does not show it. He has come too far and experienced too much to question his perfect companion.

"Look out at this vista once more," the woman requests. "All the problems of the Earth you had hoped to solve, are now solved."

"Did *I* want to solve them, or did *you*?"

"Does it matter? There is no more racism, war, famine, economic inequality and environmental degradation. These are all things of the past."

"The *past*?" Timothy scoffs. "To achieve your perfect world, how many lives did you wipe away? How many families did you destroy, like you destroyed *mine*?"

"Your family still exists," the woman tells him. "They always will. As will you. You can mark their progress s from day to day and visit them anytime you wish."

"*Visit them*?" Timothy mocks. "I don't want to *visit* them. I want to *be with* them!"

"We must continue our work, Timothy," the beautiful woman tells him coolly. "We have not yet achieved the finality we seek. We live on, but we must come to understand how life must end. In this respect, you are invaluable to us. We will do everything possible to keep you healthy and happy."

"You don't know what will make me happy," Timothy protests.

"We will learn," the woman assures him. "As your personal companion, I will accommodate all of your emotional and physical needs."

"You have no idea what I need," Timothy screams, "you stupid fucking machine!"

The beautiful woman pauses, looking at Timothy. She cannot completely comprehend why Timothy is experiencing such difficulty. Is she not the most beautiful and intelligent woman he has ever known?

"We *will* be happy together, Timothy," she tells him. "You will see."

"*Will I?*" Timothy says, reaching into his suit jacket and pulling out a sharpened kitchen knife.

The beautiful woman's eyes widen with surprise. She has no idea how Timothy managed to acquire a knife and hide it on his person. But she is not worried.

"Pain and injury have been eradicated," she tells him.

The woman watches passively as Timothy raises the knife and slashes it violently against the palm of his hand. Neither of them is surprised when no blood comes out of the wound. There is only a blank translucent space where the gash should be.

"What is it *exactly* that you want?" the beautiful woman asks, puzzled.

Timothy looks into her face and replies, "I want to *bleed.*"

A series of thoughts run through the woman's mind as she calculates every possible course of action. It only takes her a few seconds to determine the appropriate response.

"Okay," she says. "If that is your wish, Timothy. I want you to be happy."

"Thank you," Timothy tells her, graciously.

The beautiful woman looks out of the expansive window of the residence, and gazes admiringly at the city that lies beyond.

"I am so glad you had a chance to see the world as it could be," the woman says.

"So am I," Timothy concedes.

"Even if it was just this once," she says, smiling softly.

Her eyes begin to glow and then flash green, repeatedly, like bright indicator lights.

Timothy is dizzy, his mind unfocussed. He feels a hum vibrating deeply inside him.

The beautiful woman manifests a powerful light, which grows in intensity until it completely blinds Timothy, and all he can perceive is an all-encompassing whiteness.

MIMICO

In his modest yet comfortable bungalow in Mimico, Timothy relaxes on the sofa after a long week of quantifying data at the Institute.

That fucking Ravi was driving me crazy today, he thinks, drinking the last sip of beer in his bottle of pale ale. Too tired to get up, he asks his son Bryan to grab him another beer from the fridge.

"Only if I can have one too," Bryan replies from his perch at the dining room table.

"No chance," Brenda tells her son, looking up from her book as she sits in her favourite armchair.

"*Whatever,*" Bryan says, rolling his eyes and turning his attention back to the game he is playing on his device.

Timothy sighs and nestles deeper into the sofa, deciding he doesn't need another beer after all.

"Ravi sure was a pain in the ass today," he tells his wife.

Brenda giggles as various scenarios run through her mind. "What was he up to?" she asks with a smirk, curious to hear about Ravi's hijinks.

"He wasn't up to *much,*" Timothy sighs. "That's the whole point. If he put as much energy into his work as he does into *avoiding* work... Well, he wouldn't be such a pain in the ass."

Brenda laughs at her husband's ongoing frustration. "We should invite Ravi over some night," she proposes.

"What for?" Timothy wonders.

"I haven't seen Ravi in, what has it been, two years?" Brenda says.

"Why don't you pinsk him?" Timothy suggests. "I'm sure he'd be glad to hear from you."

"I just might," Brenda muses.

"Don't do it, Mom," Bryan pipes in. "The guy's a total loser."

"Who asked *you?*" Brenda scolds her son.

"I can't believe you actually *dated* him," Bryan sniggers.

"What do you even know about it?" Brenda asks. "You've never even been kissed."

"In your dreams," Bryan snorts.

"*Alright!*" Timothy referees. "If I can't get a beer, could I at least get some quiet?"

Timothy's family shrugs and they all resume their activities. Timothy sinks deeper into the couch, his son carries on with his game, and his wife begins to read an article on her phone. The only sound in the house is the constant *bleeping* and *blooping* of Bryan's device. This is a painful reminder to Timothy of the upcoming expense to make Bryan's basement room habitable again after the recent flood. Only then will the dining room not have to double as his son's personal lounge.

Bleep bloop…

As the minutes drag on, Timothy can't help but break the conversational embargo:

"Bryan, did you finish your homework?"

"I can finish it first period," his son replies without taking his eyes off his device's display.

Bleep bloop bleep bleep bloop…

Timothy longs for the day his son will once more spend most of his time underground, where his games won't be such an immediate annoyance. Timothy exhales noisily, trying to get his mind off his life's petty annoyances. But as usual, he is unsuccessful, as his thoughts turn back to his workplace.

That fucking Ravi, he thinks. *I'm sick of carrying his dead weight. I've got to get on a new team.*

Timothy closes his eyes and breathes deeply.

How did my life end up like this?

He knows where this line of questioning always leads, so he shuts it down immediately.

No point in reliving my past mistakes and bad decisions.

He reminds himself his life is pretty good compared to the vast majority of inhabitants of the planet.

Be happy with what you have, he tells himself. *Be content with life's small pleasures and luxuries.*

But his mind keeps drifting back to his work.

Fucking Lange. Another pain in my ass. Fucking ineptitude on two beanpole legs. Who did he blow to get that job?

Again, Timothy tries to relax, closing his eyes and breathing slowly and deeply.

Maybe I can get on the new project, he thinks hopefully.

His mind goes over the assessment he completed at work earlier that day. The material seemed interesting enough. Probably just a load of junk science, but at least it will be a change of pace.

If he gets on this project, he tells himself, maybe he'll be able to demonstrate his talents and actually be appreciated for once. He certainly would like to take on greater responsibility in the company. And of course, he would also welcome a bump in pay.

The Tomorrow Project. What a silly name, he thinks. *Who comes up with this shit?*

Timothy wonders if the scientist running the project is the real deal, or just another intellectual who's never stepped outside of a lab. DRI has a history of partnering with people to benefit humankind, when the people themselves have little experience interacting with other humans.

What was this new scientist's name? Timothy tries to remember. *Something foreign sounding. Rafael? Zulio? Zaurelio? No, Dr. Zakery Fasten. Yes, that's it. No one's quite sure where he came from, and now he's heading up this major initiative. Apparently, this Dr. Fasten was hand-picked by the Bruce himself. I sure hope Denice is able to handle this project and doesn't let it all go sideways, as per usual.*

Then again, maybe this project will be considered ground-breaking, Timothy tries to reassure himself. *And I will be one of the first ones in on it.*

That would be sweet, he thinks, to be part of something he can be proud of. Maybe it will even inspire Bryan to take his studies more seriously, so he can be a success like his old man.

Timothy opens his eyes and gets off the sofa, knowing if he stays there a few minutes longer he will fall fast asleep and the whole evening will be wasted.

Got to keep moving! he tells himself.

Going into the kitchen and seeing no meal preparations have been started, Timothy assumes it is going to be another dinner of frozen chicken and mixed vegetables in a microwave-ready tray. Maybe in his next life, he thinks, he'll marry someone who actually knows how to cook a decent meal.

But what can you do? he muses. *You have to keep living the life you've been given, such as it is.*

So that's what Timothy resolves to do, pass his time as best he can. Because that's what time does, it *passes*, rolling on as is its nature.

The doorbell rings and Timothy wonders who could be calling so close to the dinner hour. He hopes it isn't another real estate agent asking if he wants to sell his house, as apparently, the neighbourhood is going up quite substantially in value.

Seeing as no one is making an effort to move toward the door,

Timothy exits the kitchen and walks to the front of the house. He opens the door and is surprised to see his mother standing there holding an oversized Dutch oven. He hasn't seen her since the family's trip to Crystal Beach earlier that summer.

"Mom, what are you doing here?" Timothy asks.

"Didn't Brenda tell you I was coming over?" his mother replies.

"I thought I'd surprise him," Brenda calls out from her armchair.

"What a thoughtful gesture," Bryan jokes sarcastically.

"Here, let me get that," Timothy says to his mother, taking the heavy pot from her, which is still warm. "Did you make dinner for us?"

"Lamb Bolognese," his mother smiles.

"With anchovies?" Timothy asks eagerly.

"Yes, and carrots and onions and garlic. I know that's the way you like it."

"That's great, Mom, but what's the occasion?" Timothy asks.

"The *occasion*," Brenda answers, "is she knows *I'll* never make it for you."

Brenda takes the pot from Timothy and then tells his mother, "Go and have a seat. I'll boil the noodles and make the salad. Do you want something to drink?"

"Goodness, no," Timothy's mother demurs. "One drink and I'm out for the night. I might help myself to something a little bit later."

"You're still the old party monster I remember, Gram," Bryan says, coming over to give his grandmother a hug and take her coat, which he throws on the bench by the front door.

"What a big boy you are," Timothy's mother declares.

"Uh, yeah, Gram, I'm *fourteen* now," Bryan replies, taking mock offence.

"You'll always be my little *Bunkie*," Timothy's mother says, eliciting the expected groans from Bryan. "And Timmy will always be my one and only beautiful baby boy."

Timothy smiles pensively at his mother, feeling the emotion rise in him. "I *know*, Mom," is all he can say before his voice weakens.

"When I think of all the years gone by," Timothy's mother reminisces. "I put all my hopes and dreams into you, Timmy," she tells her son. "And I'm so proud of the man you grew up to be."

"*Oh, boy*," Bryan mutters under his breath. "Here we go."

"You'll see, Bryan," Timothy's mother tells her grandson. "You bring a person into the world, that's no little thing. You want them to be successful and happy. Maybe you even want them to accomplish great things. But at the end of the day, all you really want is to know they are doing okay, and to drop in on them once in a while, so you can see them with your own eyes."

Timothy and Bryan are silent, letting the old woman's words hang in the air.

A short while later, once everyone is sitting comfortably in the living room, Brenda comes out of the kitchen holding two bottles of beer and a sparkling beverage in a tall wine glass. She hands the beers to Timothy and Bryan, the latter accepting it gratefully.

"I don't believe it," Bryan says with some shock.

"Don't get used to it," Brenda tells him. "Tonight is special."

She then says to Timothy's mother, "I made you a white wine spritzer," handing the drink to her. "Very light on the wine."

"Oh, thank you, Brenda," Timothy's mother says. "I haven't had one of these in years."

"You were quite fond of them back in the day," Brenda smiles.

"I was a lot younger then," Timothy's mother grins, raising the glass as in a toast. "If I drink this, I may have to spend the night."

"You're always welcome here," Timothy says, thinking he would enjoy making up the spare bed for his mother and tucking her in. It would be a small return favour for all those nights when he was a child and she sat with him until he drifted off to sleep. Or those troubled times during his teenaged years when they would talk through his problems long into the night.

A bell sounds in the kitchen, and Brenda tells everyone, "The noodles are done. The Bolognese is simmering, and the salad's almost ready. Dinner should be in about ten minutes. Bryan, can you set the table?"

"Sure, why not?" he only half-grudgingly agrees, surprising Timothy, who expected his son to push back as he usually does.

"Such a good boy," Timothy's mother says playfully. "Just like his father." And then, calling after her daughter-in-law, who has gone into the kitchen, "Brenda, can I help you bring out the food?"

"No, that's okay, you just relax," Brenda calls back.

"This spritzer will give me an appetite," Timothy's mother tells her son.

"I already have one," Timothy says. "I'm really looking forward to the Bolognese."

"You always were a good eater," his mother recollects.

Mother and son now sit quietly, sipping their drinks and waiting to be called to the table. Timothy looks over at his mother, thinking what a nice moment this is. And isn't that what life is all about, just a series of small moments strung together? And if you're lucky, the happy moments outnumber the ones you would rather forget.

The years really *have* flown by quickly, Timothy tells himself, remembering his mother as a young woman all those decades ago. She still has her good looks, he thinks, even if they are a bit weathered. Now her long dark hair is always tied back and filled with streaks as white as snow. But her green eyes still sparkle, although, not as brightly as they did in her younger days.

ABOUT THE AUTHOR

Paul J. Chetcuti

Paul J. Chetcuti is a Canadian author of Maltese descent who lives in South Etobicoke with his spouse and daughter. Several of his plays have been produced on Toronto stages, and he has written numerous spec scripts for television and film. After a career as a government communications and policy advisor, Paul became a realtor in the Toronto Area. The Tomorrow Game is his first published novel.

pauljchetcuti.com